CORPORATE CATHARSIS

THE WORK FROM HOME EDITION

Published by Water Dragon Publishing
waterdragonpublishing.com

Cover design copyright © 2022 by Niki Lenhart
nikilen-designs.com

ISBN 978-1-957146-83-6 (Hardcover)

10 9 8 7 6 5 4 3 2 1

FIRST EDITION

FOREWORD

B ACK WHEN WE PUBLISHED THE FIRST EDITION of *Corporate Catharsis*, we were focused on giving people a creative outlet in response to the ridiculousness of the corporate shenanigans we're all so familiar with. It was meant to be a way to get something positive out of the negative, and also to support my personal contention that everything that happens to you is just novel fodder.

Fast forward two years, and the world has been irrevocably changed by the COVID-19 pandemic. Nothing is where it was when we published the first edition. Over 6,500,000 souls are no longer with us, globally, and despite trying to ignore that or put a silver lining on it, it's impacting us in new ways, both physically and psychologically.

We're stressed out, and it shows in our creativity.

There were so many differences between the submissions for the first edition, and those for the second. The first edition had a lot of comedy submissions; this one, very few. The first edition had no dystopia or apocalypse; this had more in those categories than any other. Stories in both editions rely a lot on magical solutions to seemingly intractable problems.

This edition had a preponderance of demons running amok in our world and ruining everything, which makes sense, given that the coronavirus is also an evil monster over whom we have no control, changing our world in profound ways. We're seeing sleep deprivation as part of the new normal, and that's coming out in our stories too.

There are new ubiquities — everyone knows about Zoom calls. Everyone knows that we're all wearing our pajamas under our on-camera suit jackets. Everyone has a new understanding of the problems with office buildings and office jobs. And with the time no longer wasted by long commutes and longer hours, we're all reaching out to rediscover parts of ourselves that we shelved when we entered the corporate churn in the first place.

It's in that light that we'd like to invite everyone to consider that in changing our world, COVID-19 also gave us an opportunity to use our creativity to respond to unimaginable pressure. To respond to an upheaval of everything with the power of our ability to imagine a new normal. And to keep in touch with that which makes us most human, our ability to tell stories to make sense of the unexplainable.

With that in mind, our insanely hard-working team welcomes you to *Corporate Catharsis: The Work From Home Edition.*

Laureen Hudson
Co-founder and Editor in Chief, Paper Angel Press

CONTENTS

CORPORATE CATHARSIS

CATHARSIS

THE WORK FROM HOME EDITION

Jack Nash was raised in the deserts of the American west and now lives in the forests of Virginia. As a communications consultant, he has ghostwritten speeches for former heads of state, global leaders, and a Nobel Peace Prize laureate. Under his client's names, Jack wrote essays or op-eds appearing in *The New York Times*, *The Economist*, and other publications. His fiction work has appeared or is forthcoming in *Kairos Literary Magazine*, a horror anthology titled "Dracula's Guests", and the *Magazine of Fantasy & Science Fiction*. Find him at *@jacknashstories*.

•   •   •

The koi pond in this story is real. It is home to thirty or so fish, who swim just yards away from a private lake. Fond of a view, I take my Zoom calls from a window where I can watch them. It made me wonder what artificial ponds I live in, and what lakes are just beyond my field of vision.

I REGRET TO INFORM YOU THAT OUR OFFICE BUILDING IS HAUNTED

JACK NASH

TO: Ms. Angelica Ingles, Head, Human Resources and Talent - AG&I Consulting Group
FROM: Jared Hess, Consultant
DATE: March 5, 2022
SUBJECT: Report on Property Damage

Dear Ms. Ingles,

I regret to inform you that our office building is haunted.

Earlier today, I called corporate HR to inform them of what happened. I also tried to explain why the office's award-winning koi pond is now devoid of fish. However, HR insisted upon a formal, written statement, hence this letter. I apologize for its length, but I want to give some context to the event. I hope you will agree that anyone in my situation would have done the same.

And I really am sorry about the koi.

You'll permit me to go back a bit, for context, to August 31st — my first day at the company's satellite office in Fairview Park. After a year of networking and cajoling, I had finally been transferred to the consulting team. I thought my career was finally taking off. You see, I have a passion for writing, and even dreamed of being a novelist one day. At the time, I had a few small works published online and a novel being reviewed by a handful of literary agents. The key to my success, I thought, was our firm's contracts with major publishing houses in New York and Boston. I believed that if I could get on those projects, I could make the connections that would one day open doors to a better future. That was my hope anyway, foolish as it may have been.

I wanted to make a good impression, so I arrived to work half an hour early. I got out of my car, I straightened my cornflower blue tie that said, 'this guy is confident but pleasant,' and entered the building.

The office was already full and bustling. Consultants have a reputation for being over-achievers, and it was true. Even early I was late. My coworkers read emails, tapped keyboards with vigor, and gazed at me only long enough to determine I was neither client, boss, nor bearer of coffee.

One woman came up to me. She smiled, shook my hand, and introduced herself as Kate Warkowski, my new manager.

We went through the usual pleasantries. She spoke of how everyone was delighted to have me onboard, I spoke of how grateful I was for this opportunity, so on and so on. A quick tour followed. Here, the conference room. There, the kitchenette (please no fish in the microwave, and label your food). Down this way, the open office space (just pick any desk).

"And out there," Kate said, "is the koi pond." Face beaming, she led me to the windows. She pointed to a shaded aquatic garden where thirty or so gigantic koi swam. Each was a variation of gold, orange, or crimson, speckled with black and white flecks, like fire imprisoned in water.

"Last year it won the award for Fairview County's Best Water Feature," Kate said. She leaned in as if to confide a secret. "When I take calls, I like to stand here and just watch the fish. Aren't they gorgeous?"

I nodded, but my attention had shifted to just beyond the pond. A housing development of condos and townhomes sat across a small lake. A miniscule dock with rows of white canoes indicated the water belonged to the property. Nature had reclaimed it to some degree. A pair of Canadian geese nibbled at plants on the water's edge, and a perch breached the surface to snag a passing insect. A gravel path, a bench, and some holly bushes were all that separated the two bodies of water.

I chuckled. "How sad for the fish."

Kate's professional smile wavered.

"What do you mean?"

"Well, there's only what, ten, twelve feet separating the koi from a lake? It's ironic."

I swallowed at how Kate's eyes narrowed.

"I mean, the way the fish are stuck in that tiny pond when there's a massive place they could be swimming. It's almost cruel."

Her mouth puckered. "It's an award-winning pond," she said.

"Right, sorry," I said. Heat rose to my cheeks, and I wondered if I had ruined my career before it even took off.

Kate turned away from the windows. "Well, let's get you started."

I followed her, trying to weaponize my enthusiasm.

"I'm really looking forward to the communications workstream. I read the white paper that came out last month, and being a writer myself —"

"That's great," Kate said, not turning to me. She pointed at an empty desk. "But what we need right now is help with data entry."

"Oh." Data entry. Just thinking about the miles of Excel rows was a needle of Novocain to my brain. But I could not afford to be picky on my first day, especially not after my *faux pas* with the fish. I conjured a smile. "Happy to help, however I can."

That became my life for three months. I came in before eight-thirty, sat, opened my computer and entered data line by line, row by row, sheet by sheet. I watched others take the calls I wanted to be on, hobnob with publishing executives I had hoped to get to know. I ate lunch by the windows overlooking the pond, just to be away from a computer for a moment. I admit I thought about leaving. This wasn't the work I imagined. It didn't help that five literary agents and two small publishers rejected my novel during those months. But the hope that one day — in a few weeks, in a month, or two months — I would find success, kept me going.

Perhaps a slow death by Excel was what gave me some second sight, some way to pull back the curtain to see the spirits of the building.

I wish it hadn't.

I saw the first one on Jenny's birthday. Sorry, HR asked me to be precise — it was Friday, November 5th. We brought her a cake, sang "Happy Birthday" in so many different keys we somehow created our own harmony, then wished her well for the many years ahead.

"And I hope most of them will be with us, right here at the company," Kate said. We tipped our red plastic cups of boxed wine to that. The party ended, cake was divided up, bags slung over shoulders, and everyone went home. Except for me. I stayed late to finish a few more rows of Excel hoping that extra effort would lead to a more challenging assignment.

After an hour or so I took a break to get some coffee. As I walked past the restrooms, Jenny came out, nearly hitting me with the door. I almost dropped my drink, and Jenny gasped. I think each of us thought we were alone in the office.

She must have been crying. Her long black hair was mussed, and wet lines cut streaks through her makeup. I tried to mutter an apology, unsure if it was for scaring her or for

4

seeing her tears. She pushed past me before I could finish. Her sniffles traced her path past desks, the front lobby, then out.

I returned to my desk, blushing at my inadvertent transgressions. Tears anytime were a private affair. But ones on your birthday were something else entirely.

It happened while I was staring out the window. The sun, setting behind the condos of the artificial lake, cast ribbons of gold and crimson over the water. While I gazed at the pond, a white something flashed across the window. A reflection. Perhaps Jenny hadn't left at all.

I turned. And stopped. She — it — I don't know which, can't tell, even now — looked like Jenny. Younger, though, and leaner, wearing a ballerina's tutu. With a leap, she flitted across the office to execute a perfect pirouette between the copier and the paper supplies.

"Jenny?" I said.

It turned to me, then smiled, bowed, extended its arms, and twirled. Like any ballerina, it had kept its head still as its body spun, like an owl. But as its neck reached its limits, it snapped around to restart. That's when the face changed. Jenny's brown eyes turned cloudy, her cheeks sank beneath cadaverous cheekbones, and her dress birthed moths and the perfume of decay. It spun again, and the face was normal. Sweet, youthful, vibrant. Another spin and the corpse thing returned, then back to the smiling dancer. On and on it went, faster and faster. Limbs doubled, the dress whirled, and the faces, one of death and one of life, merged.

I stumbled back. My foot tangled with the leg of a chair, and I fell. When I looked up, all that remained was a white, fuzzy moth fluttering against a fluorescent ceiling light. It melted into smoke and was gone.

I ran to my car and drove home.

I tried to sleep, but couldn't. What had that thing been? Had anyone else seen this dancer before? If they had, they would have told me. Right? Or maybe I was insane. Too much data entry, too many mind-numbing days. Mostly, I wondered why it looked like Jenny.

When I walked in the following Monday, everything was as it should be. Employees sat at desks typing emails and chatting over coffee. I wanted to tell someone, but I knew I couldn't. Being the most junior employee was hard enough. I could not afford to also be the crazy one who saw spirits or ghosts or whatever it was.

The day passed without dancers. Jenny sat, attended meetings, and gossiped with her desk mates. All normal. At lunch, she got up, grabbed her purse, and announced she would be back in thirty minutes. When I was sure she was gone, I walked to her desk as casually as I could. No one paid me any attention. I glanced at her belongings. A laptop, a pink coffee mug embossed with *Dance Like No One is Watching*, a potted cactus, and a photo of two people — a mother and a girl of ten or eleven.

The girl wore a tutu.

In the weeks that followed, I researched everything I could about the office building. The Fairview Park office was built in 1983. It is 12,000 square feet, has a suite of offices, a lobby, a parking lot, and of course the koi pond. It was refurbished in 2010, which added larger windows and overhauled the air duct system. As far as I can tell, only one employee has ever died there. Craig Masterson, aged fifty-seven, in 2001. Further digging proved he did not actually die at the office. While he had a heart attack at his desk, he passed away in a hospital three days later from complications of a bypass operation.

Of course, the problem with this is that the ghost — that is what I decided it had to be — was of Jenny, who was very much alive. Everything I was reading about hauntings happened in ancient homes steeped in history and tragedy. Fairview Park had neither. It was simply where we spent the day and conducted our work. It was as far removed from death as any building could be.

How wrong I was.

Just when I was deciding that I had imagined the whole incident, that the ballerina truly was a product of my data-dulled mind, January 22 happened.

Brett Clark came into the office late that day. He flung his bag down at his desk, flopped to his chair, and glowered at his computer. He seemed to have imported the winter chill from the outside.

I noticed Kate staring at him from the copier. I joined her, though I had no paper to print.

"Is Brett okay?" I said, keeping my voice low. We pretended not to look at him. His scowl cut deep canyons on his brow.

"He bought a house," she whispered.

"That's a good thing, right?" I said. "Why does he look so ... angry?"

"Have you seen interest rates? And in this market?" She leaned back with an expression of mock horror. "He wanted a four-bedroom home with a backyard and had to settle for a two-bedroom condo in a shitty neighborhood at twice the price. It's enough to make anyone furious."

I caught snippets of rumors throughout the day. Fights with his wife over financing, the months of searching with so little success, his desire to transfer to the company's Denver office now dead.

The atmosphere warmed when Bret left early at four o'clock. The trickle of employees to cars began an hour later. I joined them, but realized I had left my keys behind. Cursing both myself and how early it became dark this time of year, I dashed back to my desk.

That's when I saw Brett, or a ghost that looked like him. It wore climbing gear, complete with ropes, a harness, and helmet. It stood at a window, its hand searching the pane for somewhere to grasp.

I did not stumble back this time. I held my ground and my breath. Fighting the urge to turn, to run, to dash to my car and never come back, I stepped forward.

My voice cracked when I spoke. "Brett?"

The thing turned. Where Brett's stomach bowed outward against button-down shirts, his ghost had hints of muscle rippling underneath a t-shirt. Instead of Brett's paper pale face, its jaw was carved stone dappled with freckles. It was Brett, if he had spent the last eight years on a mountain instead of writing business reports.

The climber smiled at me. For an instant, it had the grin of simple pleasures freely enjoyed. I blinked, and it transformed to a grimace. Its eyes rolled back, its lips split, and yellow fluid oozed from the spaces between its teeth. Skin bronzed by the outdoors became gray and bloated with damp. I recoiled and squeezed my eyes shut. Nothing happened. I dared a glance, and Brett's spectral twin was back at the window, the glass reflecting its amiable smile. I blinked, and the rot returned.

I don't know how I got home. I must have run to my car, because the next thing I remember, I was on the street outside of my apartment. My knuckles ached from gripping the steering wheel.

I called in sick for the next three days.

It wasn't courage that forced my return to the office — it was the need for a paycheck and the fear of losing my health insurance. However, I vowed I would never again stay after dark. The dancer and the climber had both appeared after sunset. If I left before then, perhaps I would be spared further horrors.

A month passed with no incident. I left promptly at five o'clock each day, finding any excuse to leave earlier if I could. I know my coworkers whispered that I was not as engaged in my job as I should be, or there was some personal emergency I had to take care of. I didn't care what they said. Those weeks were blissfully free of hauntings.

It all came crashing down on Friday, March 4. We sat in the conference room for our weekly wrap-up meeting. I eyed Brett, dull-eyed and pale, and Jenny, chipper and sipping coffee. Neither turned to corpses when I blinked.

Kate was going over items for the week when my phone buzzed. An email from a literary agent. I didn't need to click it open. The preview said enough.

Jared,

Thank you for your submission. We regret that ...

So that was it. A neat, solid sum of thirty submissions, thirty rejections. My novel was uniformly unwanted. Dead.

"Jared?" Kate said.

"Sorry?" I looked up. The room seemed miles away.

Kate pursed her lips.

"I said, can you take care of the analytical section of the report? You're our data guru and we need someone to make sure all the infographics are accurate.

Eyes swiveled to me.

"Data guru?"

"Yeah, that's why we hired you," Kate said, flashing a rattlesnake smile that dared a contradiction. "It's due tomorrow. You may have to stay late but I'll approve the overtime, 'kay?"

She moved on to other business before I could respond.

Data guru. I was supposed to be a writer. I thought I was a writer. Maybe all I was good for was entering numbers one on top of each other. The rejection stung enough, why did Kate have to rub salt into my wounds?

I returned to my desk but found no motivation. Even with a report due, I couldn't analyze any more numbers or create yet another chart. A dim future stretched before me, one where numbers replaced words, calculating data murdered prose, and my novel contained only spreadsheet formulas.

Perhaps that is the way it was meant to be. I wasn't cut out to be a writer. I couldn't even get onto the projects that would make me writer-adjacent. I was the numbers guy, and I should just get used to it.

Evening approached. I watched the sun nestle behind the artificial lake. I waved goodbye to my coworkers. If I simply vanished, eaten by a ghost of whatever would happen when the sun set, would they even care? I had been here a year and they still saw me as an analytics employee. None of them had even asked what I wanted from my career, or even allowed me to have a say in its direction. Let the dark come, then. It didn't matter anymore.

The sky faded from violet to black. Sensing no motion, the fluorescent lights of the office clicked off, leaving me alone in the pale green illumination of an exit sign.

The chair next to me creaked. Holding my breath, I turned. Would it be the dancer, or the climber?

The eyes staring back at me were my own.

Ms. Ingles, I cannot adequately express all the thoughts that raced through me at that moment. I doubted my sanity, but at the same time, I knew that this was me. The soft brown hair, the stubble on his cheeks, even the cedar-wood cologne he wore, were all mine. Except the smile. He rippled his cheeks and crinkled his eyes. I hadn't grinned like that in a long time.

For a moment we stared at one another, neither moving. Then he looked down. A book lay open on his desk. He pulled a pen from his pocket, clicked it, and wrote his — my — our — name in a book, in long, looping script. Finished, he shut it and handed it to me.

I looked at the cover. The title was indistinct and fuzzy, like an out of focus picture. Only the subtitle and attribution were clear. *A Novel by Jared Hess. The #1 New York Times Bestseller.*

"You're me," I said.

He — I — nodded back and set the book down.

"But I'm not dead."

It shook its head. With a voice the whine of wind over ice, it whispered three words.

"Dreams die, too."

The grin grew. Tendons popped and flesh tore to reveal gangrenous and festering muscles. The book withered and turned to dust.

I spent the rest of the night with myself. He signed the book, over and over. Its text eluded me. I watched as he

10

transformed from the beaming novelist I wanted to be, to the dead thing I feared I now was, then back again.

When the sun tinted the sky blue, he vanished. My coworkers found me staring out the window at the koi pond. The fish traced lazy circles in the water, each a swirl of gold made flesh.

"Were you here all night?" Brett said. "Want me to grab you a coffee or something?"

"Did you ever want to be a climber?"

The pang that flashed across his face told me I was right.

Kate entered the office and made a beeline for me. "Jared, I still don't have that report, it's due now." Perhaps it was seeing me in my clothes from yesterday, or that I didn't smile politely at her, that made her hesitate.

"You okay?" She looked me over.

"I need to tell everyone something," I said. "About the office."

So I told them, Ms. Ingles. I started talking and they gathered around my desk. I recounted the whole thing, just as I've written it down here. From my first day, to seeing Jenny's ballerina, to seeing Brett as a mountain climber, to myself last night. All of it.

"Ghosts aren't real," said Alex, a senior partner who handled financial accounts. A ripple of agreement went through the office.

"And Brett and I aren't dead," Jenny said. "Neither are you. So how can we be ghosts?"

I rubbed my eyes. "No, that's not what I'm saying. It's what we gave up on that is haunting the office, not us." I looked around and sighed at their confusion. It was so clear to me, why wasn't it to them? "Look, if someone loses a leg, or an arm in an accident, they will still get itches or aches for a limb that is, by all definitions, dead. The limb lingers with them to remind them of what they lost. Phantom limb syndrome, it's called. But what if when our dreams die, they stay around to haunt us? Dreams are a part of us, as much as any limb."

They gave me blank looks.

I turned to Jenny. "Did you ever want to be a dancer, a ballerina specifically?"

She glanced down. "A long time ago, yeah."

"Why didn't you? What stopped you?"

She didn't say anything for a long moment. "I got too old. Ballerinas start their careers young, and I was on track for a while, but then school got so busy, and my mom ..." Her voice trailed off. She looked away. "Before I knew it, I was thirty-five. Most dancers retire by then, and I hadn't even started."

"What about the rest of you?" I said. "What dreams have you given up on? It can't be just be me, Brett, and Jenny. You all wanted to be something once, something that you aren't now."

"I was going to play pro football," Sam said. His chair groaned under his weight as he chuckled at the memory. "Even played a year in college. Those were good times." His face tightened. "*Good* times."

"Scientist," someone said.

"Painter," chimed another.

"What about you, Kate? What have you given up on?" I turned to her. She stepped back, blinking at the direct question. Then her face soured.

"This is all bullshit," she said. "Utter nonsense that has no place in a professional work environment."

"Then prove me wrong," I said. "Let's all stay here until it gets dark. If nothing happens, I'm crazy. If it does, I'm right, and our office is haunted."

"You're not right," Alex said. Kate nodded.

From the exhaustion or the simple absurdity of it all, I laughed.

"Fine. Let's wait and see."

In the end, I think curiosity won them over.

We watched the clock more than usual for the rest of the day. I dozed off my desk several times. I was exhausted after the night of staying up with the ghost of my dreams. Kate woke me when she found me, demanding I either work or leave. I stayed.

Five o'clock came but no one left. Pleasant work chatter shifted into whispered conversations. I knew my coworkers were all glancing at me when they thought I wasn't looking. They wanted to know what I would do when no ghosts came. I wanted to know what they would do when they did.

A silence settled on the office as the rooftops of the condos across the lake broke the sun's profile. Clouds flared orange, then purple, then faded to black.

Nothing. My mouth dried with each passing minute. Every time I stayed late, I had seen something. But now: no dancer, no climber, no me.

"Well, this was fun," Alex said. He stood, stretched, and checked his phone. "I'm gonna head out."

"Wait, please," I said. "Just a few more minutes."

Alex rolled his eyes.

"Get some help." He walked to the doors and out. Others joined. A few smirked as they passed me, but most simply ignored my pleading gaze. I willed my chair to swallow me. Maybe I was crazy.

The office emptied until only Kate and I remained. I steeled myself for her reprimand. I was going to be fired, I was sure.

"Jared," she said. I swiveled to face her. She stood over me, arms folded, smirking.

"I, I thought," I put my head in my hands. Exhaustion wrapped around me like a blanket. "I'll go now. Sorry, for this. For all of it."

"Jared," she said with more insistence. I looked up to her pointing across the room.

My ghost entered. A smile of perfect joy lit his face. Seeing us, he darted over, signed his book, and handed it to Kate.

"Best-selling author, eh?" She said as the book withered in her hand. She raised an eyebrow as the ghost's face split to reveal the rot underneath. Then she turned to me.

"I didn't take you as someone who gave up so easily."

For a moment, my head seemed disconnected from my body. She knew? More than that, she knew, and it didn't bother her?

"Oh, good, the rest are here." Kate said.

Jenny's ballerina flitted in on pointed toes, followed by Brett's climber, who strode to the windows and adjusted its harness. I turned to the kitchenette where a doctor muttered as she pressed a stethoscope against the microwave. Mold sprouted on her white coat as she walked.

"I object, your honor, I object," said a lawyer in a pinstripe suit. He burst from the conference room waving a hand at an invisible judge. His hair grew white, his teeth fell from his mouth, then he collapsed to the ground in a pile of sludge. After a moment, he reversed back into a man.

More came. A painter with no canvas, a singer strumming a guitar, a dozen more. The office buzzed with unsung songs and un-lived lives.

"Why didn't you say anything?" I said. "You called this was nonsense, bullshit."

Kate looked past me. I followed her gaze. A woman in a white dress entered from the lobby. She was Kate, carrying a bouquet of roses. As she walked, the flowers knotted themselves and fused to form a baby. It reached up with pudgy fingers to play with her veil. Then, like an apple left to the sun, the child's flesh wrinkled and cracked. The woman dropped the child, where it bounced against the carpet. Kate stood still as her abandoned dream came to her. They stared at one another as the roses reappeared, fresh and sweetly scented.

"I've stayed late a lot more nights than you, Jared," Kate said. "And what did you think I was going to say? One crazy person in the office we can tolerate. But not two, especially when one is the manager." She pulled her gaze away as the roses transformed into the infant.

"It wouldn't have mattered," she said. "I don't think anyone else will admit to themselves that their dreams are dead. They couldn't handle it."

14

"I don't understand," I said.

"Yes, you do." She gestured around the room. "You can see them because you're quiet and introspective. You know yourself. I think most writers are that way. Me, I can because I know what is possible," she stared back at her ghost, then reached up to touch the child just as its flesh withered. "And what is not. Not anymore."

"We can't be the only ones," I said. "They have to know. Dreams just can't die like this. It's so ... so," I fought the fog in my head for the right word. "Pathetic."

Kate turned to the window, but not quick enough for me to miss the look of wanting that passed over her features.

"Sorry," I said. And I was. The implication wasn't my intent.

Kate was silent for a long time. When she spoke, she kept her eyes trained on the koi pond. Its internal light lit her face in waves of rippling yellow.

"I think if they admitted it to themselves, they wouldn't be able to go on. Who are we if we can't dream of being something more than we are? Of holding on to what we wanted to be, even though we know it will never happen? It's the lies we tell ourselves that let us get up, go to work, and get through the day."

I joined her at the window. The pond, warmed by electric coils under rocks, set up curls of steam that drifted over the lake.

"You ruined calls for me, you know that?"

"What?"

"Your first day. You said it was cruel to put a pond so close to a lake. At first, I thought that was stupid." She glanced at me, a smile twitching at the corners of her lips. "The fish can't know that there's something better just a few feet away. They can't see it, I mean. But the more I thought about it, I realized it wasn't the landscaper or whatever who was cruel, we are."

"Us?" I wasn't sure if I was following. Exhaustion was taking its toll, and the continued noise of the ghostly aspirations tugged at my attention.

15

She turned to me. "We come here every day, watch the koi, and we know there is something better for them. We have a different perspective. But we don't do anything. We just let them go on believing their little pond is all there is in the world. And I used to love watching them when I was taking a call, but now when I look at the pond, I just feel sad. For them, myself. For everyone in the office."

That's when I got the idea, Ms. Ingles. We may not have been able to help our coworkers, and I'm not even sure if we should. I think Kate was right that they wouldn't have been able to accept the truth. But we could help the koi.

"Want to do something about it?" I said. Kate looked at me with a raised brow, then smiled.

We spent the rest of the night catching koi. It's surprisingly easy, and the water was warmed to keep it from freezing. We found an old net with some of the gardener's tools nearby. Kate would push the fish into a corner, I would scoop up the fish, then we would both run over to the lake and toss them in. They would stay at the surface only a moment, miniature suns in the murk, before vanishing into dark water. It took hours to free all thirty or so koi. When we were done, we were wet, exhausted, and laughing.

I helped Kate out of the pond and shivering we ran to our cars. She paused as she opened her door with shaking hands.

"Are you coming back tomorrow?"

I looked over the lake. Its surface reflected the sky's first hints of approaching dawn.

"No, no I don't think so. You?"

"Probably. It's haunted, but it's not all bad."

With that we embraced. She got in her car, I got in mine.

So, Mr. Ingles, that's how the fish got out of the pond. Kate called me later to say that people had complained to HR about my comments of the office being haunted. A few might have been genuinely concerned for my mental health. I assure you I am of sound mind and no danger to anyone, much less myself.

But, given my resignation, it's not really any of your business anyway. Not anymore.

Regards,
Jared Hess
Former Consultant, Aspiring Author

Kimberley Wall has been a project manager, a program manager, an office manager, and a caregiver. Now in her fourth professional decade, she is learning to balance work with play, science with art, and attachment with release. She is currently brewing tea, studying witchcraft, and promoting grace and dignity at the end of life. She is continually adding book ideas and changing which will take priority, resulting in none of them being anywhere near submission for publication. Kimberley lives in Northern California with her clowder of devoted cats and too many hobbies.

•   •   •

Hard work, the slow climb, a quality product, and constantly building your reputation; that's how you gain success. But what do you do when a global pandemic shuts everything down and erases you from popular thought? Do you start over, bitterly slogging through yet more years in the climb to the top, at an age by which you were sure you should have achieved your dream? Unbearable! But there is no fast track to success ... or is there?

MESSAGE IN A BOTTLE

KIMBERLEY WALL

K ANE ADAMSON HAD ALWAYS WANTED to be Something. Someone. Have a Title that people respected. After years of hard work, he ran a diner but still wanted to be a Michelin-Starred Chef. He'd been sure he was on his way when COVID hit and restaurants had to shut their doors. Not many work-from-home opportunities for a chef, and a stalled rise is as good as a fall. He had to find his fast-track to success. He'd been trying to achieve The American Dream for a long time now, and the conventional path of hard work, especially starting over, was just too ... hard.

Then he found the job opening that could be his ticket. An "old-folks home". This should be a breeze. If he got an interview, he knew he'd land the job. He had that certain indefinable something, that suave charm and confidence of the middle-aged white man seeking a position in management.

•　　•　　•

He was in, and this job was a dream. Well, a good stepping stone on the way to the dream, anyway. Chef Kane, Culinary Director and Executive Chef. That's going to read well on the résumé, indeed. But the job wasn't quite the "breeze" he had imagined. He hadn't counted on this management position having quite so many responsibilities. So much ... management. Tedious administrative tasks were not how he envisioned spending his time. He was destined for so much better; he felt it in his bones. Ah, well, he'd be fine. He knew how to work the system. "Weaponized incompetence" they called it. He snorted in amusement. Whatever works, baby. All he had to do was make that bro-connection with the CEO and the rest would fall into place. He could claim that his talents lay in cuisine, not computers. In soufflés, not staffing. In petit fours, not paperwork. He'd soon have all the other directors and sundry staff doing the tedious stuff so he could focus on, you know, the important things, like career advancement.

•　　•　　•

First day, settling into his new office. An office! The plaque read "Culinary Director". The white, double-breasted chef coat hanging just inside the door read "Executive Chef" under his name. The door had a big glass window in it, but he would cover that. A man's office should afford him some privacy. He unpacked his few personal effects and arranged the workspace to his liking. Time for his first morning management meeting. Time to charm the troops. He slipped the flask out of his messenger bag and took a fortifying swig. Self-confidence in liquid form. He strutted down the hall.

Back in his office, lounging in his comfortable leather chair, he mused that, while he felt the meeting had gone well, a bit more charm might be necessary to establish dominance. He was idly surveying his new domain when he noticed The

Bottle. Where had that come from? He was sure it had not been there earlier that morning. He asked a few staff members if someone had brought it in while he was in the meeting, but no one he asked knew anything about it. Oddly enough, no one he asked seemed to remember him asking just moments after they spoke. Even more odd was the fact that no one seemed to notice The Bottle even when they seemed to be looking right at it.

It was a big plastic jug of what looked like bourbon, and bottom-shelf bourbon at that, or so the front label seemed to indicate. Kane decided he must have just missed it that morning, rationalizing that it must have been left by his predecessor, probably for safe keeping. Perhaps it had been purchased to use in a recipe. It certainly wasn't for drinking; he had more discerning taste than that as evidenced by the quality hooch in his flask. But, well, you can't just leave cooking alcohol lying around for the staff to get to. He decided there was no harm in leaving it in the back corner of his desk for now. And so The Bottle sat, as if it had always been there, as if it were not there at all.

But it called to Kane. A deeply spiritual melody, just sub-audible, filled him with desire, wonder, lust for its magic. Sparks of golden light, emanating from the warm amber liquid rather than reflecting the fluorescent office lights, tugged at the corner of his eye as he worked at his desk.

Intrigued, he lifted the large bottle from its corner and cradled it in his lap to really look at it. He had the fleeting impression that it didn't feel as it ought to — weight? temperature? consistency? — but he lost the thought before it really took hold. Raptly reading the back label, he never noticed the subtle strands of light around him weaving themselves into a glimmering mesh. The label told an enticing tale of success and power gained one ounce at a time until The Ultimate Prize was attained. But there were Rules. No more than one ounce per week. A full seven days between doses. The Bottle must be left where it was found. Every drop of The

Elixir must be consumed by The Chosen One. Any deviation from The Rules would deny him The Ultimate Prize. It was a slow process, a long-term commitment, a recipe for Heart's Desire that demanded patience and sacrifice. In accordance with Chaos Theory, it warned, as The Chosen One's world became more perfectly ordered, all around him would devolve into an increasing number of accidents, arguments, and escalating disasters that he would have to manage in order to maintain the illusion of normalcy.

The label described The Ultimate Prize, the coveted words of enlightenment, in vague but enticing terms, promising that it lay at the bottom of The Bottle, unreadable, unknowable until the last ounce was drunk. By the time he finished reading, he was caught in a web of excitement. He had found his fast-track to The American Dream.

Well, no time like the present to get started, right? Kane twisted the plastic cap, broke the seal, and ignored the impression that he was hearing the distant squeak of disused metal hinges opening. He paused, sniffed at The Elixir, and felt that sudden, familiar bliss that the aroma of high-quality booze induced. He almost took a swig straight from The Bottle but stopped when he saw the shot glass that had been hidden in the shadows behind it. There was only one line on the glass, and it marked 1 oz. OK, he thought, The Rules are serious, but at least the tools you need to do the job are provided. He carefully poured the first dose and then knocked it back. Euphoria! It spread to every cell in his body, making him feel like he could fly. He never even felt the enveloping net of shimmering light as it sank into his skin. Contract sealed.

•   •   •

Days went by and Kane's colleagues welcomed him and offered him support as he learned the ropes here. Maintenance rearranged the dining room tables for him. HR reviewed his department timesheets for him. AP taught him how to process his invoices by letting him watch while they do it. With each victory, he felt a tingle just under his skin.

Days went by and small things began to go wrong. Dishes broke at an unusual rate, the ice machine repeatedly jammed, the water spout for the ice cream scoop began to leak on the floor.

•   •   •

Weeks went by and Kane walked through the community like a rockstar. He told everybody what they wanted to hear and rode the wave of popularity. He felt like he was glowing. Red hot, baby.

More weeks went by and it was no longer just small things going wrong. Incomplete food deliveries that cause last-minute changes to the menu, spoiled food in the pantry, recipe mishaps, broken equipment, and the staffing issues! Would he never be free of these infuriating staffing issues?

•   •   •

Unbeknownst to him, there is one who sees everything that goes on in the community. The true root cause of the current chaos in the dining department remained undetectable, but HR knew Kane was at the heart of it. They were constantly having to clean up his messes, all too often in the form of processing resignations for people who just wanted to escape, not complain. Rumor had it that all three female cooks had stories they were afraid to document about Kane's inappropriate jokes, unnecessary physical contact, and backhanded compliments on their job performance. And why was the white male cook allowed to slack off on the performance of duties he didn't care for, resulting in the Mexican-born female cook having to work harder to pick up his slack? When she got into an argument with him in the kitchen over the inequity, Kane reprimanded *her* for causing a disturbance. Again, no formal complaint, but the young Muslim woman Kane hired as a dining room server left quietly, telling HR she had to find a job where the manager would not require her to remove her head covering "because it wasn't part of the uniform". A very personable young man, much liked by the diners, who happened to start life as a female, never could seem to get enough hours on the schedule to make ends meet, so he moved on. Then there was the single mother whose childcare ended at 3:00pm whom Kane constantly pressured to work overtime or her hours would have to be cut. And the newlywed woman who kept getting called in to cover empty shifts on her days off, giving her no shared days off with her new wife.

Since no complaints were filed and the CEO didn't recognize any wrongdoing, HR was powerless to act.

• • •

Months went by and the Culinary Director at their sister community suddenly departed. Kane was offered a promotion, to rule, er "supervise", the dining departments of both communities.

Months went by and the chaos became noticeable to others. Vendors not paid, deliveries suspended, inaccurate timesheets, arguments, accusations, blame, resentment, good staff quitting, lazy and incompetent new hires, complaints from the diners.

• • •

HR was still watching, and the incidents were getting worse. Even if individual staff members would not file formal complaints, something had to get documented. HR started a file.

ADAMSON, KANE
INCIDENT REPORT 001
DATED ■■-■■-■■■■
Kane showed up in the kitchen with half an hour remaining in the lunch rush and heard that they had

run out of the special. He upbraided the cook in front of everyone in the kitchen, telling her she's incompetent and should have made more food. She tried to defend herself by swearing she prepared all the food provided for this meal. He warned her that if she can't do her job right, maybe she shouldn't be rewarded with the good shifts. The cook was afraid to point out that Kane is the one who plans and provisions the specials. He stormed back to his office after telling her it was up to her to think of something to serve the diners.

ADAMSON, KANE
INCIDENT REPORT 002
DATED ■■-■■-■■■■
Kane showed up just after the lunch rush to find his kitchen staff throwing away almost two full pans of that day's special. He berated the cook in front of everyone in the kitchen, telling her she's incompetent and shouldn't have made so much food. She tried to defend herself by reminding him that he ordered her to prepare all of the food provided for this meal. He warned her that if she can't do her job right, maybe she shouldn't be rewarded with the good shifts. The cook was afraid to point out that Kane is the one who plans and provisions the specials. He stormed back to his office after telling her she'd better quit wasting company money or he'd have to cut some waste, if she knows what he means.

ADAMSON, KANE
INCIDENT REPORT 003
DATED ■■-■■-■■■■
Kane entered the kitchen through the Out door, swinging it into a fully laden tray being carried out to the dining room by one of the servers. She managed to recover her balance and save all but one dessert plate,

which hit the floor with a crash. Kane snarled that he's tired of clumsy servers and maybe she can't be trusted to work the busy shifts. He stormed back to his office, leaving the server to clean up and plate a new dessert before delivering the meals.

ADAMSON, KANE
INCIDENT REPORT 004
DATED ■■-■■-■■■■

The loss rate on forks is unbelievably high. Kane repeatedly orders dozens more forks and yet there are never enough forks to get through a meal. Promising an irritated diner that he would get her a fork right away, he stormed in to berate the dishwasher — who keeps up a constant, diligent flow of dishes and utensils through the dish machine — for being lazy and incompetent. Maybe he shouldn't be trusted to work the busy shifts if he can't keep up. The dishwasher was afraid to point out that there are no forks currently being washed or ready to be washed. There are no forks. Kane stormed back to his office, leaving the diner with no fork.

ADAMSON, KANE
INCIDENT REPORT 005
DATED ■■-■■-■■■■

Kane told HR that he wants to fire "that Mexican kid" for not showing up to work his scheduled shifts. HR checked the official schedule online and saw that no schedule has been entered for this person or any other on Kane's staff. HR explained, again, that verbally informing or texting staff that you want them to work a certain shift is not proper company procedure, and no case can be made to terminate an employee based on job attendance if the online schedule and timesheet do not document the problem. Kane regaled HR with a tale of how overworked he is, that he just can't find time to enter the schedules, that the program is so confusing for someone who knows cuisine not computers (a favorite quip of his, apparently), and couldn't they help him out just this once? Just this once. Just this once. Just this once. He brings candy the next day.

ADAMSON, KANE
INCIDENT REPORT 006
DATED ■■-■■-■■■■

Kane planned a spectacular buffet dinner for the holiday. He told Maintenance to bring him the folding serving tables he'd need, and to make sure they're thoroughly cleaned and set up as he has directed. Maintenance reminded him that the serving tables are stored where the dining staff can easily get them, and providing and cleaning tables for a dining event isn't actually a Maintenance responsibility. Kane slumped into the guest chair in the CEO's office to impress upon him how exhausting it is trying to put on a great event and keep up with all of his own work, much less having to do someone else's work, too. He said he doesn't understand why Maintenance refuses to be a team player, shirking their responsibilities especially as they relate to Kane. The CEO called Maintenance in for a chat about teamwork, especially for big events like this. He brooked no argument, and Maintenance went to fetch and set up the tables. When the event was over, Kane told his staff that Maintenance would deal with the tables so they didn't have to, and he went home. The following morning, the CEO brought Maintenance in for another chat, pointing out that they didn't clean up, break down, and stow away the tables brought down for the event. Maintenance didn't think it would do any good to point out that their staff all go home by 4:00pm, whereas dining staff are on site until 7:30pm.

There was still plenty of room in the file folder. The watch continued.

Although HR couldn't put it into words, there seemed to be some kind of resistance, some kind of protection around Kane, that they were unable to overcome. And nothing could be done as long as the CEO was unwavering in his support.

•   •   •

Kane walked the razor's edge between confidence and anxiety, faking the confidence when he didn't actually feel it. But every ounce consumed brought more trouble. On the other hand, every ounce consumed brought him a sense of euphoria and the unshakeable belief that he was smarter and cleverer than ever. Better than everyone else and one step closer to his dreams. Yeah, his creative explanations would keep it all together. He was sure of it.

•   •   •

Only one ounce each week. A full seven days between doses. It was maddening. By his calculations, it would take 59 weeks to consume all of The Elixir. As the weeks stretched into months and the months stretched into a year, balancing his desire for The Ultimate Prize against the strictures of The Rules began to take its toll on Kane. To get him through the days in between, he began to draw more heavily on his private stash. His staff and some of the other directors noticed gaps in the day where Kane could not be found. He had an endless supply of excuses. It was a good thing The Elixir made him more creative. He didn't realize that the supplemental booze didn't have the same effect.

Worried, the CEO began keeping an eye on Kane. He wanted him to succeed, wanted to believe him when he explained away all the incidents, staffing problems, and strange disappearances. He gave Kane the benefit of the doubt right up until he walked in on one of his visits to his flask. There was no explaining this away. He was noticeably impaired in the middle of a work day. What the hell had he been thinking?

Kane was offered the choice of completing a recovery program in order to return to his job or tendering his resignation. He wasn't really interested in the "recovery program" but he'd be damned if he'd give up now. Six months he spent following a new set of rules, being on his best behavior, vowing that he'd changed his ways. Six months playing the good boy to get his job back, to get back into his office, to get back to The Bottle. He had to get back to The Bottle. That's what kept him going. He had to finish what he'd started. He had to finish The Bottle. After all he'd been through, he had earned The Ultimate Prize and no one was going to keep him from it. When he came back to the job, he made all the right speeches, he played well with others, he stayed within the lines. He did everything their way until at last he felt that their eyes weren't on him every moment of every day. Back in his office, he played by The Rules there, too.

Now he felt himself in a maddening race. Every week seemed to take longer to end, and the chaos and resentment built around him ever faster. Anxiety began to eat at him. Would he really be able to hold it all together long enough to finish The Bottle? Some people use cupcakes for self-soothing, but sweets had never been Kane's security blanket. He pulled out the flask. He'd been doing this for more years than he could remember. He knew how to use the booze to quell the anxiety, relax, feel more confident. He wouldn't overdo it this time. Or get caught.

He knew now, however, that he could not safely imbibe The Elixir and the contents of the flask in the same day any more. Every ounce of The Elixir had gotten stronger than the last, until now, with less than an inch of liquid left in The Bottle, each sip spun his thoughts and slipped him further out of the reality of the workplace. The euphoria was intoxicating in itself. It induced vivid visions of his fabulous future: wealth, accolades, and plenty of time to sip handcrafted umbrella drinks on a private beach somewhere while his servants, er "staff", kept his empire running. The sound of footsteps in the hall outside his door snapped him out of his daydream and plunged him into anxiety and paranoia again.

His mind scrambled for creative excuses and workarounds to hold it all together until the end. He knew, he just knew, that the moment he drained The Bottle and achieved The Ultimate Prize, all these troubles would fall away and never bother him again. The label had promised that the whole world would be structured to serve and support him, whatever he wanted he could have with no consequences to himself.

•   •   •

The end of another week. There was so little left in The Bottle now that he thought he should be able to see the message at the bottom, but there didn't seem to be anything there. He worried for a moment that there was no Ultimate Prize but shoved that horrifying thought aside and reminded himself that the label said the message would only appear after the last ounce had been drunk. But he was so close now! Surely there was only one ounce left! Today was the day, it had to be! He picked up The Bottle, twisted off the cap, and poured another dose into the shot glass. It wasn't the last. There would be one more. Only one more. Just one more week to wait. One more week. He broke down in tears. He was so tired of having to wait, of having to deal with all of these burdensome mundanities weighing him down and holding him back from greatness: managing the staff and all their petty problems, making the schedules and checking the timesheets, creating the menus and buying the food, inventorying and ordering the supplies, reviewing the invoices and forwarding them for payment, balancing the department's budget, planning events, attending meetings, hiring new staff members to replace the ones who fell victim to his machinations. He was better than this! He deserved better than this!

The old desire pulled at his veins, the fiery addiction, whispering rationalizations in the back of his mind. He didn't dare break The Rules of The Bottle, but he would damn sure break the rules of recovery. He pulled out the flask and took a long pull. He had forgotten his own rule about not drinking from the flask the same day he took The Elixir.

The effect was immediate and devastating. He fell into his chair in a stupor. His door was open and people walked by, pausing to try to rouse him. Eventually, someone notified the CEO. By the time he looked in the door, Kane was awake and trying desperately to act normal. His movements were carefully controlled to look casual, his answers enunciated to prevent slurring. It would have made a great comedy routine in the tradition of Foster Brooks if it hadn't been so tragic. It was clear to the CEO that Kane wasn't tracking what was going on, the seriousness of the situation. The man seemed to think he had everyone fooled. Kane, of course, thought he did. He believed The Elixir made him untouchable.

·　　·　　·

The CEO looked at the sad figure of a man who had wrestled with his demons and lost. With as little drama as possible, he had Kane escorted from the building. Gone. He was gone. It was all gone. Kane's carefully constructed world came apart. For want of a week, it was all gone in an hour. He never felt the tendrils release him, but he noticed their absence once he sobered up. He felt empty, abandoned. When the CEO cleared out Kane's office, he poured out the last ounce of the cheap bourbon the man had apparently sacrificed his career for, and he recycled the plastic bottle.

Kane never got the message.

Dominick Cancilla pays his bills by working in a tiny box in a big company in Southern California. He's sold a few novels, but much prefers working on short stories. If you run into him in public, be sure to ask how his wife's lizards are doing.

•   •   •

My little sister once received a Holly Hobbie doll that was almost as big as she was. It's been almost fifty years, and my sister now has a husband and children, but she remains my little sister and one of the most important people in my life. For Holly Hobbie's part, she has a place in my sister's home and is still as loved as she ever was, but doesn't look quite as big as she used to. As your life passes, you can never be sure which things will change and which will remain the same, but watching the world progress is the joy of being alive.

HEIDI BIG AS ME

DOMINICK CANCILLA

"AM I BEING RIDICULOUS?" Georgia asked as she completed the third circuit of her tiny apartment in as many minutes. "The place doesn't have to be immaculate. Leilani's not going to care. She's from IT, not Fastidious Central."

Heidi sat on her chair by the bed and said nothing. At a couple inches over six feet tall, she was as big as Georgia and looked as much like a real person as a thing handcrafted from cloth could be. Heidi was a good listener and Georgia took their lifelong friendship practically for granted.

"Why did I put my desk in the bedroom?" Georgia asked. "It's awkward. Do you think it's awkward?"

She dropped to sit on the bed, hard enough to bounce a little bit. The comforter was a crazy quilt Aunt Thea had made to keep Georgia warm when she moved to the city, and it still looked as good as new. She ran a hand along it for the familiar feel of stitched panels as she leaned toward the bedside table where a framed drawing of her family stood. Roman — her brother — had drawn it so she'd always know what those she'd left behind looked like.

Georgia squinted a little at the drawing. Remmi — Roman's twin — had a bandage on his hand. She hadn't noticed that before. In her desk drawer was a well-worn letter from Grandma Vesta that described in detail how the family was doing. Georgia would have to see if it said anything about Remmi's hand.

Later. She'd look at the letter later.

"I know, I know," Georgia said. "I'm letting myself get distracted. But distracted from what? Pacing and fretting?"

Heidi's supportive silence was a comfort. Georgia avoided considering how weird that might seem to anyone else.

When Georgia moved from the little logging town of Silvanus to take a job with Project Placement, she'd intended to leave Heidi behind. It was a foolish notion, an attempt to act like an adult rather than just be who she was. Dad had built her a trunk that held everything she needed for her new apartment, and sure enough, when she started unpacking, there was Heidi right on top.

Thank goodness for that.

Georgia hadn't known how lonely it would be working remotely from an apartment. When she accepted the job, she assumed that being on the telephone or video calls most of the day would be socialization enough. It wasn't. Fortunately, Heidi was an ideal roommate — pleasant company, always at hand, never in the way. They complemented each other perfectly.

If Heidi could talk, she might have pointed out that if all they needed was each other, Georgia wouldn't be feeling so aflutter about meeting her coworker in person for the first time. But Heidi couldn't talk and Georgia was terrible at introspection. Which was why she'd almost left Heidi behind in the first place.

Mom liked to say *A journey of a thousand miles begins with a single misstep.* It was funny, but it was also true. Just like when Georgia had been fretting about whether or not to take the job and Mom said *You can't drown in the same river twice.* A simple mistake can lead you far afield; chances are worth taking because at worst you will learn something.

That philosophy wasn't Mom's alone. As insular as a mountain town populated mainly by your relatives and in-laws might be, everyone in Silvanus dispensed heart-felt encouragement when it came to finding your way in life. Some people moved out and only came back to visit. Some returned with wives and husbands to log or build furniture or join one of the other businesses that had kept the town prosperous for more than a century.

Georgia was letting her thoughts distract her again.

The little bedside clock read a quarter to eleven. Fifteen minutes left until Leilani would arrive to fix the computer. Georgia forced herself off of the bed and went into the living room, if only for a change of scenery while she fretted.

She should put on some music. Should she put on some music? What would she even put on? Georgia didn't know a thing about what was currently popular or what might make a good impression. She had a mild obsession with show tunes, so those were the only playlists she had on her phone. Her favorite was *Paint Your Wagon,* but only because the song about talking to trees reminded her of Aunt Thea. Listening to it always made her cry.

Forget that. No music.

She re-straightened the throw pillows on the couch; octuple-checked that the home-decorating books on the trunk she used as a coffee table were stacked regularly and aligned with the trunk's edges. She supposed she could check her hair again, but it wasn't important. Realistically, people either couldn't get past her height or didn't much care about her appearance at all.

The clock on the DVR warned that there were two minutes left. Assuming that Leilani wasn't late. Or lost. Or flakey. Or dead.

Georgia had a moment of panic when she patted the pocket of her jeans and didn't find her phone. How was she supposed to buzz Leilani in without her phone? Hadn't she had it when she was thinking about her playlists? Where had she put it?

Calm. She willed herself calm. What was there to panic about? Atop the shelves under the wall-mounted television was a hardback-sized box Dad had made to hold things she'd lost. Georgia opened it, took out her phone, closed the box again.

And then just stood there.

Phone in her hand.

Like a performing robot waiting for the show to start.

"I'm officially an idiot," Georgia said, loud enough to be heard by Heidi in the next room.

Saying that didn't inspire her to do anything, though. Thankfully, just when panic was starting to build itself up again, the phone rang.

"Hello?" Georgia asked. She answered so quickly that it was obvious she'd been waiting with a hand on the phone. Embarrassing.

"This is Leilani from Project Placement IT," said a voice that Georgia recognized from Zoom meetings and tech-support calls. "Here to fix your computer?"

"Come on in," Georgia said. "Up the stairs on the right. Unit 201."

She was supposed to push the star on the phone to buzz the door open but hit zero twice before getting it right, subjecting Leilani to a couple phone tones before the door unlocked.

Georgia was just starting to berate herself for that particular act of brilliance when another problem came into focus: Would opening the apartment door before Leilani got there seem weird? Or would it seem weird to wait for her to knock when Georgia obviously knew she was there? Why hadn't she figured that out instead of spending the whole morning tidying an apartment that was already immaculate?

Georgia settled on listening at the door and then opening it right as Leilani got there. It was supposed to look like humorously perfect timing, but Georgia remembered too late that someone of her height suddenly appearing in a doorway would be startling to some people.

Fortunately, Leilani didn't seem to be one of those people.

She had jeans and a chambray shirt, hair just orange enough not to be natural, and a workmanly backpack slung over one shoulder. Leilani was about a head shorter than Georgia and had a glorious variety of earrings, particularly impressive to Georgia, whose squeamishness made her the only one of her siblings without pierced ears.

"Georgia, right?" Leilani asked, looking genuinely happy to be there.

"Georgia," Georgia said, only realizing that made no sense when Leilani's eyebrows went up and her mouth and eyes made a *you want to try that again?* expression. "I mean, yes. You're Leilani?"

"Got it in one," Leilani said.

"Come on in," Georgia said, standing back from the door. "Sorry about the mess," she added, as if she was in a bad sitcom. Where had that come from?

Leilani took it in stride. "Oh, please. I just came from a house where it looks like they did oil changes in the living room. You do remote customer support, right?"

Georgia nodded. Project Placement offered remote one-on-one consultation for people doing home-renovation projects, and she was one of their highest-rated "craft-sultants." Like everyone else in her family, she'd been brought up helping fix things, which made her a natural for the job.

"Interesting," Leilani said. "Most of you guys, your place is a mess. Half-built projects, repairs in progress, a big workbench covered in dust and chaos — that kind of thing. This place looks like a princess lives here."

Had she just called Georgia a princess? Georgia blushed at the possibility. "Thanks. There's a storage facility a block down and I rent a space there to use as a workroom. That's where my mess is." It was actually pretty tidy, but Georgia didn't want to sound pretentious. "I mostly make furniture," she added.

"Really?" Leilani asked, sounding genuinely interested. She looked around the room again, as if trying to see it with new eyes. "You make any of this?"

"The end table, the bookshelves, the table and chair by the window, racks in the kitchen, picture frames — things like that. My dad and uncle made the sofa. I don't enjoy upholstering."

"But you could do it if you had to?"

"If I had to."

"Impressive."

Georgia shrugged. "I guess. It was like tools were my toys growing up, so that stuff's second nature."

"Mine were mostly plastic horses, but that didn't really pay off vocationally. You're not so much into computer repair, I take it?"

"Nope. Not my thing."

"Fortunately, it's mine. So where's the beast I'm here to paper train?"

"On my desk," Georgia said.

"Okay," Leilani said.

"In the bedroom," Georgia said.

"Okay," Leilani said again.

Then they just stood there.

"It might be easier if we got closer," Leilani said after a moment.

"Right! Of course. I zoned out for a minute there."

"It happens."

They went into the bedroom. Georgia indicated the desk in the corner, where a laptop computer sat centered between two large monitors, one displaying a login screen.

"Go ahead and log in," Leilani said, dropping her backpack to the floor next to the desk.

Georgia sat in the desk's chair, logged in.

"Show me what happens when you try to get online," Leilani said.

Georgia launched the web browser and waited for the corporate intranet to auto-load. She was confronted with the same error message as when they'd gone through troubleshooting steps on the phone.

"Got it," Leilani said. "Sometimes there's some subtle thing you're doing wrong that I can't tell unless I see you do it, but that all looked right to me. Go ahead and log out. I'll take it from there."

A few moments later, Leilani was seated at the desk, logged in with the administrative account, checking system settings.

"What kind of things do people sometimes do that you can't tell over the phone?" Georgia asked.

"Lots of things," Leilani said, her fingers continuing the work as she talked. "Since you don't have an internet connection, I couldn't remotely share your screen, so that makes it harder to detect problems. I used to live with a woman who read an article on cybersecurity and convinced herself that she had to keep her computer's Wi-Fi off so she wouldn't get hacked. We talked about possible reasons for her lack of internet, but it wasn't until I saw her disconnect Wi-Fi after startup that I realized what the problem was. I'd assumed she was using the wired connection."

"But she wasn't."

"Nope — for security reasons, of course."

"That's pretty crazy."

"Pretty Crazy? That was my stage name!"

"What?"

"My stage name? Get it? It's like — it's a joke. Like 'Hot Yoga? That was my stage name!' 'Nipple Shields? That was my stage name!' 'Hippo Critical —'"

"Oh! Got it. I get it. For a second I thought maybe you did improv or something."

"Nope. That's just a thing my girlfriend and I used to do. It's a habit."

"Your girlfriend?"

"Ex, really. The woman I used to live with."

"Used to."

"Right. She was nice, but maybe too nice, if you know what I mean?"

"Not really."

"She didn't know how to turn people down or put them off. There were all these guys who hounded around her because she wouldn't just tell them she was gay and in a relationship. I called her Hotel California because guys would check her out and then never leave."

Georgia barked a laugh and slapped a hand over her own mouth to stifle it.

"Liked that one, did you?" Leilani asked.

"It sort of got me by surprise."

"I caught that. Better than you not getting it at all." She pulled the chair a little back from the desk. "It's going to run a diagnostic for a few minutes. You don't have to hang around if there's other stuff you need to do."

"Not really."

"This part isn't exactly fascinating."

"That's okay."

Leilani's gaze drifted around the room, finally settling on Heidi in the chair on the other side of the bed. "Whoa — that is one large doll."

"That's Heidi," Georgia said. "My grandmother made her and gave her to me when I was born."

"Impressive. How big is she?"

"She's as big as me."

"That's insane."

Georgia had allowed herself to become so relaxed in the conversation that the insult almost felt like a slap. "What do you mean?"

"It's crazy tall."

"You think my height is crazy?"

Leilani turned quickly from Heidi to Georgia. "No! I'm sorry. I didn't mean it like that. I mean it's an unusual height for a doll. I didn't mean you."

Georgia relaxed, relieved. "Oh, right. That's true about dolls. I thought you meant the other thing because — well, I get a lot of comments on my height. I'm kind of sensitive on the subject."

"I bet you are. I get some of that about my hair, but that's not really the same thing. I like your height, though. It works for you."

"Thanks."

"But the doll — Heidi?"

"Right."

"That's amazing for a doll. And she was literally a birthday present? Crazy gift for a newborn."

"Not really. She was like a sister. My older brothers are twins, so it's like she was my twin."

"More like a big sister."

"Why do you say that?"

"Well, when you were a kid, Heidi was what — four times your height?"

"No. Heidi is my height."

"She is now, but I mean when you were a kid."

"She's always been my height."

"You mean you had a little doll when you were little but got bigger ones as you grew?"

"No, just Heidi."

"Then your grandma altered her?"

"No."

"You don't mean she changed on her own."

"She didn't change. Heidi was my height when she was given to me; she's my height now. She's always been my height."

The computer beeped. Leilani turned back to it. "There's your problem. Your ethernet port isn't responding."

"Am I going to need a new computer?"

"No need to bring a gun to a pie fight. It's probably just an old driver. We've been having an issue with automatic updates not catching everything." She picked up her backpack, got out a thumb drive, plugged it into the computer, typed some commands.

When it seemed like Leilani wasn't needing to concentrate so much, Georgia said, "I liked the pie-fight comment."

"Thanks," Leilani said, smiling. "It's one of my dad's."

"My mom says things like that," Georgia said, happy for the distraction from Heidi. "She once said my cousin was such a pessimist that he couldn't decide if a glass was half empty or half full of poison."

"My dad said, 'It's the thought that counts, but you can only count so high.'"

"There's clearly a chance our parents are related."

"I hope not." Leilani took her hands off the keyboard and relaxed against the back of the chair again. "More waiting while the computer does its thing. Just for security reasons, can you tell me if anyone else uses the laptop?"

"It's just me," Georgia said. "I moved here right when everyone started working remote, and I found that after sharing a room with a cousin most of my life, I enjoyed the solitude."

"I get it. Wish I'd learned that lesson so easily. After the ex I told you about left, I felt like I needed to get that void filled immediately and basically hooked up with the first person who showed any interest. Big mistake. Ex-two and I barely got along and her cooking tasted like a vacuum cleaner smells."

"Sounds like a nightmare. The cooking, I mean. I've got nothing against living with someone."

"Me either. I'll just be more selective next time."

"Right."

The computer plodded through its task; the moment stretched.

Had silence always felt so uncomfortable? Georgia wished she had more experience with people and less with dolls and furniture. Right when it was almost too awkward for Georgia to stand, the computer beeped.

"Good to go," Leilani said. "Just got to reboot and we'll see if that did the trick." She clicked a couple icons and the machine started to cycle off.

"I know making house calls is a pain," Georgia said. "I appreciate you coming out."

Leilani looked like she was going to say something but let it go. "We may be the only women working out of this office," Leilani said instead. "If we don't support each other, nobody will."

"I get that," Georgia said. "When I went in to sign my paperwork on the first day, the HR guy was practically giddy when he realized I checked off two boxes on his diversity scorecard."

"More like a bingo card. It's all a government-regulation game to that clown. He thinks Diversity is a city full of divers."

"Oh, that — that was truly terrible," Georgia said, grinning far more than the pun warranted.

"Can't argue there," Leilani replied with a grin of her own. She looked back at the computer, which was showing the login screen again. "Go ahead and log in," she said, getting up from the chair.

Georgia did.

While they waited for the initial programs to load, Leilani asked, "Do you mind if I ask about the doll again? I don't think I'm getting it."

Georgia shrugged. "I'm not sure what there is to get. Heidi is my height and has always been my height. It's like my scarf. My brother knitted it for me for my eighteenth birthday. It's my favorite color."

Leilani looked confused. "I don't see how that's the same."

"When I got the scarf, my favorite color was sky blue."

"Your brother made you a sky-blue scarf."

"He made me a scarf that's my favorite color." She gestured to a spot by the bedroom door where a set of hand-made coat pegs was attached to the wall. From one of these hung a deep burgundy scarf. "See?"

"I don't see a blue scarf."

"There is no blue scarf. There's a scarf that's my favorite color. These days, my favorite color is burgundy."

Leilani turned back to her. "That doesn't make any sense."

"I'm not sure how to explain it any better. When I moved out here, my father gave me a locket to wear in good health, so I never worried about the pandemic. One of my brothers made me a little leather purse with lunch money in it so even if my luck soured, I'd never go hungry."

"Unless you had to spend the money."

"I have spent the money, lots of times."

"What about when it runs out?"

"What do you mean runs out? It's a purse with lunch money in it."

"You can't have infinite money in a purse."

"I don't. I have enough for lunch." The home page of the Project Placement intranet popped up on the computer screen. "Look! You got it working!"

"Glad I could help," Leilani said. She picked up her backpack, put her thumb drive back in it, slung it over her shoulder. "This has definitely been interesting. You need anything else from Planet IT?"

"No, but can you hang on one second?" Georgia asked. She pulled open a drawer in the desk, rummaged around for a moment.

"What's up?"

"I want to show you something. I really enjoyed talking to you."

"I liked talking to you, too. I don't think I completely get where you are coming from, but I feel like something was clicking in there somewhere."

Georgia pulled a little book from the drawer. It was thin with a marbled cover on which embossed letters read *Important Contacts*.

"Oh, wow. You have a phone book?" Leilani asked. "I don't think I've seen one of those since I was a kid."

"My grandpa made it for me. He makes paper and binds books for a hobby."

"He made that? From scratch?"

"Yes. He even made the paper using wood from the first tree I helped fell."

"That is some serious stuff. Do you actually use it as a phone book? I mean, instead of using your phone contacts?"

"This is easier," Georgia said. She opened the book, began to flip through the pages.

"You have incredible handwriting," Leilani said.

"Mine's terrible," Georgia countered. "Grandpa has always been proud of his penmanship." She stopped flipping pages toward the middle of the book, held it open, and pointed to an entry.

The entry was for Leilani, in the same handwriting as the rest of the book, carefully nestled between two other entries in alphabetical order.

"That's me," Leilani said.

"It is."

"That's my phone number and email address."

"Right."

"Why is it in your phone book?"

"It's in my book of important contacts."

"Why?"

"Apparently, it's important."

They looked at each other, things moving unsaid between them.

Georgia closed the book and put it back in the drawer. She got up, smiled, gestured for Leilani to move toward the living room.

"You mind if I call you sometime outside work hours?" Georgia asked.

"I'd like that," Leilani said. "You're weird, but in a good way. I don't get to say that about a lot of people."

"Me, too," Georgia answered, unsure whether that had made sense. She opened the front door.

"You know," Leilani said as she walked into the hall, "I changed my personal phone number after my last breakup. I haven't even had that one for a month. How long have you had that book?"

"I'll call soon," Georgia said, ignoring the question; not wanting to lose the moment.

"You do that," Leilani replied before turning toward the stairs.

Georgia watched her go, then closed the apartment door, leaned against it, and hugged herself tight with a squeal of delight. That done, she practically ran to the bedroom. There were a thousand thoughts rushing through her head and Heidi needed to hear every single one.

Jon Hansen (he/his) is a writer, librarian, and occasional blood donor. He lives about fifty feet from Boston with his wife, son, and three pushy cats. His short fiction and poetry have appeared in a variety of places, including *Strange Horizons*, *Daily Science Fiction*, and *Apex Magazine*. He enjoys tea and cheese, and until recently spent entirely too much time on Twitter.

•   •   •

The idea for this story was a combination of events. I'd moved to the Boston area with my family not long before COVID hit, and, as a result, I'd had trouble finding a new position. It got to where I was considering TaskRabbit work to pass the time. During this time, I was walking a lot, exploring our new home, and, in my wanderings, I discovered this ornate brick house that looked like it would be a good house for a wizard. Naturally, a wizard would need really weird odd jobs done, and things grew from there.

EASY MONEY

JON HANSEN

L ARS LOOKED AT THE GPS and frowned. Yep, this was it. Set among the apartment buildings lining the edge of the Boston fens, his destination looked like a decayed castle: walls covered in winding ivy around a six-sided tower flying a tattered banner. The whole thing was surrounded by a brick wall topped with spikes, and a heavy wooden gate. Were those gargoyles on top?

"Easy money, my ass," he muttered to himself.

Lars was used to ugly jobs. He'd worked security at Lucky Nick's for years, tossing drunks getting handy. Now too many didn't take him seriously, and wouldn't give up until he got extreme. The third time an ambulance hauled someone off, Nick gave him a drink, then let him go. "It's bad for business."

"So now what?"

Nick sighed. "Tell you what. If you can raise the dough, you can buy a share of the club. Pays good dividends. Easy money." Lars's mom had always said there was no such thing, but that never stopped Lars.

Lars opened up the ChoreBadger app. His cousin Erik used it, said it'd be perfect. Weird jobs, but paid well. Lars felt like a robot's errand boy, but money was money. He was most of the way there, he just needed a bit more.

The cartoon mascot snarled its slogan at him ("Tough guys for tough jobs!") and then opened to his queue. He slipped on his cheaters to read the tiny print.

DO NOT LEAVE OUTSIDE GATE. RING BELL AND WAIT.

Lars checked his watch. Half past three. Plenty of time to make it to his sister Tina's place in Quincy for dinner.

He got out and popped the trunk. Inside sat the package, a small thing covered in butcher paper, one side covered in foreign stamps and weird alphabets. Lars was 100% sure it hadn't gone through customs.

The app had sent him to a rundown house in Queens near the bay, where a stone-faced woman handed it over. Lars wondered if she was getting paid too, but didn't ask. First rule of easy money was not to ask questions. A six hour drive later and now he was almost done.

He carried the package to where a large brass button was mounted beside the gate. He pressed it. Far off behind the wall, a faint buzz sounded. Satisfied, he stepped back to wait.

Half an hour later, Lars was pretty sure someone had screwed up somewhere, and it wasn't him. He'd triple-checked the app for the delivery date, called the client direct only to be pushed straight into voicemail, and pressed the button at least a dozen more times. Lars got a weird flutter at the pit of his stomach. He recognized it. Something had gone sideways.

If it was up to him, he'd just keep waiting. Tina would be mad, of course, and would serve him up a helping of guilt. He'd let her down before, of course. He didn't want to do it again, but he would if he had to. No delivery, no money.

The bigger problem was with him hanging around here. Across the street sat a row of brownstones, and he'd noticed a couple people notice him. He knew how it looked. This was the kind of neighborhood where, if he stayed long enough, some anxious citizen might call the cops. Just to be safe. Tina had said he had a naturally suspicious looking face.

Lars pulled his phone out again and checked with support. AutoHelp advised documenting everything in case of a complaint, but to otherwise follow the client's wishes to the best of his ability.

"Inside the gate they want?" said Lars out loud. "All right, inside the gate they'll get."

He eyed the wall. Lars was a big guy, but the wall stood twice his height and looked not at all climbable, even without the spikes. And in this neighborhood? Last thing he needed was to get grabbed on another B&E.

Still, there were other options. He shook the package gently, listening for anything fragile sounding inside, then gave it a few tentative squeezes. Clearly this thing had traveled a long way. Who was to say that, if something broke, it hadn't happened well before Lars entered the picture? Besides, a package like this had to be insured, and Lars couldn't see any cameras. Satisfied with his reasoning, he turned back to the wall. Then he gave the package a two-handed toss, just enough force to get it over the wall.

To his surprise, just as the package passed over, the nearest gargoyle moved. With the swipe of a clawed hand, it batted the box away back towards the driveway.

"What the hell?" Lars stared. The gargoyle had resumed its original pose, with no hint it had moved. Was that really a person in some kind of crazy outfit? Curious, he threw a pebble at it.

The pebble bounced off the gargoyle's head with the sound of stone on stone. The gargoyle didn't move. Lars shook his head.

"Can't be real," he said. "Maybe it's some kinda weird security system. Robot arm with a fancy-pants sensor." Even saying it out loud didn't convince himself. Lars picked up the package. He shook it cautiously, listening for anything broken. Nothing.

"Okay, look," he said up to the gargoyle. "This package is supposed to be delivered here. See, whoever lives here is paying me but no one's answering." He held his phone up. "Just need to get it over this wall. Got it? I'm going to try again, just ... let it go, okay?"

Lars felt eyes upon him as he stepped back. Holding the package like an aging quarterback, he felt like an idiot. He shook it off. What counted here were results.

He gave the package a couple test pumps, then threw it in a high arc with plenty of force. Up it sailed, high enough to pass over the gargoyles by several feet.

To his shock, the gargoyle stretched itself out to its full length. Huge batwings unfurled to block the package's flight. As Lars gaped, the gargoyle seized the package with its claws and hurled it back to the ground. This time it bounced. Before the package landed again, the gargoyle had dropped back into place, once more an unmoving statue.

Lars swore. A corner of the package now looked torn, most likely from the gargoyle's claw. "Great," he muttered.

As he bent to grab the package, it moved. Not much, but it definitely moved. Lars straightened up, instincts on alert. He took a step back, then another.

Something exploded out of one end, a small blur charging straight at him. Pain exploded in his ankle as the whatever-it-was wrapped itself around his foot. Lars fell backwards, landing hard on his ass.

Lars kicked at the thing, whatever it was, to no avail. All he could tell was it was small and mean. It kept attacking his ankle, jabbing at it over and over with what felt like red hot needles, tearing at the skin. If this kept up, it'd strip his foot to the bone.

He half-crawled, half-stumbled to his car, and flung open the door. The needles had started moving up his leg, towards more sensitive areas. He fumbled open the glove compartment.

Inside was a Kevlar glove. He'd picked it up for jobs where the homeowners had guard dogs. Rottweilers and German Shepherds, not Tasmanian devils. He yanked it on and grabbed at the thing. Clothes and flesh tore as he gripped it by its neck and pulled. He gasped for air as he looked at it.

It looked like a little man made from gray clay, but without a face. At the ends of its little arms, in place of hands, were sharp metal hooks. It thrashed with rage, tearing at the glove, but it couldn't work free. Lars just held it, and after a minute, the clay man stopped. It seemed to be waiting for Lars to do something.

Keeping his grip tight, Lars picked up the box. Inside it was filled with inflated plastic balloons. A weird smell wafted from the opening, and he felt dizzy for a moment.

"Be grumpy too if I woke up from my nap," said Lars. "I don't suppose you'd be willing to go back into your box?"

The little person began ripping at his hand again with those hooks.

"Would it help if I said I was sorry?"

The creature ignored him, only kept struggling.

As Lars wondered how he'd get paid now, he heard a sound. He turned.

In the still-closed gate, a small door slid open. Through it stepped a three-headed dog. It was medium sized, covered in black fur. The three heads looked to be a Doberman, a German Shepherd, and, of all things, a Chihuahua.

"Okay," said Lars. "This is some real Addams Family bull crap."

The three heads turned and growled at him in unison. Then it charged.

In a flash Lars dropped the box and scrambled up on the hood of the car, an impressive feat considering his size, the agony radiating from his ankle, and that he still gripped the little clay man. The dog barked up at him in a variety of tones, all promising bites.

To hell with it. His best option now was to cut his losses and beat it.

He threw the clay man at the open doggy door. Still waving its arms, it hit the ground and bounced through the opening. With luck it would head to the house, and whoever ordered it could deal with it. Now he just had to get in his car.

Easier said than done, however. As Lars started to jump down, the dog ran over, its three sets of jaws snapping at anything in range. Lars jerked back. Could he get down off the other side and then in the car without getting bitten? The Chihuahua head looked particularly angry.

As he weighed the odds, the clay man charged back through the doggy door. Lars tensed. It could probably use those hooks to pull itself up the side of the car, and then he was screwed.

To his surprise, the clay man instead went for a closer target. It leapt on the three-headed dog and seized hold of its fur. The dog made an alarmed sound, heads whirling to see what had happened. The clay man started tearing at the dog with its hooks. Fur flew as the dog's heads howled in unison.

As Lars watched, the dog twisted and writhed, trying to escape, as the clay man held on like a bronco rider. No matter what the dog did or how it struggled, it couldn't escape. Finally, it ran back through the doggy door, whining in protest.

As quick as he could, Lars hopped down and scooped up the box. Before the doggy door could close, he shoved the torn end of the package inside to wedge the door open. As he hoped, the address label was visible but the torn side not. "Good enough," he said. Grim satisfaction filled him as he took a picture and uploaded it to ChoreBadger. A green checkbox appeared, and he smiled. That done, he gave the box a kick, nudging it free, and the doggy door slid shut.

Lars looked up at the gargoyles. "Hope you enjoyed the show," he said. Now that it was over, the adrenaline holding him up drained away. He limped back to the car, exhausted. He needed bandages, a soak and a meal.

He felt eyes on him as he drove away.

•   •   •

Lars dabbed at a bit of sauce on his chin with a napkin. Around him sat Tina and her kids, chowing down on another of her pasta concoctions. "What's this one called?" he said.

Tina paused, smile lines crinkling around her eyes. "Smaldino sauce. You like it?"

"Magical," he said, and she beamed.

Tina often experimented when cooking, adding all sorts of spices and extra ingredients, and then naming the results after people. Flavors she liked got named after friends. Mrs. Smaldino lived up the block and sometimes came by with coffee cake.

In his pocket Lars's phone bugled, Nick's ring. "Sorry, gotta take this." Tina rolled her eyes, but said nothing. His ankle pain had faded to a dull ache, present but ignorable, and a moment later he had slipped out the back door to stand in the night air, phone at his ear. "Hey, Nick. What's up?"

An unfamiliar voice answered. "So nice to speak to my deliveryman."

Lars pulled his phone away from his ear. The contact did say LUCKY NICK. He hung up.

The phone rang again, still reading LUCKY NICK. Lars pressed Ignore Call. The phone kept ringing, but the ID changed to ALWAYS ANSWER. Finally, Lars did. "How'd you do that?" he said.

"Not important," said the voice on the other end. Lars couldn't tell anything about its owner, only ambiguity. "I have some comments about your delivery methods."

"Yeah?" A spark of his old anger flared. "Well, I got a complaint about your package, considering it tried to rip off my foot."

"You did try to throw it over the fence. Twice." The voice chuckled. "That makes homunculi rather irritable. I had quite a time getting it away from my dog."

"They deserved each other. Look, this isn't FedEx. Next time do what you said you'd do and be there." Lars set his jaw. "What do you want? Your money back?"

"Oh, no. I'm not unhappy, not at all." Lars thought he could hear a smile in the voice. "Your persistence and ingenuity are impressive. I've sent you a bonus."

"Enough to cover the doc's bill, I hope?"

"Of course." There was real amusement now. "I'll be in touch. I have other … chores for someone of your skills. Easy money." The line clicked and went dead.

Lars pulled up his bank account and whistled. Twice the original fee, with no cut taken out by ChoreBadger. That much closer to the buy-in, but still.

He looked up at the night for another moment, and sighed. "Mom was right. No such thing as easy money."

N.L. Sweeney has been writing since they were old enough to spell (poorly). Some of their works have appeared in *Flash Fiction Magazine, Unbound III: Goodbye Earth, Sublunary Review*, and *Clamor*. When not writing, they busy themselves with escaping into video games, cuddling their puppy, and drinking ungodly amounts of Earl Grey tea.

•　　　•　　　•

I wrote this after my brother, Ben, and I had a conversation about an app that streamlined demonic possession. The development of this story owes a lot to the state of things during the COVID-19 pandemic. Like so many people, I felt powerless. I tried working on other stories during that time, but I kept coming back to that conversation about surrendering responsibility, stress, and control to a lower power. Ultimately, I decided to put the concept to paper, and "Connection Established" was the result.

CONNECTION ESTABLISHED

N.L. SWEENEY

"WHAT I DON'T GET," said Austin, for perhaps the third time that day, "is why you won't at least give the app a try."

I got that squirming feeling in my stomach again. The kind I always got when I had to defend my decisions to someone who didn't want to listen. But that wasn't the only reason I felt that way. InfernaList was a special case.

Austin sat back in his chair, giving the coffee sleeve a little spin. "You don't even have to pay anything," he said. "The UI design alone makes it worth checking out."

Beside me, Heather shook her head, the purple curls of her weave shaking into her face. She tossed the strands aside with a flick. "Look, Austin, if Beth says they don't want to try, they don't want to try," she said. "Stop being such a man and actually listen to what they're saying."

Austin furled his brow in defeat, casting one last glance my way, the promise that this discussion wasn't over.

Austin had been my roommate since high school — one of the few who knew me before I started going by Beth. He was a good guy — smart too. But he was also an expert mansplainer when it came to new apps.

Ever since InfernaList had popped up, Austin had been hounding me to try it. It wasn't anything religious that stopped me. I'd stopped believing in the Christian white man in the sky a long time ago, though with the implications of this app, maybe I'd been too quick to reach for my atheist card.

InfernaList officially came out two weeks ago, developed by a guy named Fahad Remberra, who, if the stories were true, had been contacted by a demon four weeks ago. The copy on the app store promised to match users with demonic specialists who could "take the wheels" for "the necessary but unpleasant tasks that bog down life." In other words, the app was a glorified possession matchmaker.

Austin had opted into the beta three weeks ago. He'd used one of the demonic specialists to to help him play the stock market and had made two grand that first week. His Instagram page had looked fresh, too, but he claimed that was inspiration and not one of the demonic specialists.

Austin set down his empty cup, hands pressed together in a plea. "Can I just say one more thing?"

I rolled my eyes. But nodded.

"You shouldn't encourage him," Heather chastised. She pushed up from the table, holding a hand in front of Austin's face before he could speak. "You want anything? I can't sit through another pitch."

"I'm good," I said. I'd been nursing the same cup of iced white chocolate mocha since we'd arrived. The ice had melted during Austin's second monologue.

"I'll take a chocolate chip cookie," Austin said, poking his head up over her hand. Heather frowned down at him, but he just smiled. "Warmed up, if you could."

She shook her head, stepping into the line and pulling out her phone.

Turning back to him, I said, "She'd probably like you more if you weren't so pushy."

Austin shrugged. "I prefer things this way," he said. "It keeps me sharp."

Sipping my watered-down white chocolate mocha, I motioned for Austin to continue.

"At least give it a try while it's still free," Austin said. "Word is the developer is looking to move to a subscription model for 2.0."

"Who was it that said if you aren't paying for it, you are the product?" I asked.

Austin waved his hand. "Some asshole, probably," he said. "There's nowhere for them to even send your information. You think cosmic creatures care about your demographics?"

"They made an app, didn't they?"

"Everyone makes apps these days," Austin said, throwing up his hands. "My grandma made an app to sell sewing patterns. You think she cares about her followers' data. Besides, all that stuff is in the cloud already." He pointed an accusatory finger at my chest. "This is about Christian shit, and you know it."

"Dropping the Christian god for the literal Devil sounds pretty similar," I said. "It's the same service, just a different provider."

Austin's hand slapped the table like he was a contestant in a gameshow. "There it is," he said. "You're still thinking of the specialists in the heaven and hell way. They aren't that kind of devils. They're more like imps or ifrits. The point is, they offer a service that can literally make you a savant at whatever task you have them take over for."

"At the cost of all the time they spend doing it," I said.

Austin narrowed his eyes, his smile quirking up. He always got that look when he knew he had me on my back feet. Austin had been in the debate club in high school. Technically I had been there, too, but that had been to avoid taking an art class.

"Do you actually enjoy the time you spend doing the dishes or balancing your taxes?" he asked. "Is that time actually precious to you?"

I pressed my lips together. "It could be."

Austin was already shaking his head. "Why not have someone else take over for you for a bit on those tasks you don't like."

I sighed. "Why do you even care so much?"

"Because I care about you, Beth," he said, his hand going to his chest. "You know that."

"He's also bought three thousand dollars in shares," Heather said, setting a cookie down on the table and placing a kiss on my forehead.

The barest hint of a smile pierced Austin's self-righteous visage. "I only backed the company because I thought it could use the support," he said. "And it's going to be big, Beth."

"I'll think about it," I said.

Austin's shoulders sank forward, and I sat back.

The conversation shifted to Heather's job and the dick manager who only complimented her when she'd straightened her hair. I let the two of them talk while I worked over what Austin had said. I was lucky enough to have a copywriting job I didn't hate, and I'd always been a sucker for that endorphin hit of finishing a task. Was that why I didn't want to use it?

Heather was meeting up with a friend that night, so I kissed her at the bus stop and rode home, listening to the lo-fi beats coming from the commuter in front of me who had their ear buds in but had skipped the critical step of plugging them into their phone.

Was this a time I would have handed off to one of those devils? There certainly wasn't anything special about this time. If I'd had the foresight to download something before I'd left the cafe, I would have just passed it with a podcast I didn't really care about.

Some of the other riders had nodded off in their seats, likely listening to mediocre podcasts of their own. Even the coach driver yawned at the red lights. "It's just like a dreamless nap," Austin had said.

I was so focused on my own thoughts, that I ended up getting off a stop late and walking an extra 10 minutes down the street. A cold wind whipped my jacket hood and fluttered the golden leaves of the trees on my street.

At home, I heated up macaroni and cheese leftovers from yesterday's date night and turned on the TV, pointedly avoiding the calendar above my desk informing me that two more pages of my graphic novel were due today.

A small man with greased down hair pointed out storm clouds on the screen. I ate my mostly heated noodles, tapping likes and hearts on my phone until a message from Heather popped up. She and her friend flashed peace signs at the camera in front of the only queer bar the straights hadn't managed to invade yet. "Going out dancing," she said. "Be home late. Love you!"

I sent a heart emoji and turned back to hear a man finishing a report of another school shooting to a woman with an appropriately furrowed brow. She faced the camera, hand going up to her earpiece the way it always did when she wanted to get the audience's attention. "This just in, we have reports that Fahad Remberra, creator of the controversial InfernaList app, has just donated one hundred million U.S. dollars to cancer research," she said. "This comes after several religious groups have had outcries about the 'evil forces' this application employs. Ryan."

The co-anchor, Ryan, shuffled his papers. "When asked for a comment, Remberra replied, 'InfernaList was always about finding ways to help people. This is just another way for me to do that.'"

"It is reported that this latest donation has removed Remberra from billionaire status," she said. "This makes the young programmer one of the quickest billionaires to gain and lose the prestigious title."

The news program shifted to talking about stocks and

the meteoric rise of the company, and as their voices droned on, I slipped off to sleep.

I woke up to the creak of the front door and keys rattling onto the countertop. I blinked up at Heather. The TV appeared to be advertising a three-in-one jewelry set with interchangeable REAL PRECIOUS JEWELS.

My phone said it was 4 a.m. Heather slipped out of her shoes and crossed over to me, tsking. "Your chiropractor said to stop falling asleep on the couch" she said, helping me up. She smelled like weed and floral perfume, and she had that after-party glow to her cheeks.

"I didn't mean to," I said, following her to the bedroom. "I was just watching TV."

She pressed a kiss to my cheek and guided me to the bed. I was asleep before she had even undressed.

Next morning, I woke with a sharp pain in my neck and the smell of bacon and butter wafting through the air. I shuffled into the kitchen and found Heather busy at work.

She sashayed around the kitchen, her headphones in her ears and her weave swaying to a silent beat. Heather said it made me a creep, but I enjoyed moments like these, when I could just watch unobserved as the people I loved lived their lives. Heather only danced like this when no one was looking. She flipped a couple slices of bacon onto a plate and drummed a few beats on the counter.

She smiled at me as I pulled out a chair. "One sec," she said, flicking off the stove. It wasn't just bacon she'd made. A full plate of golden brown hashbrowns sizzled in a skillet, and she pulled a pair of omelets out of the oven that were practically overflowing with cheese.

She set the feast down on the table, tapping her phone, turning to me, and pulling out her ear buds in a fluid movement. She paused, her grin widening. "Tadah!" she said, waving her hands at the table.

I chuckled. Apparently last night had gone well. "What's the occasion?"

"No occasion," she said. "It just seemed like a full breakfast kind of day." Heather pulled a pair of plates from the cupboard and set them down. Her eyes gleamed as she sat.

The eggs were fluffy and buttery, and the cheese melted in my mouth. She'd cooked onions and mushrooms and spinach into the egg. She raised her eyebrows at me over her own mouthful. "Right?" she said. "Isn't it great?" She shook her head.

I furrowed my brow, looking down at my plate. She seemed as surprised as I was. It wouldn't have been the first time Heather snuck in a surprise ingredient. After she'd found out the health benefits of turmeric, she'd found ways to work it into all the meals she made until I was pretty sure she'd single-handedly turned our insides yellow.

Another bite brought a rush of flavor, sharp cheese, sweetly caramelized onions, smokey bacon. "What did you add?" I asked.

She grinned between bites, punctuating each with a low moan in the back of her throat. "Nothing different today," she said. Then she considered, resting her fork on the edge of her lip. "I don't think so, anyway." She pulled her phone out and after a moment gave a confirming nod of her head.

"You don't think so?" I said. "Are you high?"

She shook her head. "God, can you imagine how good this would be if I were? But no." She lifted her phone, and I recognized the logo immediately. It was the same one that had been on the news last night next to Fahad Remberra's name. A pointed red tail kinked into the shape of a checkmark. InfernaList. "It was like magic," she said. "One moment I'm tapping in the meal, and the next it's all ready. Casey, the woman I was with last night, she uses it to help her run to work. This app is awesome." She narrowed her eyes in mock annoyance. "Don't tell Austin I said so."

I swallowed, an icy feeling spreading through my chest. I glanced at the kitchen where she'd been cooking just minutes ago. My stomach curled around the oily cheese and bacon. Who — *what* — had I been watching dance around the kitchen?

Her hand settled on mine. "I'm sorry, Beth," she said. "I didn't think you would care. Should I have told you?"

"It's fine," I said, forcing myself to smile. And judging from her frown, I didn't do a convincing job. I lifted another fork full of omelet into my mouth, trying not to think about the demonic force that had put this meal together. Had they put something in the food? I played the image of her dancing over in my mind. Had she been dancing differently than before? Had her voice sounded normal?

I nodded too many times then stood, grabbing my plate. "It's really good. Thank you. I'll finish it at my desk. Early start today."

Heather's frown deepened, but she didn't say any more. Setting the plate as far away from me as I could, I sank into my chair and pulled up the workspace app to log that I was online. Heather ate the rest of her meal in silence. She kissed my head as she walked out the front door.

As the door clicked shut, my gaze wandered from my computer screen to the omelet on the corner of my desk. I sank into my chair. Heather had been trying to do something nice, and I had shot her down. Regardless of whether it had been her at the wheels when she made the meal, the thought behind the gesture was the same. And yet ... "It's just an omelet, Beth," I said into the empty apartment. "You're being an idiot."

Gritting my teeth, I shoveled another bite of lukewarm omelet into my mouth. Even cooled down, the bite was heavenly but that somehow made it worse. I forced another bite into my mouth, and another, and as the plate clattered down onto my desk, I waited. It felt like something was supposed to happen when you ate a meal prepared by a devil. Was this how Persephone felt when she ate those pomegranate seeds?

My hands clenched on either side of my keyboard. I listened to the low hum of my computer's fan and watched the display of blue lights flickering across my motherboard. Normally it would have comforted me, the way displays of ordered symmetry often did, but needles of anxiety prickled through me.

I had never considered myself brave. When you're queer, there's an expected level of obstinance you're expected to build up. Heather had it, and so did her friends, but all I'd gotten from my roll of the identity dice was willfulness. When something scared me, when I couldn't put logic to the way I felt, I embraced it. It had worked out for gender, for the most part, so why not an app that let a demon hijack my body?

I lifted my phone. I didn't have to search long in the app store, had barely typed in that first letter when it popped up. One circular progress bar later, I was staring at a login page. The agreements page would have put the Illiad to shame. I tapped through it.

A welcome message popped up on my screen. A chibi demonic cherub bobbed alongside the text.

> Welcome, HopeForTheBeth! Thank you for choosing InfernaList. Let us walk you through how our application works!

I unchecked the tutorial box. If I was going to win against the part of me that wanted to throw my phone across the room, I needed to get this over with quickly. A series of dropdowns and checkmarks rose before me. I glanced up at my monitor and back at my phone.

> Employment >> Remote Work >> Marketing >> Copyediting, Proofreading, Content Creation (mult. Platforms), Social Media Management, Email Interaction, Digital Correspondence.

A heavy feeling settled into my stomach, the same one that happened whenever I looked over my resume. Six hours a day, five days a week, over three years, all categorized into a handful of checked boxes.

I adjusted the time slider at the bottom of the form to six hours. A warning popped up as I clicked the next button. The chibi demon cherub waggled a cautionary finger beside the message.

This exceeds the recommended duration for sedentary work. Would you like this time to include regular bathroom breaks and other bodily necessities (e.g., eating).

I stabbed my finger on *YES*. One last message popped up.

Would you like to specify what foods you would like to intake? If left unspecified, InfernaList will optimize caloric intake and preparation time.

I tapped *Decide For Me.*

My hands trembled. My chest felt tight. If I had a heart attack would the demon continue to work? If I came to six hours from now, would I even realize if I'd had a heart attack? An arc of blue light spiraled in an unending circle.

Matching you with one of our experienced specialists.

After a few agonizing moments, a name flashed on the screen accompanied with a bespectacled cherub behind a desk.

NAME: Renaldo, 8027 years old.
TITLE: Marketing Specialist.
PROFESSIONAL EXPERIENCE: 2090 Years.
USERS SERVICED: 9108.
RATING: 4.89 Pentacles.

My eyes unfocused on the years but it was the name that my gaze kept coming back to. I'd been prepared for Asmodeus or Baphomet, something ancient and unknowable. I glanced back at my screen, peering over the circular icons I associated with each of my fellow employees. How many of them had worked with Renaldo?

At the bottom of a CV that listed every conceivable platform and program, was a blue *ACCEPT* button. I pressed my pointer finger to the screen before I could stop myself.

Establishing connection.

A progress bar spread across the screen.

Connection established.

I was hungry. The coworking app for my job sat open in front of me. The clock read 2:35. My hands completed their movement to my lap. My chest tightened. It had already happened. Six hours gone faster than I could blink. What had I done?

I took stock of my surroundings, focusing on the details, trying to get my heart to stop pounding in my ears. My compression gloves sat beside my desk where I'd left them. My shoulders felt stiff, but they weren't as tight as they usually were. Whatever had taken over my body had better posture than I did. I imagined a pair of taloned hands gripping my shoulders and forcing them back.

Tendrils of worry wormed their way into my stomach. Analysis could wait, I told myself. Focus on the details. An apple core sat in the waste bin beside my chair. I skimmed the coworking app and found my icon beside a message:

Signing off for the day. *WaveEmoji*

The rest of my tabs were closed, no other programs were running, the journal beside my keyboard lay where I had left it, my pen safely tucked into the spiral. With no details left to distract me from my thoughts, they washed over me. It didn't take six hours to eat an apple and log in and out of work. What had I done? But it hadn't been me at the helm, had it? It had been him. Renaldo.

A gentle chime sounded from my phone, and the InfernaList icon rose to the top of my notification list.

Progress Report.

I took a breath and pressed the notification. A blue icon floated up.

Would you like to view an itemized list of our services?

My fingers trembled. A bulleted list took over my screen.

8:35-8:48 — Responded to emails and messages.

8:48-9:23 — Gordon's Grill content creation.

9:23-9:25 — Responded to Google Review.

9:25-9:35 — Gordon's Grill content creation.

9:35-9:40 — Required stretch break.

9:40-9:43 — Drank 8 oz of water. Urinated.

9:43-10:13 — Drafted analytics for Gordon's Grill ad campaign.

And the list went on. It looked like a normal day, only Renaldo had been faster. Much faster. I tended to be pretty focused, with only the occasional social media break or text to Heather or Austin, but Renaldo had outperformed me on even my most focused day.

I combed through the day's emails to find next week's content. The Gordon's Grill social media posts were perfect. The images were crisply cropped, and the pictures were so well photoshopped I could almost hear the burgers sizzling.

The door to the bathroom creaked open, but it still made me jump. Had Renaldo come to collect his fee? Instead, Heather smiled at me from a cloud of steam. "You're finally up," she said, a smirk spreading across her face. "How was your first time?"

I blinked at her. "How did you ... When?"

"About an hour ago. You didn't even look up when I walked in," she said. "Your fingers were flying, and I don't think I've seen you eat an apple in months. So what'd you think?"

I shook my head, closing the app. "It was like nothing happened," I said. "I'm sorry for ignoring you. It wasn't me." I shivered.

Heather shrugged. "It's alright. I needed the shower anyway," she said. "Check the interruptions box next time. We're lucky it wasn't an emergency." The anxiety tentacles writhed in my stomach. Heather patted the air. "Sorry. That was supposed to be a joke. I'm still tired. Want me to show you how to optimize your session for interruptions?"

I pushed my phone away. "I'm not doing it again," I said. "I feel like I just woke up from sleepwalking."

"If you're sure," she said, scrubbing her hair with her towel. "I mean, maybe it's a matter of degrees. I used it for the run home and got the post-workout shower without having to stick it through the workout."

I wrung my hands. "Anyway, what brought you home from work early?"

"I finished up my coding for the day," she said. Her gaze softened. "Also, I wanted to check in on you. You seemed pretty rattled this morning."

"Yeah, I guess it just weirded me out," I said. "I thought I was watching you dance around in the kitchen and then you told me it wasn't you. It felt like I'd been admiring a stranger."

"A stranger with these hips," she said, slapping her side. She sighed at my lack of response. "No more surprise omelets?"

I shook my head, pulling down a box of macaroni even though it felt like I'd only just finished my omelet. While the water boiled, I went and grabbed my phone and found a message from our team's copy editor. "Putting that Communications degree to work! No edits from me. Nice job, Bethany."

Jennifer always had edits for me. A sick feeling coiled inside me, the same feeling I got in high school when I stole my desk neighbor's answers and got an A on my Chemistry test, my first and only A of the year. I tried skipping school the next day until Dad told me to "man up" and made me bike to class.

I knew better than to confess now, but that didn't change the feeling. I'd cheated, and now they would expect better of me, better than I could do, apparently. I had always thought Jennifer was nitpicky, but it turned out it was my copy that was the problem.

"Your macaroni's overflowing," Heather said from her seat at the table. I dashed over and lifted up the pan, water sizzling on the glowing burner.

I sighed. Never again.

• • •

True to her word, Heather didn't surprise me with any morning omelets, though she continued to run, and I would often find the dishes done before I rolled out of bed, something she'd despised doing before.

Jennifer was disappointed by my work the next day, but she got over that eventually, returning to her curt, "Edits below."

Our team was radio silence about the app, but other companies that made the news started asking employees to hand in their phones before their shifts. Several schools reported a record number of perfect SAT scores. Several colleges decided to omit test results entirely from the application process.

Some old white men who had very little understanding of how apps worked — and didn't realize they had no authority to summon someone from Indonesia — called Fahad to appear before Congress.

It wasn't clear if Fahad heard the summons or if he even cared. When a reporter asked him about it, he seemed understandably confused. InfernaList transitioned to an optional paid subscription model. Even with the subscriptions being optional, Fahad told that same reporter he was having trouble donating money as fast as it came in. According to a statement from the company, he had plans to set up a medical foundation and youth resource center at the beginning of the next fiscal quarter.

Austin gained over 400,000 subscriptions on his channel overnight for his video game playthroughs. I watched a few episodes of it at lunch. The content was so-so, and Austin was mediocre at video games at best, but the edits made things look fresh and playful.

Three weeks after the day I tried InfernaList out, he sent me an invite for coffee. I thought about canceling, but Heather made it clear I needed to get out of the apartment, so I hopped on the bus and listened to my podcast, so I could pretend I didn't see the red checkmark tail flash on the coach driver's phone.

Austin was waiting for me when I arrived, dressed in a sleek suit and purple t-shirt like a new age CEO. He clapped me on the shoulder and insisted on paying for my coffee. When I asked for a 12-ounce, he shook his head. "They'll have a 20-ounce."

He held up his hands when I cast a look at him. "Might as well take advantage of the offer," he said. "I'm not exactly hurting for cash right now."

I rolled my eyes. So that's how it was. This was a "look how successful Austin is" coffee. He'd done the same thing after he got the scholarship for law school. For the umpteenth time since I walked out the door, I wished that I hadn't let Heather convince me to leave the comfort of my spot on the couch.

"Congrats on the YouTube channel," I said. "I didn't know you were thinking about streaming."

He smiled at the barista as he took our drinks, sitting down at a table directly beside the door. "I didn't," he said. "I just figured it was an easy task that I could do to make some extra cash while I figure out my next step. But honestly, it's a dream."

"Who did you get to do your editing?" I asked, but by the gleam in his eye I already knew the answer.

"An 800-year-old demoness named Claire," he said, grinning. "Best choice I ever made, honestly. I get to do the fun part, and she helps me look good."

"Isn't that cheating?" I asked.

He smirked. "Would it be cheating to ask an editor to do it?" He shook his head. "Of course not. This is the cheaper option. I'm just using my resources."

I stared down at my mug. Just how fast I could chug a latte? I wondered. I silently cursed myself for ordering a hot drink. But I didn't have to change the subject. A young woman walked up to our table, hands fidgeting at her sides. She had purple hair and a sweater with a band name I didn't recognize.

"Excuse me, I'm sorry. Are you Austin Sidler?" she asked, her eyes widening.

Austin glanced up, smile wide but not too wide. He tossed his hair out of his face. "I am," he said. "Can I help?"

The teen seemed to melt under the weight of his gaze. I sipped my drink and burned my mouth. Neither Austin nor the girl seemed to notice. "Yes ..." she said. "Well, I was wondering ... You see, I'm a big fan. Would you ..."

His smile widened a centimeter. "I would love to take a photo with my number one fan," he said. "There's just one thing I need you to do for me."

If her eyes could have widened any more, they would have swallowed her face. She nodded.

"Could you wait until after my friend and I leave to post it on your social?" he asked. "You understand how it is, don't you ...?" He paused, holding out his hand.

"Samantha," she said.

"Samantha," he repeated.

Without taking her eyes off Austin, Samantha thrust her phone in my direction. I was tempted to let it fall into my coffee, but I took it. Austin flashed a grin, and the girl turned the color of a cherry when he put an arm around her shoulder.

She took her phone, gaze still glued to Austin's face.

"Remember," he said, pressing a finger to his lips. "Our little secret until we leave, okay?"

She nodded, seeming to glide back to her seat, phone pressed to her chest.

"Well, that was something," I said.

"What was?" he asked. Austin's phone vibrated. "Oh." He pulled his phone out, nodding down at it. "Sorry, I'm on the beta for supplemental input when I get recognized in public," he said.

Now that I thought about it, there had been subtle shifts in his demeanor. Austin had always been quick, but he'd never been smooth. It was just like watching Heather chassé around our kitchen. I tried to keep my voice from quivering. "Supplemental input?"

"Claire, actually," he said, setting his phone face down. "She's good at PR. Keeps people from getting those bad in-person reputations tabloids love writing about. She hops on if someone recognizes me from the streams. It won't go live for a month or so." He sipped his cappuccino. "Before you worry, I have it disabled for our conversation."

I felt a tremble beneath the surface. It felt small, the same way I'd felt watching my mom drink and wondering when she was going to start yelling. How many drinks until she started telling me I was a disappointment? How many until she started screaming?

"Anyway," Austin said. "How are things for you? Heather told me you gave the app a test run."

"Things are fine," I said. "I deleted it."

Austin sighed. "That's because you're using it wrong," Austin said. "You have to be strategic. Assign it the stuff you don't want to do but have to do. Then fill in for all the fun stuff." He leaned forward but another person tapped him on the shoulder. This time a twenty-something-year-old with a face full of piercings.

Austin turned, grinning before he even saw them. But that wasn't Austin, I had to remind myself. Austin was asleep. The person — if you could call her that — smiling at the unwitting fan was Claire.

I pushed my chair back. How many other people around the café were actually people? How many were just hosts for demons? One of the baristas cleaned the steam wand; the script writer came up from his laptop for sips of coffee like a diver rising for air; a man across the room barked confidently into his phone; a pair of friends spoke in the corner of the room where we usually sat. Steam hissed. Voices rolled over one another. Fingers tapped out a staccato rhythm on a keyboard. Their movements were mechanical, efficient, clinical. Perfect.

The same way Heather had looked when she danced around in our kitchen.

My lungs tightened. I couldn't get enough air into my chest. The air felt too thin. My heart hammered against my ribs. Sweat streaked my brow.

The young person with the piercings lifted their attention from Austin to furrow their brow at me. "Hey, bro, you okay?" they said, their lips forming the words but losing their sound in the cacophony.

"Don't worry about them," Claire said. Austin's face flashed a grin my way. "Bethany is just a little shy."

I pushed my chair in, mumbling something that might have been an apology but was probably gibberish. I stumbled out of the café and into the street. I needed air. My heart drummed a hellish beat. The streets blurred into a stream of flashing lights and blaring horns.

Someone called my name as the bus doors rattled closed. Either Austin or Claire. I couldn't be sure anymore. I sat in the seat with the window that wouldn't close. I could feel the other people watching, feel their gazes settling on me from the corners of their demonic eyes. "Don't scream," I said. "Just don't scream." I just had to make it home, somewhere where I didn't feel like the only human left, the only one still present in their own body, the only organic vehicle with a human brain behind the wheel.

It felt like hours later when I pushed into my apartment and fell against the cold metal door.

I didn't realize Heather was there until her arms wrapped around me. I breathed in the musky smell of the lumberjack deodorant she wore. It felt like someone had flicked off the mute button. Sounds rushed in around me. The drip of our faucet, the low hum of our refrigerator, and Heather's voice.

"Why didn't you answer your phone?" she asked, her voice raw and strained. Her arms shook. "Austin and I were worried sick. Hold on, I'm going to let him know you made it home safe. He about had a conniption when he called."

"I'm sorry," I said. "I didn't know you called."

She let out her breath, deflating. She set her phone aside and pushed it away from her. Then, Heather crawled over me and sat beside me against the door, a gentle weight against my side. "Do you want to be held?" she asked.

I nodded, leaning into her embrace. Her arms were stronger than I remembered, but that was comforting in a way. It was like having a guardian beside me, someone I knew could fend off whoever — or whatever — came knocking at our door. We sat like that for a long time, Japanese words from one of Heather's anime shows blaring in the background.

"Do you want to try sitting on the couch with me? We can talk about it," she said. I nodded again, swallowing. "Let me get you a glass of cold water," she added.

I didn't quite feel ready to go to the couch by myself, so I watched her pour a glass from our pitcher in the fridge. Lacing my hand in hers, she walked me to a seat, handed me the glass, and paused her show. "Drink," she said, firmly but not unkindly.

I did as I was told, annoyed at how immediately my body responded to the water. My pulse evened out. My breathing slowed. Heather shifted to face me, her stance open.

"Tell me what happened," she said. She locked my gaze with hers. "Austin said you ran out of the café?"

I took another sip, and the cool water slid down my throat. My neck loosened and my shoulders lowered, and I told her how it had felt, surrounded by what felt like a hundred lifeless shells being piloted by strange creatures.

Heather was silent, nodding along, her gaze focused but not sharp the way she sometimes looked when she had a problem to solve. She offered low "mms" and affirmations in response, and when I fell silent, she said, "That must have been really terrifying for you. Have you felt this way before?"

I frowned. She was talking the way she had after her first college psychology class. "I mean, I haven't had a panic attack in years," I said. "This app stuff has really gotten to me."

She nodded. "You haven't said anything about it since a few weeks ago, but I can tell how uncomfortable you are when I come home from my runs," she said. She paused, then lifted her eyes. "I wish I could say it was all going away, but from the look of things, the app is only going to get bigger over time."

I shook my head. "When did I become an old person?" I said. "I'm supposed to be hip and trending. First to get all the new gizmos and gadgets."

Heather chuckled. "I hate to break it to you, love," she said, raising an eyebrow, "but you've never been hip or trending. It's what I love about you."

I smiled, clenching my heart in mock pain. "You wound me, Heather."

She returned the smile, but she had that look in her eye that told me she wouldn't be distracted by jokes. "My point is, you won't be able to stay inside and avoid moments like today. The amount of people using InfernaList is only going to grow," she said.

I sighed. "You want me to see a therapist," I said.

Taking my hand in hers, she leaned in. "I want you to get the help and support you need," she said, "because I won't always be here to give you glasses of water when you get home." She flicked a finger toward the TV, her lips quirking up. "I have priorities. Lots of anime to catch up on."

"Well, I'd hate to get in the way of anime," I said.

"See, now you understand," she said. Heather scooted up against me, laying her head on my shoulder. "You don't have to say yes right now, but at least consider it. I'm worried about you."

I kissed the top of her head. Maybe she was right. Maybe I did need to start seeing a therapist again. But right then, in that moment, everything felt like it might be alright. "I'll think about it," I said. "I promise."

For the remainder of the evening, we watched her anime, which turned out to be a *yaoi* retelling of Gawain and the Green Knight, which admittedly wasn't far off from the original story. Heather ordered us delivery pizza from my favorite place, and we snuggled on the couch until it was time for bed.

Heather was already asleep by the time I finished washing my face. My cheeks felt warm watching her curled up, her weave safely tucked into her silk cap. She snored softly into her pillow.

Outside, a gentle wind rattled our bamboo wind chimes. I made my way around the house, flicking off the lights in the living room. Heather had forgotten her water, so I walked into the kitchen to refill her glass and almost stepped on her phone.

Another wave of warmth rolled through me. She'd been so intent on making sure I was alright that she'd set her phone away for the entire night. I reached down to grab that, too, and the phone buzzed in my hand. On reflex, I spun it around and glanced down at the notifications and froze.

A red tail twisted into a checkmark. I should have set it down, just pretended I hadn't seen it. It could have just been a notification about her run earlier. It could have been an ad or promotion. My hands trembled as I pressed the notification and entered Heather's code.

> Session complete. Would you like to see an itemized report of our services?

I flicked on the light to our bedroom and Heather groaned. "Heather, what is this?" I asked.

She blinked up at me, eyes going to the phone in my hand. She raised her hands as if I were a rabid dog preparing to charge, but she had it all wrong. All I wanted to do was run away. "Beth, sweetie, you were so distant, I didn't know what to do, so ..."

"So you handed me off to a stranger?" I demanded. The phone slipped from my hand, and my hands covered my face. Those warm feelings I felt leaning into her, the kiss on my forehead, the weight against me. Bile rose in my throat.

I felt Heather's arms settle around me, but I pushed her away. "No!" I said, stumbling back.

"Beth, you needed a professional," she said. "You needed a doctor."

My jaw trembled. "I needed you," I said. I couldn't stay there. I couldn't be in the room with her anymore, if it even was her.

Before she could say another word, I rushed to the front door, flinging it open to the cold night air. Cars rushed past, buses screeched to a halt, people strolled past, staring down at their phones. I tried to take another step out the door, but my legs refused to move. There was nowhere safe left. No one left to trust. A sea of demons waited on both sides of my front door.

Manny Frishberg was born in the shadow of New York City but has lived on the West Coast for the past 40-plus years. His stories have been appearing in anthologies and magazines since 2010. Before that he held jobs shaping wood, sheet metal and words (not all at once). His current work includes book editing and coaching, science reporting, and writing short stories and novels.

•   •   •

Years ago, I worked at a community health clinic, and the doctors and nurses were among my friends; after a health crisis that landed me in the hospital, I got to know some LPNs and orderlies. For those of us living through it, the Covid pandemic has been a source of sorrow, but for the monsters whose sustenance is human life, I imagine, it must all be a moveable feast. I want to thank the members of Sound on Paper, who have helped me hone this and dozens of other works, and especially Laura Staley, from whom I "borrowed" the idea of a Day-thief.

TAKE YOUR TIME

MANNY FRISHBERG

"T HIS ONE CODED IN THE WAGON," the EMT reported as I met the gurney with the dead man coming through the automatic doors of the Emergency Department. I shuddered when he said it and stepped back to let him pass. I could tell by the gleam in his eye that he was a 'pyre.

Reading the name on his chest, I decided to give Jones the benefit of the doubt, assume he waited 'til the last seconds, that the patient was circling the drain when he took her. I guess I was feeling charitable, this being Christmas night. After all, it's not like I'm one to judge.

Mostly, 'pyres that become EMTs have some thread of morals left. Long as it doesn't get in the way of their draining away people's animating force. Bloodsucking is just a metaphor.

I can abide a 'pyre better than I could the soul-eaters: scavengers, they do jobs where they don't draw any notice, nurse's aides and orderlies, always hovering like buzzards circling their prey. The soul-eaters don't kill, but what it is they do take makes them worse than the vampyres to my mind. Thank the Lord, at least I'm not one of *them.* The time I take would go unused if I didn't harvest it.

This was 2019, my first time in New York. I'd just moved from San Francisco after Thanksgiving — when you don't age much, you can't be spending too much time in one locale. Or stay on one job. And an ICU nurse is always in demand.

I'm not religious (to say the least), so I volunteered to work the holiday, and they were short-handed in the ED that night. Otherwise, I would likely have never met that EMT. And, if I'd known *anybody* else in town, I would not have spent Boxing Day with Theophilus Jones. Hell, I didn't know anybody this side of the Atlantic celebrated Boxing Day 'til he asked.

I don't know if I was dreaming of a white day-after-Christmas, but what we got was a gray one. Piles of snow pushed up against the curb by the snowplows melting into Henry Moore sculptures edged in soot, pretty in their own degraded way. That's how Theo looked at them.

I wasn't used to the wet cold, or how the wind felt like it was blowing around tiny ice crystals that stung your nose and cheeks as you walked along. But that was evidently Theo's idea of a first date, a walking tour of the Upper West Side. The Somme in 1917 had been winter enough to last me a lifetime, maybe more than one. After that, I stayed by myself to keep away from the Spanish flu. No sense taking a chance on catching it; there'd been no shortage of men in the trenches not living out their allotted three-score-and-ten.

I told Theo he'd better be planning on buying me lunch, and we ducked into this burger bar at Broadway and 84th Street. I ordered up a cheeseburger, fries and a vanilla malted and waited for Theo to pick up his menu, but he just sat sipping his ice water like he hadn't had enough of the cold already and looked straight through me with those chocolate-brown eyes, and I felt like I was the only one in the room. I still didn't like that he didn't order, and I gave him a quizzical kind of look. And that's when he told me:

"I don't eat." That's it. Not that he wasn't hungry just then or that he was on some kind of cleansing fast. He looked at me, waiting for a reaction, a small, almost hidden smile said that he could tell there was something about me, too, and he was testing the waters.

"Yeah, you just about skinny enough for me to believe that," I said, letting my eyes do the laughing. "But you're wiry, too. You've got some muscles on your bones. You're surely not what I'd call undernourished."

"I never said I don't take sustenance, just not the kind they serve here." And there was that twinkle in his eye, same as the night we met.

"Oh, you're a vegetarian then?" I said, half-serious, but also testing the waters for myself. Then, it was his turn to laugh. He chuckled in a way that made me want to shrink down to a dust mote and blow away, but then he turned his smile on and I forgave him for my embarrassment.

"I'm not laughing at you," he said. "For real," he added when I didn't look convinced. "It's that you're right in a way I ever thought of. What I hunger for isn't meat. You've got a funny ... I mean unique way of seeing things. If you *are* seeing me for who I am."

I could see we had stopped playing games.

"You mean, you being a va—" He put a finger to my lips, very gentle.

I don't like being touched first, usually, but he brushed them just like a feather's breeze and his hand was gone again. Barely a touch but enough to hush me.

"It's an ugly word, we prefer not to use it. It conjures up some revolting myths."

"So, then, what do you call yourselves?"

"*Opiri.*"

I tried it out myself, and it didn't feel bad on my tongue.

"What does it mean?"

"The same thing, really. It's the Old Slavonic word that the modern 'V' word comes from. Only, when you say it, people don't immediately think of Bela Lugosi in white-tie and a cape, turning into a bat and drinking people's blood. Which we don't, by the way." I felt my cheeks flush because I already knew that. I smiled.

"You're telling me this because ...?"

"Because I could tell, right in the ER, that you saw the real me, and I don't meet too many of our kind. Don't know that there are very many. Not like we're settling down to have families." He laughed again, only this time it was cold, sardonic, and I could feel that it was aimed at himself. "Can you imagine? If we started breeding — talk about overpopulation. We'd overrun them in no time. Then what?" And that dark laugh again. There was a deeper sadness to it. I have known it myself.

"I'm ..." I was afraid of how he'd react. "... Not like you," I said. Theo just nodded once and listened. "Not exactly. I don't take their life. Or, I don't draw the Breath of Life out of them to absorb their life energy, or consume their soul, whatever that may be." Theo tried not to show it, but I could tell my words had cut him. I hurried to say more.

"I collect their remaining days, the unused time left to them. Before it goes to waste. "Of course," I confessed, "there's always an element of uncertainty — as long as someone's alive they've got a chance of recovering. But as a CU nurse, I'm not playing the long odds. It can be sad, too. A patient will hang on for days sometimes, and you can't help but get attached." I'd been telling that tale to myself so long, I believed it was true.

"How old are you?" It was a rather brazen question for so early in a relationship, but I wanted to change the subject.

"I was born in 1713," he said. "For the first time. I died and was resurrected, to borrow the Catholics' phrase, in 1742."

I did the math quickly in my head, two hundred and eighty years, almost. I tried not to figure how many lives he had to take in that amount of time. Theo looked at me expectantly, like it was my turn. His eyes never left me. It made me want to open up.

First time in I don't know how many years, how many decades, I decided to be honest with him. It'd been a long time since I'd talked about myself — my real self.

"I grew up in Philadelphia in the 1840s, mostly — I was born in '43." I was half expecting him to say something about the difference in ages but he just turned those lovely eyes on me, like what I had to say next was the most important piece of news in the universe. "I was lonely a lot. There were always other kids around, but they always treated me as kinda' strange, and I guess I was, 'cause I always had a book, and I preferred bein' around older folks. They just all had more interesting things to say, know?" I didn't even realize I had started to talk that way until he smiled.

"So, how do you come to be here today?" It was an innocent enough way to phrase it. Subtle, I liked that. I looked around the restaurant: one guy on a stool halfway down the counter, a man and his kid at a table close to the kitchen door, none paying us any mind. I stood up and put on my coat, even though we hadn't gotten — that is, I hadn't gotten my order. Theo followed my lead, dropped a twenty on the table and walked out ahead of me.

"It's just not something I talk about in public," I said, pulling my coat tight against the wind off the Hudson. No one else was fool enough to brave the weather for no good reason, so we had the street to ourselves, for at least a block or two. The wind whisked past my ears and seemed to blow my words up toward the rooftops as I spoke them, making it feel all the more private.

"Like I was saying, I had an affinity for older people, but really, one in particular. Mademoiselle LaForge, that was the name on her dress shop window, but to me she was Mémé. She would tell me stories about life growing up in Haiti, where she was from. It was a desperately poor country then, just like it is now, but her family did okay. Her auntie was a Voudon priestess, 'so there was always gonna be sometin' t' eat,' she'd say, and laugh, 'long as some fool want' her t' see his future in chicken's guts.' Like it was all some game they'd been playin' on the rubes.

"Only it wasn't. On account of some real voodoo magic got passed on to Mémé. And got passed on from her to me, I guess 'cause, she said, it had to go somewhere, and I was the only one that bothered to listen to her. Anyway, she taught me to take the time people leave behind when they die too soon."

I felt a lightness after I said that, like some great weight had been lifted off my soul, and I felt like laughing right out loud. So, I did, standing there in the middle of the sidewalk, a pile of sooty snow piled up against the fire hydrant, and the wind whipping past me so's I could barely hear myself. And I'm howling like a damned banshee. Just making a damned fool of myself. And, what does Theo do then? That lovely man — or *opiri*, or whatever damned thing you call him — started laughing and howling in the wind in harmony with my hysteria until we both kind of collapsed into each other's arms.

And it was just like that, spontaneous in the moment, no plans, no promises. But he made the cracks in my ceiling dance all night.

After that, we spent time together as much as we could, given our schedules. My weekends were usually Monday, Tuesday, when I got two days straight off work, so I had New Year's Eve off, but Theo had already signed up for double shifts that day.

"Too many people goin' out, gettin' stupid and winding up in a meat wagon," he explained it to me. "It's a moveable feast, so to speak." And those eyes of his set to twinkling. I laughed, then. I don't know how he did that, whether it was just natural to him when he got excited or was it some *opiri* trick. Or maybe it was just the way the light would glint sometimes and catch him, and I wanted to see some kind of magic in it. I've always strained to see the magic in the world — that's how I landed myself in my predicament in the first, captured by an old woman in the web of stories she wove for me.

Theo and I decided then that we would celebrate the Chinese New Year instead of the American one, and we made a date to go down to Mott Street for the Lion dance on January 26. We'd heard about a virus outbreak in Wuhan, China in the late fall, and a few cases were popping up in the States, almost all people who had traveled to China recently. Some of the folks in the Department of Public Health started raising the alarms, which just made sense, knowing how many Chinese people live in New York and, you know, they all have relatives.

Well, but Theo and I didn't think much about it. After all, we were immortal, or the next best thing in my case. I never asked him exactly how that worked for his kind, whether they got hungry and how often or how much they needed to eat? Let alone all the myths about sunshine and stakes-through-the-heart, and the like. Not even whether he'd age, if ever so slowly, or was he stuck forever at what age he'd become when he died the first time. We had much better things to talk about — when we found time to talk at all, when we found need to talk.

Things were that good for a while. I began to see it as something to last forever, although truthfully, when forever is an actual possibility, it's more like, for the indefinite, foreseeable future. (Now, that's irony! I don't think that I ever really appreciated irony; not like I do.)

In March, the first case of what they'd started calling Covid-19 hit New York and in the following weeks, it exploded. By a month later, the city was a ghost town, bars and restaurants all closed down, stores shuttered and anyone on the streets 'cause they had to be, trying to keep six feet away from everybody else — and good luck doing that on a bus, let alone the subway. People everywhere just trying to cope with the hot-and-cold-running stay-at-home orders. They started bringing refrigerated trucks around in front of the hospitals because they ran out of room in the morgue. By the first of April, three of the nurse's aides working on the new Covid ward had got it and died.

I was running myself ragged, but in that, I was no different than anybody else. I worked twelve-hour shifts, went home to collapse on my bed and shower before heading back for another. And sometimes, I'd work on through a double — twenty-four straight hours; a third of the nursing staff was getting sick and winding up chasing the same respirators as everybody else. I was tired — drained, really. Most of the patients in those first months were old, like really old, or sick with other things that had weakened them already. Even so, there were so many coming every day, I was racking up months, years every shift I worked.

Now, you know that kind of schedule didn't really allow for much of a social life, not that there was anywhere to go out and do anything. Theo didn't need to eat — well, not food — and he preferred not to. After the gas he passed after he did indulge me and swallow a morsel, I preferred he didn't either. That put the lid on ordering in.

We kept it up through the spring like that. We texted, sexted a few times but we're both a little old for that new trick. We Facetimed and Zoomed, which I had to admit was a sight better than writing long, florid love letters that demanded even longer and more impassioned responses. But long-distance relationships suck, even when you're in the same town. Especially when you're in the same town.

We managed to sync up our schedules finally and got together in the middle of May. So many people were getting sick by then that they had to shut down the subways overnight. By the beginning of that week, the temperature dropped below freezing and even snowed and hailed, which was weird for May. I told Theo that they started putting the homeless on buses parked in the yard just so they had a place to stay warm.

He said, "Yeah, we picked up four popsicles just the last week." And he smiled at me; his eyes had that same glimmer — those laughing eyes that had been so mesmerizing, that still were. Yet this time I felt a chill rise up my back that wasn't like the usual excitement I got, looking at him — didn't know just why at the time. I knew his kind of gallows humor. Surrounded by all that sickness and fear and grieving, even the mortals fall back on it sometimes.

"I could use some plain old hypothermia cases," I said. "Or a myocardial infarction. Hell, just a damned case of MRSA. All this fuckin' Covid ..." I just shook my head. I didn't have the words, all of a sudden.

And Theo, sitting next to me on the couch, just looked at me — no laughing glimmer in his eyes now, but not the understanding I was searching for in them, either. Not for a second or two, then it was like some kind of light came on in his head and he took my hand and caressed it in his. His hands were always so cold — goes with the territory, I suppose. But his touch was reassuring, just like it was supposed to be, and I drew my breath again and tried to finish.

"It's just all too much, sometimes," I said by way of apology. "Not that they're dying. Everybody dies some time." I didn't mean to be ironic, didn't realize I had been until Theo smirked at it. *Fuck him*, I thought. But I had to smile for a second.

"It's when they got hope. They come into the ICU fighting for their breath, and if they're lucky, we got a ventilator for them and an ART tech to run it, so for a few days, they start getting better. Then, it's like somebody's pulled the plug and they go swirlin' around and down the drain before the shift's over." Theo put his arm around my shoulder and pulled me in close, my head resting on his chest. I could almost imagine hearing his heartbeat inside his chest. I could tell he felt for me, but I could tell, when a siren and flashing lights went past the apartment windows, he was thinking about the meals he was missing.

Riding home on the F train to shower the next morning our conversation kept repeating in the sound of the wheels clicking along the tracks. For me, it wasn't just that Covid was relentless — so many dying every day it was hard to keep count, let alone remember their names.

People all around were dropping like flies. And, so their deaths were so damnably capricious. They were lining up in front of the Emergency Department entrances three and four deep and stretching down the block — of course, the worst thing you can do with a deadlier-than-flu URI running rampant. But just try tellin' people that; they're sick and they're scared and nobody seems to have any good idea what to do about it.

I thought about quitting. The sheer scope of it was overwhelming, and I had plenty of money. That's just one of the things about living a very long time, the stock market will always go up if you give it a few decades. War feels like you're on the road to the Apocalypse; it's relentless and indiscriminate, but there's a logic to it: blow them all to Hell and let God sort 'em out. Pestilence isn't like that other horseman. I felt I was needed here.

Theo *was* one of the decent *opiri*, one that had some sense of morality and so didn't prey on the hale and hearty, waiting until there was no real hope. But he'd been who he was — what he'd become — for long enough to have grown a thick, tough carapace around his soul. None of it ever seemed to touch him, though. And why should it? He had sympathy for the people he took, the sympathy you might have for the fly you had to swat.

•   •   •

Near the end of June, I got off late one night, tired but too ragged to sleep, too hot to stay home. I took the subway to Whitehall Street and walked to the Staten Island Ferry Terminal. Nobody, really, is on their way to Staten Island on a Wednesday night at 3:30 a.m., so I had it pretty much to myself, except for the seagulls coasting on the bow wind. The air temperature was still up near 80 but the breeze from off the bay felt good on my face. Skimming past Lady Liberty out there in the middle of the water, I heard that old Byrds song in my head, about her dancin' 'neath the diamond sky, her one arm wavin' free, until I was pleading at the top of my lungs, "Let me forget about today/ Until tomorrow."

Mémé tried to tell me, said that every skill you pick up, every gift you learn to wield, comes with a price. I was young, too young to listen, and too full of myself to pay attention, let alone to ask what made her let herself get so old? In the end, though, I learned it for myself.

You see, for me, it's not all from the outside. It's like when you harvest the unspent days, you live 'em, you experience every last one. Including *their* last one. It makes it like you die each time. And these deaths being quiet, almost gentle, somehow made it worse.

I called Theo from the boat back to Manhattan and got his voicemail. I really didn't feel like I could see him again just then. I felt bad about breaking up with him in a phone message, and I tried to tell him it wasn't him, which is a damned stupid thing to say, ever, let alone in a breakup voicemail. Especially because, of course, it was him.

After that, I quit taking time, though. At that point, I think I'd begun to understand Mémé a little better. Besides, I had all the time in the world. Until I didn't.

See, at least my kind of being immortal doesn't guarantee you won't get hit by a truck. My truck was named Covid-19. They moved me up to the ICU yesterday and found a ventilator for me this morning. Nurse's aides and orderlies stare through the glass to see how I'm doing — soul eaters masquerading as concerned coworkers. But I got the last laugh on them.

I texted Theo, telling him to come to see me one more time. I've taken decades, probably centuries. I hope my time can keep him from being hungry for a while.

Adrienne Canino lives in South Central Alaska and indulges in cozy winter habits most of the year. She has loved sci fi and fantasy since meeting the characters of Ellen Ripley and Daine Sarrasri in her youth, and probably even before. She escapes her day job wrangling research by skiing and camping and writing and reading.

•   •   •

This story is inspired by my friends who started programs in wildlife biology during the pandemic. Throughout our hikes and outdoor socializing, they humored me with tales of lab experiments in their kitchen and whether or not the sink counted as a safety station. I found myself laughing at how it contrasted starkly with my own experience as a teaching assistant, once upon a time.

WHEN THE LAB IS CLOSED

ADRIENNE CANINO

Date: 09/19/2021 9:55 PM
From: barberw@stu.arcana.edu
To: farmswortht@arcana.edu, desantom@stu.arcana.edu
Cc: flores-purgezm@stu.arcana.edu,
carpenterr@stu.arcana.edu
Subject: MBIO 115 Lab 3 - mandrake root safety procedure
help

Dear Professor Farmsworth, Micah,

Hope everyone is doing well!

Can you please advise us? We're trying to run our lab, and
we completed the setup per the safety video (New 2021 At
Home Procedures for Magical Biology Students), but it
seems our mandrake sprout has escaped the dental floss-
chopstick staking system. We think it has been in the
apartment the whole time, because the cat's been missing,
and Marco got hit with a sound-wave this morning. It's
playing in the shower right now (keeping the water on is
distracting it).

How can we get it back into the pot? Our apartment super
has provided a Class A bucket, in case we need it, as well.

Also, can we have an extension on the lab? The ER said
Marco should rest for 48 hours, and we haven't even tried
to get the hair sample off the little guy yet.

Thanks in advance,

Willow Barber
Magical Biology Department
Arcana University
Clouds, IN

Date: 09/19/2021 10:27 PM
From: desantom@stu.arcana.edu
To: barberw@stu.arcana.edu, flores-purgezm@stu.arcana.edu, carpenterr@stu.arcana.edu
Cc: farmswortht@arcana.edu
Subject: RE: MBIO 115 Lab 3 - mandrake root safety procedure help

Hi Willow,

Thanks for your question. Good thinking with the shower. A Class A bucket is a great start for a trap. Try some peanut butter or chocolate (or both!) in the bottom, slide it into the bathroom and sooner or later the mandrake will get curious and eat until sleepy. If you've taken your Physical Magic 105 and can manage the stun charm, it would be useful to have at the ready.

Once in the bucket, it's scream cannot harm you, but please continue to wear all the safety equipment from your lab kit, including earplugs, earmuffs, and safety goggles. Cover with a coat of soil to induce its long-term sleep behavior, and quickly repot into the lab container. The safety manual recommends menthol dental floss; double-check that is what you are using. Red pepper flakes sprinkled on top sometimes works as extra incentive to keep them underground; too spicy for their tender roots.

Please do also be careful with your shower for a few days. As you know, mandrake makes a powerful ingredient in various fertility, sleeping, anti-inflammatory, and aphrodisiac potions.

Professor Farmsworth and I can give you a 48 hour extension. Marco, we hope you feel better soon!

Let me know if I can answer any further questions,

Micah Desanto
Teaching Assistant, MBIO 115 Fall 2021
PhD Candidate
Magical Biology Department
Arcana University
Clouds, IN

Date: 10/25/2021 1:33 AM
From: barberw@stu.arcana.edu
To: farmswortht@arcana.edu, desantom@stu.arcana.edu
Cc: flores-purgezm@stu.arcana.edu,
carpenterr@stu.arcana.edu
Subject: MBIO 115 Lecture Monday

Hello Professor Farmsworth, hi Micah,

Thank you for an interesting lecture video from Monday. I know a few students and I have noticed what seems to be a hiccup in the middle? The section about terroir in magical herb growth jumps through a lot of dark smoke and music that seems to know our names and demand some sort of payment. Maybe the video platform got hacked?

I wanted to let you know (though I did get through the rest of the lecture after). Can I double check that the content was complete despite the spam, so that I can be prepared for the midterm?

Thanks, hope you're enjoying the halloween festivities,

Willow Barber
Magical Biology Department
Arcana University
Clouds, IN

Date: 10/25/2021 6:43 AM
From: desantom@stu.arcana.edu
To: barberw@stu.arcana.edu, flores-purgezm@stu.arcana.edu, carpenterr@stu.arcana.edu
Cc: farmswortht@arcana.edu
Subject: URGENT RE: MBIO 115 Lecture Monday

Willow, Marco, Rufus,

Please be advised this is not a spam attack on the platform. The video lecture is fine, you seem to be the target of a Curse.

As you know, Arcana University has a strict anti-harrassment policy, in addition to priding ourselves on being a community of ethical magic-workers.

I reported the incident to Student Affairs, and they'll be contacting you soon. I suggest you run a standard detection wand over your laptops in the meantime, on the off chance you can sever the connection.

Take care, and be extra careful on Samhain, unless you know for certain the curse has been resolved. Maybe get ahold of some holy basil?

-Micah

Micah Desanto
Teaching Assistant, MBIO 115 Fall 2021
PhD Candidate
Magical Biology Department
Arcana University
Clouds, IN

Date: 10/25/2021 6:45 AM
From: Student-Affairs@arcana.edu
To: barberw@stu.arcana.edu, flores-purgezm@stu.arcana.edu, carpenterr@stu.arcana.edu
Cc: desantom@stu.arcana.edu
Subject: Hex-event via MBIO115-2 BlackCuldron site

To Willow Barber, Marco Flores-Purgez, and Rufus Carpenter,

Please be advised you are under magical monitoring as of 6:45 AM, the 25th of October, due to an official report regarding your safety from a concerned university member. The monitoring spell will operate under all the terms and conditions you agreed to in your student code of conduct booklet, and all questions can be answered by the First-Year Experience Team.

I need to set up an interview with you, which may or may not be conducted in person or via mirror spell, or a phone call or the school's video platform Mirroom, and anyone affected by the curse must be present unless they cannot be due to the pandemic.

Please call our number at 1-800-555-2203 at your earliest convenience, but no later than 10:00 AM the day of this notice. The magical monitoring spell will provide you with a notification an hour before the deadline.

Best,

Sgt. Poppins
Security and Anti-curse Department
Student Affairs
Arcana University
Keeping you, and your broom, safe

Date: 11/29/2021 2:03 PM
From: barberw@stu.arcana.edu
To: farmswortht@arcana.edu, desantom@stu.arcana.edu
Cc: flores-purgezm@stu.arcana.edu,
carpenterr@stu.arcana.edu
Subject: MBIO 115 Lab 12 - DandeLionesses escaped?

Hi Micah, Professor Farmsworth,

So, over the fall break, it seems that our cat and the pride of
Dandelionesses we raised for Lab 12 have escaped and are
stalking the neighborhood dogs (really just our super's
Chihuahua, they're not that big yet). Apparently they were
seen just this morning around the garbage bins, so we
know they're not far, and not fully grown, and no one has
gotten hurt. We did tie thread to their stems, and our cat
Nala is microchipped, but so far our Trace spells haven't
come up with anything.

As you know, we need sign-off from a staff or faculty
member to work a bigger magic, or the police will come to
interview us again, and we really want to keep this
apartment for next year.

Can we set up a meeting today or tomorrow morning in the
patio area First-Year Experience has set up for outdoor
office hours?

Thanks!

Will - also my number is 333-1978

Willow Barber
Magical Biology Department
Arcana University
Clouds, IN

Adrienne Canino

Date: 11/29/2021 2:31 PM
From: desantom@stu.arcana.edu
To: barberw@stu.arcana.edu, flores-
purgezm@stu.arcana.edu, carpenterr@stu.arcana.edu
Cc: farmswortht@arcana.edu
Subject: RE: MBIO 115 Lab 12 - DandeLionesses escaped?

Hi Willow,

I'm on campus today, in the office all day. Come over as soon as you can, we'll file the paperwork, and I can come back to your neighborhood to help you catch them.

If I remember correctly, Rufus is allergic, right? They can always tell, it may make for a good lure.

See you soon,

-Micah, 433-8791

Micah Desanto
Teaching Assistant, MBIO 115 Fall 2021
PhD Candidate
Magical Biology Department
Arcana University
Clouds, IN

Date: 11/29/2021 2:38 PM
From: carpenterr@stu.arcana.edu
To: desantom@stu.arcana.edu, barberw@stu.arcana.edu,
flores-purgezm@stu.arcana.edu
Cc:
Subject: RE: RE: RE: MBIO 115 Lab 12 - DandeLionesses
escaped?

Not so sure I want to be bait.

-R

Rufus Carpenter
Magical Theory Department
Arcana University
Clouds, IN

Date: 11/29/2021 2:48 PM
From: flores-purgezm@stu.arcana.edu
To: desantom@stu.arcana.edu, barberw@stu.arcana.edu,
carpenterr@stu.arcana.edu
Subject: RE: RE: MBIO 115 Lab 12 - Dandelionesses
escaped?

Ha! Rufus, you're so 'a lure' ing!

Marco Flores-Purgez
Magical Biology Department
Arcana University
Clouds, IN

Date: 11/29/2021 4:31 PM
From: farmswortht@arcana.edu
To: desantom@stu.arcana.edu, barberw@stu.arcana.edu,
flores-purgezm@stu.arcana.edu,
carpenterr@stu.arcana.edu
Subject: FWD: Are your students doing a lab?

Is this handled?

-Terry

T. Farmsworth
Associate Professor and Class 3 Mage
Magical Biology
Arcana University
Clouds, IN

Date: 11/29/2021 12:39 PM
From: terracottapotta@beemail.com
To: farmsworhtht@arcana.edu
Subject: Are your students doing a lab?

Hey Terry,

I noticed some wild Dandelions over off Fox street today, not far from campus. I wanted to let you know, in case it was your students and something went wrong. Hopefully not though!

Anyway, I reported it to Creature-Control, just in case.

Hope you're doing alright with this crazy surge, we hope to have a semi-normal holiday party, with our bonfire in the driveway technique, so you'll be hearing from me soon.

Cheers,

Maddie

Follow @TerraCottaPotta on Pentagram

Date: 11/29/2021 6:31 PM
From: desantom@stu.arcana.edu
To: farmswortht@arcana.edu, barberw@stu.arcana.edu,
flores-purgezm@stu.arcana.edu,
carpenterr@stu.arcana.edu
Subject: RE: FWD: Are your students doing a lab?

Yes, Professor, we got the Dandelioness pride back into
their thread-rows. Nala, the cat Lab group 3 has, is back,
and my understanding is the lab report will be turned in on
time, by midnight tonight.

We did run into Creature-Control while herding them, but
we had them under spell by then, and the CC team left it to
us after I explained it had in fact been an at-home biology
lab.

See you tomorrow,

Micah

Micah Desanto
Teaching Assistant, MBIO 115 Fall 2021
PhD Candidate
Magical Biology Department
Arcana University
Clouds, IN

WIZAPP: CHAT ROOMS
Bio Lab & TA
Micah D., Will'o'da'Wisp, Marcoooooooooh, Me

2:03 PM: Will'o'da'Wisp: So Micah, Lab Group 3 here again. Is it possible the Chimera we have for the Bisection Final are 3 creature blends, not just 2?

2:18 PM: Micah D.: Willow, is your creature still in suspension?

2:19 PM: Will'o'da'Wisp: Well, yes and no.

2:19 PM: Will'o'da'Wisp: Two pieces of it are.

2:19 PM: Will'o'da'Wisp: Is it possible they were not just lion-snakes, but goat-lion-snakes?

2:21 PM: Micah D.: It's a super rare mutation, but, yes, technically possible.

2:22 PM: Marcoooooooooh: It's possible. It's in our apartment right now.

2:23 PM: Me: I am not being bait again.

2:23 PM: Micah D.: Is your salt line broken?

2:25 PM: Micah D.: Guys?

2:29 PM: Micah D.: Willow? Should I come over again?

2:32 PM: Micah D.: I'm on my way.

2:34 PM: Micah D.: You got any of that Holy Basil left? Or the Class A bucket still?

2:40 PM: Me: Dude, it won't fit in the bucket, you better come over here and see this. Willow gets like, an A++.

2:40 PM: Marcoooooooooh: Can we keep it?

2:41 PM: Micah D.: DO NOT TOUCH ANYTHING - FLYING NOW.

Date: 12/08/2021 09:32 AM
From: desantom@stu.arcana.edu
To: barberw@stu.arcana.edu, flores-purgezm@stu.arcana.edu, carpenterr@stu.arcana.edu
Cc: farmswortht@arcana.edu
Subject: Lab group 3 MBIO 115 Lab 15 - Chimera Bisection resulted in three

Good morning Professor Farmsworth,

I'm writing to update you on Labgroup 3's final lab. Their labkit Chimera was actually a Mythos class — lion, goat, and snake. They alerted me as soon as they found out, but unplanned for as it was, the goat escaped. It caused quite a bit of ruckus before Willow successfully netted it.

With the supply issues, I cannot re-issue them an at-home kit. I think we had hoped that folks could be back on campus to complete this lab by now, but alas, Memorandum 2021-17 prevented that. Given that it is a mistake of the lab supplies, rather than any fault in the execution of their Bisection charm, I would like to grade them on this lab as it was executed, and according to the same rubric.

What do you think?

-Micah

Micah Desanto
Teaching Assistant, MBIO 115 Fall 2021
PhD Candidate
Magical Biology Department
Arcana University
Clouds, IN

Date: 12/08/2021 10:47 AM
From: farmswortht@arcana.edu
To: desantom@stu.arcana.edu, barberw@stu.arcana.edu, flores-purgezm@stu.arcana.edu, carpenterr@stu.arcana.edu
Subject: RE: Lab group 3 MBIO 115 Lab 15 - Chimera Bisection resulted in three

Micah,

Yes, that's fine. Grade as you see fit.

Willow, Marco, Rufus: I know we're not supposed to reference THOSE movies, but seriously, why is it always you three?

-Terry

T. Farmsworth
Associate Professor and Class 3 Mage
Magical Biology
Arcana University
Clouds, IN

Graham J. Darling of Metro Ottawa Canada designs molecules such as the universe has never seen and demonstrates medieval science and technology to school kids and passers-by. His singular hybrids of diamond-hard Science Fiction, mythopoeic Fantasy and unearthly Horror have escaped through *Dark Matter Magazine* and *Sword & Mythos* (eds. Silvia Moreno-Garcia & Paula R. Stiles) — residents are advised to lock their doors and windows, then tune in for survival tips at *Fiction.GrahamJDarling.com*, Twitter.com/GrahamJDarling or Facebook.com/GrahamJDarling.

•　　　•　　　•

Against Death and the Devil, against tyrants and wars, against the crazes and phobias infecting their own audiences, storytellers have invoked the power of Comedy to belittle the Overwhelming enough to see past it and so hope to cope; to slay giants and build worlds from their bones. So let it be with this presumptuous virus: after all, it isn't as if there weren't still plenty of other things out to get us. For now.

THE NEW SEASON

GRAHAM J. DARLING

A SHARP DOUBLE TOOT SOUNDED from the street outside. I rolled over and peered between the curtains: up, first, at the pole in my front yard, where a few tatters at the top stirred weakly in the dawn's early light; then between bushes at bits of receding rusty vehicle until it turned a corner and vanished.

Then I took a minute to check over my ravaged carcass. With COVID-34, the spots were purple. They itched like blazes and left scars like bullet-holes, but at least we weren't shambling about, eating brains — that had been COVID-29.

I crawled out of bed and hand-pumped my scuba gear, went out and got the day's food from the blue box at the curb, and then flipped it back over to show to whom it may concern that I was still alive. There hadn't been any recycling or garbage collection for a good ten years, but that's what backyards are for; nor was anyone still paying the farmers who came around in crop-spraying masks and biodiesel pickups, but their daily deposits of apples and beans and corn meant we in town wouldn't have to come knocking on their doors, coughing in their faces.

Then, because it was a Wednesday, I went back out and walked down the middle of the street, high-powered rifle at the ready to enforce social distancing, and maybe bag the odd three-eyed crow (their corvid COVID wasn't contagious to humans, this year, yet). From a block away, I waved at the house of my fourth wife — the one who'd lasted the longest, so far — and she blinked her shutters twice in return, and we were good for another week.

Then I came back to collect my crowbar and axe and went out to chop wood to cook breakfast. The current timber supply was starting to show its foundations and I'd soon need to start on another. There'd be little to fear from the people inside: virus doesn't live long on corpses.

I scooped a pitcherful of water, ready to boil, from the rain-barrel on the way back in, and that was that for my outings for the day.

After a spell of paperwork, I fired up the solar sat-phone and called my Cabinet to review the state of the nation. There hadn't been an election in years, but with every president having died in office, eventually the succession had passed to me, ex-postmaster in these parts.

"Good morning, Mister President!" shouted the Secretary of State, still somewhat deaf from COVID-24, and my own successor until I could recruit a new vice-president with their own phone, or find anyone left from Congress.

"Oh, what's the use?" mumbled the Attorney General — there hadn't been any births since COVID-31, a mumps mimic. "None of that, none of that," said the Secretary of Defense, a Churchill fan — some hope remained that very young children might yet grow up to be fertile.

The pleasantries aside, we were briefed by the Secretary of Homeland Security on what she'd gathered from her phone-in talk show. Then we thrashed out the Middle East question for a while (whether anyone there was left), and finally moved on to the usual main course.

Also as usual, the Secretary of Health began there by pushing for regular check-ups (he'd been a dentist). The Secretary of the Treasury, a frustrated tax-preparer and still a bit cracked from COVID-32, shouted once more that all carriers should be shot in the head, but the Secretary of Commerce very reasonably pointed out, once more, that this would only spray more infection into the air, and even apart from that, could only end with no one left alive.

"What I'd like to know," I said, "is what next year's version will look like. Has anyone got a clue yet about COVID-35?"

"I am COVID-35," said the Secretary of Agriculture, speaking for the first time that day.

I shut my eyes with an inward groan — insanity, again. Unless ...

"Uh, pleased to meet you, Mister, uh, 35. So you've taken over your, uh, our colleague's brain? Any chance he'll, er, ever get it back again?"

"Avenues for collaboration may yet be found, if he lives," said COVID-35. The words were what the man we knew might've chosen, but delivered in a strange, clipped monotone. "But today I must speak to you for myself."

"Go on," I said. My Cabinet all leaned forward expectantly, except for the Secretary of the Interior, who had fallen asleep — at least, I hoped it was sleep. He'd been the most spotted of any of us.

"I know my own survival depends on yours," said COVID-35. "If you go extinct, so do I."

"Then why," I said, "are you killing us off?"

"Why this is happening," he — it — said, "is because your kind has been far too healthy for far too long. Fire is a natural part of forest life, so that some trees like sequoias even need the touch of flame to open their cones and release their seeds.

But if you humans start putting out every little smolder before it really gets started, then the underbrush just keeps piling up, so when the big one finally comes along and escapes control, everything gets burned to white ash: root, stem, seed and all."

I got the message, and nodded: enough with the vaccinations already — of course that's what a virus would say.

"In the normal course of things," the possessed one went on, "when faced with a new disease, those who already happen to have what it takes to survive will live to pass that on to their descendants. But the germ itself will also mutate into milder forms, that succeed through leaving their hosts alive long enough to jump to others, even protecting them by stimulating or preparing their immune systems against worse things. Thus, a guardian virus might eventually be allowed permanent residence in the human body, and even its template taken up into the human genome, much like hunters who evolve into shepherds, or bandits into an aristocracy and a State. It's that kind of co-existence we've been working towards, but you've all been just ... so ... easy to kill."

"I see," I said. The Secretary of the Interior had slumped right over — looked like I'd now have to find a replacement there, too. "What do you propose, then?"

"To study the precedents," said COVID-35, "by consulting our ancestors. That's why I've now summoned COVID-8341 BC from the depths of this body's chromosomes, to tell us how he and you people managed to make it through that earlier outbreak."

The Secretary of Agriculture's second head, a souvenir of COVID-27, usually didn't have much to say, but now began to sniffle and wheeze, while COVID-35 translated. "Never had this trouble in my day — you humans knew your place back then pineapple — sorry, that was an actual cough. You died when you were supposed to, so the rest of us could live and we could all just get along. Now it's all so complicated ... The last time things got this bad ..."

We waited with bated breath — some breaths more bated than others, if you count the Secretary of the Interior.

"I heard 35's talk of forest fires," said, arguably, the Secretary of Agriculture, COVID-35, or COVID-8341 BC. "Well, one way to stop a fire dead is to take away its fuel — to make a firebreak, by cutting out a swath downwind with axes, or burning one out with your own backfire, anything to destroy some of the forest faster than what'll destroy it all. That's what COVID-Cretaceous had to do, he told us the other day while we were all kicking back in the gene pool.

"His shtick had been to turn all the cells in a body — liver, skin, the works — into neurons. In those days, dino-brains walked the Earth. Kills 'em in the end, of course, but before they all died out, the strongest strain developed a hive mind, clairvoyance, telekinesis — it understood in time what was happening, reached out and nudged an asteroid from its orbit, and the rest is pre-history."

"My God," whispered the Secretary of Labor.

"Not really," was the reply. "But COVID-Cambrian still preaches to us on the perfect COVID of a bygone RNA World before it fell into DNA sin, and of which we are but a sorry remnant.

"But enough about us. Let's not lose track of the main issue here, or beat around the bush. Your people's population is low right now, but to break this cycle we're all caught in, it has to drop still lower, suddenly, and for years. You've got nukes: it's time to use 'em."

I did indeed have nukes: the key code I had inherited with my office, to activate and launch any part of our great nation's automated atomic arsenal, or all of it.

"What, do your dirty work for you, to ourselves? Never!" stormed the Secretary of Defense. "We shall fight you on the beaches, we shall fight you in the hills ..." The Secretary of the Treasury was also shouting again, and the Secretary of Education burst into tears. The ruckus was loud enough to wake the dead; abruptly the Secretary of the Interior sat up straight, blinking.

The Cabinet meeting threatened to dissolve into chaos. I put them all on hold and took a bathroom break.

When I got back from my bucket in the garage, things had already quieted down some, and I waited until I had everyone's attention again.

"While we all appreciate your coming forward," I said to our guest or guests, "and we stand ready to further consider your claims, I feel that my Administration currently lacks the mandate to carry out the action you suggest. The people ought to be consulted before we kill most of them off, perhaps in a plebiscite —"

"And cause a nationwide panic?" said the Secretary of Transportation, but we all looked at her in weary astonishment.

"— or an election."

An election! Smiles broke out and heads nodded all around. It was high time we had one, if only to remind the nation it was still a nation, with a government to look after it, and a flag and an anthem and everything. And this was an issue that was sure to capture the public interest, with more at stake than just who's left alive to rule. Namely, who'll be left alive to be ruled, something folks would surely take a lot more personally.

The Secretary of Agriculture immediately tendered his resignation so he'd be free to found the COVID Party and run for president and vice-president, and I was secretly relieved to see him go: we didn't want the Enemy at our inmost counsels, after all.

And after all, an election would keep it busy, keep us all busy, until COVID-36.

Pauline Barmby (she/her) is a Canadian astrophysicist who believes that you can't have too many favorite galaxies. She affirms that her proposals to use the world's biggest telescopes are — to date — entirely non-fictional. Her fiction has been published in *Tree and Stone* and *Martian* magazines, *Nightmare Sky* from Death Knell Press, and *Compelling Science Fiction* from Flame Tree Press. When not reading or writing she runs, knits, and ponders the physics of curling. Find her on Twitter at *@PBarmby*.

•   •   •

I happened to spy the PhD Comics strip "Things that could be happening outside [e.g., a zombie outbreak, world's biggest blizzard] that you wouldn't know about because your lab/office has no windows" on a colleague's office door. It got me thinking about observatories, where I used to spend a lot of time. When you go observing you're at the top of a mountain, sleeping during the day, and quite isolated from the rest of the world. So maybe the world could be ending and you wouldn't pick up on it for a while. But what if the end of the world came from more than one direction? Those ideas got this story started.

THE OBSERVATORY AT THE END OF THE WORLD

PAULINE BARMBY

Extracts from the logbook of
Mt. Watford Observatory, February 2012

FEBRUARY 18

Wind: 65 km/h.
Conditions: light flurries and blowing snow, moon 11% illuminated. Too much snow to open the dome and it's possibly frozen shut anyway.

Personal notes: Nearly got blown off the mountain walking between dorm and telescope. Took some calibration data but it's frustrating not to be observing! On the other hand, I can go to bed before dawn. And it's so quiet. No one else on the mountain, no city TV or radio. The zombie apocalypse could be happening down in town and I'd never notice.

Observing like this is just about a thing of the past. I'm keeping these notes and copying in my texts with Julia so we can show our future grandchildren what Ye Olde Days were all about.

Julia: Miss u

Marko: Miss you too. Sorry we had to miss Valentines but I'll make it up to you when I get back.

Julia: Not your fault, my stupid schedule. Love you <3

Marko: Wish you could see the view up here, so beautiful. The snow is like a fluffy blanket over everything. So quiet my ears are ringing.

Julia: Remind me again: why can't u just run telescope from home?

Marko: This place is kind of an antique — still useful but there's not enough money to upgrade it to remote operations. So: observe all night, sleep most of the day. Boring but peaceful.

Julia: Sounds amazing

Marko: Kinda lonely. Although if I get the last of my thesis data, I should be able to find an asteroid I can name after you.

Julia: Really?

Marko: Yup. If it ever stops snowing that is

Julia: fingers crossed. Night M

Marko: Night. Love you <3

FEBRUARY 19

Wind: 40 km/h.
Conditions: scattered clouds, periods of flurries, moon 6% illuminated. Conditions at sunset were looking optimistic so I opened the dome and started twilight calibrations. Maintenance note: dome shutter squeals, needs lubrication. Exposure log: on-sky for calibration observations only.

Personal notes: Managed to get a few standard stars before the clouds rolled in from the west. Baited by sucker holes, gave up around midnight. Argh. No getting the thesis done without the remaining data. Without a finished thesis, no following Julia to wherever she matches for her residency. Being away for a week is one thing, but I can't imagine being apart for months or years.

Marko: Hey sweetie!

Marko: Julia?

Julia: ??

Marko: Oh shit, forgot about the time. Sorry for waking you

Julia: NP. How goes.

Marko: A bit better but still cloudy. Go back to sleep. Love you.

Julia: Luv u 2

FEBRUARY 20

Wind: 35 km/h.
Conditions: mostly clear, moon 2% illuminated. Lost about 2.5 hours when the telescope stopped tracking. Fixed by rebooting telescope control system FOUR TIMES. Dome shutter still squeaking. Exposure log: complete calibration dataset, about half of the survey area covered.

Personal notes: Finally on the sky! What a relief, even if I did end up wasting a lot of time with the TCS. Would be nice to let J know, but I don't want to wake her up again.

Julia: Better weather tonight?

Marko: Thanks, yeah, mostly clear and finally getting some decent data. Should be some new asteroids in there.

Marko: You're still up? R u on night shift now? Sorry, hard to keep track.

Julia: Can't talk now

Marko: Everything OK?

Julia: ED is crazy. Full moon?

Marko: Um, that was 10 days ago. Trust me, I'm an astronomer.

Julia: We're busy that's all I can say

Marko: Talk later. Get some sleep. Love you.

Julia: You too

FEBRUARY 21

Wind: 75 km/h.
Conditions: clear, new moon. Dome closed per wind limits.

Personal notes: Just about finished analyzing data from last night. Some near-Earth asteroid candidates, but need confirmation of non-sidereal motion from 2 more nights. Maddening to have perfectly clear skies, no moonlight, AND BE SITTING HERE WITH THE DOME CLOSED. I'd go outside to stargaze but it's so windy I might not be able to reopen the door.

Julia: You awake?

Marko: Yeah I'm here. Too windy to observe but hoping it'll die down.

Julia: Getting worried

Marko: Not really — still have a couple nights to go. Can still get the data I need

Julia: No I'm getting worried

Marko: Are you OK? Sweetie, what's up?

Julia: Many pts w/ resp symptoms, many staff out sick

Marko: Oh no, like 2004 with SARS?

Julia: Maybe worse

Marko: J, you need to take care of yourself! Did you get some sleep?

Julia: Few hours

Marko: That's not enough

Julia: I know

Julia: How is it up there

Marko: Lonely. I miss you.

Julia: Make sure you get some sleep

Marko: Look who's talking

Julia: I know

Marko: Try to rest, OK? I worry about you when I'm not there to tuck you in after the long night shifts.

Julia: I'll be ok. Love you

Marko: You too. <3

FEBRUARY 22

Wind: 40 km/h.
Conditions: high cirrus, moon 1% illuminated. Minor issue with the camera control software, lost a few exposures when they didn't save to disk. Fixed, as always, by rebooting everything. About 30 min lost. Exposure log: complete calibration dataset, most of the survey area covered.

Personal notes: so neat to hear the deep rumble of the dome as it turns overhead, like being in the hold of a spaceship or something. Reassuring somehow. Reassuring is good, because I'm starting to feel nervous again about getting enough data — only 3 nights left in this run. And nervous in an entirely different direction, thinking about how to propose to Julia. Is that too old-fashioned and cringey? I can't imagine being without her. I just want us to spend the rest of our lives together.

Julia: Hi love, did u get a good sleep?

Marko: Not bad. Tough when the wind was so noisy. Thanks for asking. You?

Julia: No time

Marko: Covering shifts again?

Julia: Yeah

Marko: More flu patients?

Julia: So many

Marko: Can't they call anyone else in?

Julia: They're trying

Marko: You're feeling ok though? Right?

Julia: Coughing a bit. Just tired

Marko: Sweetheart, you have to take care of yourself.

Marko: Can't look after patients if you're sick!

Marko: Julia?

Julia: Sorry, quick consult

Julia: How's your thing going

Marko: Please don't try to change the subject. Promise me you'll rest. Someone else can look after the patients.

Julia: There isn't anyone else

Marko: It's that bad?

Julia: Idk. Feels like it

Marko: Stay safe, promise me.

Julia: Trying

Marko: Please, take care of yourself. Ily.

Julia: Ily too. Gotta go

FEBRUARY 23

Wind: 30 km/h.
Conditions: scattered clouds, moon 3% illuminated. Not quite photometric but close enough. The camera dewar's cryo-pump is making different noises from before, something like *squee-oo, squee-oo*. Maintenance crew please take a look next week. Exposure log: running the full survey imaging sequence.

Personal notes: Data from the two good nights so far show hints of 7 small bodies that don't match anything in the database. Plus 47 re-discoveries. Reported positions to minor planet center. Orbits are still pretty uncertain: one of the new ones looks like it might have quite a close approach to Earth in about 90 years.

Julia: How much food do you have up there?

Marko: Maybe a week's worth still. I always bring extra. Why?

Julia: I think you should stay longer

Marko: Why?

Julia: Safer up there

Marko: What do you mean?

Julia: This flu is different, people aren't getting better

Julia: You haven't seen the news?

Marko: No, mostly working or trying to sleep

Julia: I get that

Julia: It's bad tho

Marko: ARE YOU OK??

Julia: Just tired

Marko: I have one more night, but I could make the round trip tomorrow: come down to look after you, then come back up.

Julia: NO PLS DON'T

Julia: That road is dangerous. I'm probably overreacting, just tired

Julia: Helps to know you're safe up there so please stay

Marko: OK. You're scaring me a bit though.

Julia: I'm scared too

Marko: Just hang on. I love you.

Julia: love you too

FEBRUARY 24

Wind: 45 km/h.
Conditions: very thin cirrus, moon 7% illuminated.
Running the full survey imaging sequence. Crow flew into
the dome around 0200. Lost about half an hour chasing it
out. Probably left some droppings, will check later.

Personal notes: Too tired to analyze data. Checked the
emergency supplies: water, generator fuel, heating oil
(what is this, the 19th century?) tanks all full. Medical
supplies recently updated. Can't find the emergency food
stores but I've been eating too much anyway. Why did I buy
so many snacks?

Next week's observer didn't bother to come up the usual
night early, no wonder given the weather. Maintenance
crew was due today and they haven't shown up either.
Haven't been able to get hold of Julia — not answering her
phone or texts. Probably (hopefully!) that means she's
finally getting some sleep. Those hospital shifts are awful,
especially in flu season.

FEBRUARY 25

Wind: 25 km/h.
Conditions: patchy cirrus, moon 13% illuminated. Definitely non-photometric but still worth observing. Full calibration set, quadrupled exposure times to reach necessary depth. Seeing: decent at about 0.8 arcsec. Refilled camera dewar, note that N2 tank is down to about 10%.

Personal notes: After cleaning out the bird poop, lots of time to analyze the last 2 nights' data. The potential Earth-crossing asteroid is getting interesting but the orbit uncertainty is still pretty high.

Next week's observer still hasn't shown so decided I might as well keep observing. The mountain's Internet link keeps going down and then coming back up. No one's answering the phone at the base camp office. This is getting really lonely. Now I kind of wish the crow would come back. Getting more worried about Julia. I know she hates it when I fuss over her, but why isn't she responding?

Marko: Did you get some rest?

Marko: Julia? Are you OK?

Marko: Please answer, love. I'm worried about you.

FEBRUARY 26

Wind: 30 km/h.
Conditions: clear, moon 20% illuminated. Excellent transparency and seeing (about 0.65 arcsec!) Two run-throughs of the full survey sequence plus additional imaging to follow up the object of interest from 23 Feb.

Personal notes: This morning I couldn't sleep. Mountain Internet is still down. Decided to drive down to base camp to see what was going on. The upper road was okay although it seemed like it hadn't been plowed since last week. Base camp buildings also locked and apparently empty. Weird: there's always someone puttering around there, even on weekends. I almost headed into town to check on Julia. She's probably back at the hospital though, and she did ask me to stay here. If I show up she'll just be mad.

Drove back up and had a 2-hr nap, then spent some time analyzing the combined data, including last night's, and holy shit. That Earth-crosser? (Screw it, I'm calling it "Bob".) With the revised orbit, Bob's minimum distance is now down to 1000 km. Now we're talking about a substantial collision risk. I need better-calibrated photometry and a better albedo measurement to get the size, but at a first estimate, the thing is about 2 km across.

When conditions are right at sunset, sometimes you can see across the valley and tell whether the dome is open at the 4-meter on Cactus Peak. I forgot to check at sunset, but there was no answer when I phoned their landline number at about 1930 or when I tried again just after midnight. Julia's still not responding either. I tried her pager, landline, email, everything I could think of. Hospital numbers all constantly busy. I'm gonna go down to town in the morning to find out what's going on.

FEBRUARY 27

Wind: 35 km/h.
Conditions: high cirrus, moon 28% illuminated. Seeing 0.8 arcsec. Checked Cactus Peak 4-meter with binoculars at sunset; their dome is closed. Repeating last night's observation sequence.

Personal notes: Dammit, slept way later than I planned, didn't wake up until almost sunset. Endless observatory safety briefings have beaten into my head that the mountain road is too treacherous to drive alone in the dark. Julia would kill me if she found out I'd done it.

Still observing because I don't know what else to do. Running the orbit pipeline with last night's data included. HOLY MURGATROYD. Now the 95% confidence interval for Bob's closest approach has it *colliding* with Earth. The most likely collision is 90 years from now but I can't rule out 15 years either.

Found an old radio stashed in the workshop and the only thing I could pick up was a Mexican AM station. Lots of talking, even faster than usual, and the voice didn't sound like a professional announcer. Even with my lousy Spanish, I was pretty sure I got 'influenza' and 'quarantine' and 'help'. The room spun and I felt faint.

I left the observing sequence running and walked out to the edge of the road where it drops off. My tennis shoes squeaked in the slush and my feet started to go numb. Ninety years from now, the world was going to end. The signs from the last few days, that I'd been trying not to think about, implied that my world might have already ended. Julia, gone. Our future, wiped out. I thought about just letting myself fall.

Panic clenched my stomach and a gust of wind made me shiver. Automatically I looked up at the sky to gauge the seeing and guess what the clouds might do. Jupiter and Venus shone high on the ecliptic. The western sky was clearing out and I imagined I could see M31 setting even though there was no way my eyes were dark-adapted enough. Were anyone else's eyes on the sky right now? Or was everyone who was left just huddling inside, trying to make sense of what had happened? I let out a breath I hadn't realized I was holding. I might be the only person alive who knew about Bob's appointment with Earth in a few decades. *That* was a reason to keep going, to at least get the word out.

I shuffled back inside to push through the emptiness until dawn. While the telescope hummed and the dome rumbled, I assembled the critical information about Bob's orbit and the collision prediction. In the back seat of my car was a Christmas present from my brother — a ream of the expensive, acid-free paper that the university library insists on for printed copies of theses. I used it to print a hundred copies of the critical data, and wrote out another twenty copies by hand with the most permanent writing implement I could find. By the time I finished, the sky was lightening, my writing hand ached and I was woozy from the Sharpie ink. I stepped outside and breathed the mountain air, whole body shaking.

FEBRUARY 28

Wind and sky conditions: irritatingly perfect. And what did it matter? To think that ten days ago, my biggest concern had been whether I'd get enough data to finish the last paper of my thesis. No need to worry about my thesis defense any more. I safed the telescope and turned everything off except the cooling system. There was enough liquid nitrogen and generator fuel to keep it going for at least a couple of weeks.

Tackling the mountain road after being awake for eighteen hours wasn't the best idea, but I had to find Julia, had to know what had happened. The road turned out to be an easy drive, still deserted, as was the base camp. The same couldn't be said for the highway, crammed with cars heading out of town. I didn't look too closely at their insides: on the valley floor it gets hot enough, even this time of year.

I couldn't pretend the bodies weren't there once I got into town. The smell alone was enough that I barely managed to pull over before losing my breakfast. More bodies than I ever wanted to see, if fewer than I'd expected. Most seemed strangely peaceful, as if they'd just dropped in place where they were. The carrion eaters had clearly gotten to some; flocks of vultures circled in the thermals over the largest parking lots.

Chaos reigned at every hospital access road and entrance: I had to leave the car on a side street and walk the last few blocks. Here things didn't look so peaceful. There were bodies everywhere, some in small groups, some with dark stains beneath them on the baking asphalt. The stench was overwhelming. I heaved bile and spit.

My heart rose at the familiar sight of Julia's red mountain bike in the same corner of the bike cage where she always locked up. Something on the bike flapped in the slight breeze. Getting closer, I found an 8.5x11 sheet of paper tied to the top tube, my name in slightly shaky capital letters blurred by droplet stains.

> MARIO,
>
> If you're reading this, hopefully you stayed away long enough to wait out the incubation period. Best we can tell, it's only about 36 hours, so you'll likely be safe. Please maintain as much distance as you can from other people for now.
>
> It all happened so fast. I wish I'd had a chance to say goodbye. If we had to be separated, at least it happened while we were both doing what we loved. You might think that your passion was less important but that's not true: just keeping people alive isn't worth a lot if they can't also look at the stars.
>
> Keep dreaming. I love you.
>
> Julia

Stomach hollow, head pounding, I sank to my knees on the scorching pavement. My throat was dry and I could only choke out a few sobs while holding the note close to my face. I hoped that Julia's perfume might somehow still linger, but the only scents were disinfectant and death. I imagined Julia coming out to place the note, knowing we'd never see each other again. She would never have thought to get on her bike and get away while she still could. She'd have dried her tears and gone back to doing what she could, what she loved.

FEBRUARY 29

Wind: 20 km/h.
Conditions: a sparkling blue day that looks like a good night, moon 41% illuminated. The half-lit sphere winks gently at me as I turn off the highway and head east toward the observatory. I glance down at Julia's note and blink back tears.

A leap year seems precipitous: extra time, like I seem to have been given in this life. I think I've figured out what to do with it, for now.

There must be other survivors around somewhere. I'm not ready to look for them, or to be around other people, just yet. I deposited copies of my info sheet somewhere out of the sun at every location I could think of: museum, water-treatment plant, city hall, Air Force base. I've loaded up on supplies and I'm going back to the telescope. There's still work to be done on Bob's trajectory and I might be the only person who can do it right now.

I'll keep people alive the only way I know how. Maybe someday there'll be time for dreaming too.

Antaeus is a U.S. Military veteran who writes from a lakefront home in Southwest Florida. While cleaning toilets in a bar at age nine, he wrote his first poem on a sheet of sandpaper-like toilet paper. Antaeus is the author of *The Prepared Citizen*, a three-book series on Situational Awareness. Antaeus has also written numerous sci-fi and humorous fantasy novels. Antaeus can now afford to use actual paper, but his lousy handwriting forces him to write his books digitally. To view Antaeus' books and see what he's currently working on check out *antaeus-books.com*.

●　　　●　　　●

During the Pandemic, stores and restaurants were closing/downsizing at an alarming rate while Cannabis dispensaries were opening and thriving. During that time, a major call-center told all its employees they would be working from home. My neighbor was the maintenance person there and figured he was being laid off, so he applied for unemployment compensation. To his surprise, he began receiving his regular paycheck, an unemployment check, and government subsidy money. He told me he was making a lot more money unemployed than working. I asked him what he planned to do with all that extra money. He said flippantly, "I'm going to buy a pizza oven and sell marijuana pizza out of my garage." My overactive imagination ran with that, and "Pandemic Pizza" was born.

PANDEMIC PIZZA

ANTAEUS

From: James Johansen
To: Pascale, the pizza purveyor < Passonouta@bullddog.net>
Subject: RE: Pandemic Pizza

Pascale, I can't believe you turned your grandmother's old pizza recipe into a money-maker. Of course, I want in on your deal. It will be like old times. Like the time when we were seven and had a Kool-Aid stand together. Do you remember all the fun we had when we traded thirteen-year-old Jenny Buggly a glass of grape Kool-Aid for a kiss? I do, and I still break out in lip sores occasionally.

I'll be at your shop on Saturday at about 11 AM. I can't wait to taste your pizza.
Your friend,
J.J.

-----Original Message-----

From: Pascale Sonouta < Passonouta@bullddog.net>
Sent: Monday, June 6, 2022, 10:25 AM
To: James Johansen <jjohansen@cowpaddy.net>
Subject: Pandemic Pizza

Hey, J.J., how are you and your family fairing during this pandemic? I thought I'd send you this email to update you on what I've been doing during my company-required work-from-home time.

To put it succinctly, I've been getting very rich!

Since you're my best friend, I wanted to let you in on this gig and give you a taste of some of the easy bucks I've been raking in. I'm thinking of opening another store and thought I'd throw you a bone if you're interested. I know you have no idea what I'm talking about right now, so I'll explain. Here's the scoop.

When the lockdown started, we were told everyone would have to work from home. At first, I was worried they would find out I was the company maintenance man and couldn't do anything from home. You know, no light bulbs to change or toilets to fix and all that. But then the payroll department kept sending me checks every week, so I didn't say a word. Since I couldn't work, I applied for and started receiving state unemployment money. Then the government money started rolling in. Ultimately, I was making more money unemployed than when I was employed.

We were living high on the hog, but this whole enterprise started because I was bored. With nothing constructive to do, I began experimenting with an old pizza recipe of my grandmother's. It took six weeks of trial and error, but I finally created the perfect pie. Did you know that pizza means pie in Italian? The pie had an aromatic sweet-tasting crust because I used real maple syrup in the dough. When I pulled it from the oven, the freshly-cooked pizza's aroma was so appealing that it resulted in nose drools.

I named the pie "Nonna Sonata Special Pizza," after my grandmother. It's a thin-crust pizza covered with an assortment of colorful roasted bell peppers, caramelized onion, and crumbled sausage, then I top it with my "Special Ho-made Pesto."

The secret isn't so much in the dough, although that helps. It's the ho-made pesto I put into the dough that makes my pizza irresistible. I incorporate a particular combination of herbs from my garage garden in each pie. I use nothing but the best seeds while growing my herbs. Then I plant them in organic soil, bathe them in artificial sunlight, and give them bottled water to drink.

I tested the pizza on my wife and immediately knew I had a winner. After two slices, Nancy stopped nagging me about doing chores around the house. Instead, all she wanted to do was have sex, lots of sex. Whoopie!

The family in the house next door has also been in lockdown for a while. Their five kids are home from school, and sometimes I hear their head-banger music through my walls. Nancy suggested I give them a treat and test the pie on them simultaneously. Of course, I used a less intense combination of herbs because of the kids. As soon as they came out of the oven, I literally dropped three pies off at their house. Unfortunately, I had stepped barefoot on a giant beetle near their front door. It worked out okay, though, because they landed top-up.

The next day, my neighbor, Brian, the freeloader, came to our house and asked me if I had a few more pies, I could give him. He said his family went wild for the ones I dropped off and couldn't stop eating them. Instead of the kids fighting with each other or playing video games and loud music, the whole family sat around laughing or taking naps after dinner.

I told Brian that I was still in the process of experimenting with the ingredients and didn't have another pie handy. He got upset and offered to pay me a hundred bucks for each pie I made him. When I checked my stash — err, stock, I had enough herbs on hand to make him four pies. It was the most effortless four hundred bucks I ever made.

You know me, J.J., I'm not one to pass up an opportunity to make some easy money, so I began selling pizza out of my house the next day. The word spread faster than I expected. Soon I couldn't keep up with the demand, and the neighbors across the street began complaining about the traffic. They didn't like to look at all the cars parked outside my house. So, I decided it was time for me to expand.

Due to the lockdown here in Florida, most Main Street stores have closed their doors forever. So even though Nancy was against it, I cashed in our 401K and opened a pizza shop next door to "Mary Jane's." That's an herb and CBD dispensary the government considers an essential business. The best part is that MJ's has an abundant supply of the herbs I use in my pizza dough. So, I negotiated a deal with the owner to get what I needed wholesale provided I made her a free pie every day.

About a week after I opened the store, I was tossing a pie and had just placed it on the counter. My cat, Katie, knocked over a bottle of blue food coloring, staining the dough. I don't know how food coloring got on the workstation because I didn't use it. Anyway, it turned the pie an ocean blue color. That's when I had the epiphany which is making me a billionaire.

I began adding food coloring to the pizza dough. The pies now come in red, green, yellow, or blue. A slice sells for ten bucks, and a whole pie is eighty dollars. Due to the pineapple toppings, the "Mellow Yellow" is like a Hawaiian pizza. My unique green pesto adds a nice contrast. The mellow yellow doesn't sell too well because it looks like someone barfed. However, Sarasota being a circus town, the pie does have a following in the clown community.

Sarasota's surfing community is significant, and they go wild for the "Blue Lagoon" pies. The pie looks bright since its toppings include tomatoes, purple onions, yellow peppers, anchovies, and my unique pesto, which makes it colorful. They sell for fifteen dollars a slice or ninety dollars for a whole pie. I can't keep them on the shelf. The downside is that the surfers crowd around outside the store. Their bikini-wearing followers cause the old men to crane their necks to get a better view. All this rubbernecking disrupts traffic on Main Street, which, in turn, brings the deputies around to direct traffic.

I felt sorry for the deputies standing out there in the hot sun, so I gave them a slice of pizza and a bottle of my herb-infused water. Since no good deed goes unpunished, those freeloaders show up every day and won't go away until I give them a free pie.

The Gothic faction is a staple of my business. The wannabe vampires can't get enough of the red pies with extra double red sauce (hold the garlic), with blood sausages as a topping. The blood pies go for a hundred each, but the Goths don't care. Money is no object to them because they all live at home.

The Goths are also big on the impulse items like blood pudding, blood orange drinks, and Bloody Mary's. Most of them spend money like they have an unending supply of it. The problem is that they only come into the store at night, so the place has to be open from dusk to dawn, just for them. I don't mind, though. It's my busiest and most lucrative time of the day.

Vegetarians like my green pies and the vegan-friendly rainbow pies with extra herb topping. I make the crust light and buttery tasting by using plant butter, then top it with a cornucopia of vegetables. Sometimes they will order the pie with organic grass, quadruple vegetarian cheese, and the vegetables piled high. Of course, I charge extra if they want a gluten-free pie. My customers have lined up six feet apart, twenty or thirty deep, waiting for them to come out of the oven.

Following the government mandate, everyone has to wear masks, including myself and the staff. Our masks are N-95 certified and wild-looking. They're black with a yellow tongue licking red pizza-looking lips.

When the mandatory mask-wearing started, any customer who showed up without a mask had to buy one of our herb-infused face masks before entering the store. After a while, no one showed up wearing a mask, and I had to employ three seamstresses to sew and stuff the face masks to keep up with the demand.

At first, we were take-out only. However, business got so good that I had to knock down a wall and expand into the building next door. The original store is still strictly a take-out service, and the new section is for the eat-in crowd. Our tables are all spaced eight feet apart for safety's sake. The sign over the doorway says, "The Land of Nod," because most eat-in customers end up nodding out at their tables. We charge them an hourly fee for that.

Last month, the Sherriff dropped by and said he might have to close me down because of overcrowding. It was a bullshit reason. After consuming two free slices of contact-high pizza, he changed his mind. Then he asked for a horny goat weed pie to take home to his wife.

The next day I sent my delivery guy, Mephistopheles, to the Sheriff's office with ten black pies. They were decorated with a red, five-pointed star "special sugar" topping that Mephistopheles makes himself.

The day after that, the Sheriff and the Governor dropped by. The Sheriff said if I keep the pies coming, he's got no problem with me. The governor suggested I make a COVID-19 pie with my herb topping and a topping of hydroxychloroquine. "Hi-Droxy Pie" is now on the menu and seems popular with my news media and political customers.

While I'm on the subject of take-out, Mephistopheles, my delivery man (I think his name means an equal-sided triangle in Latin), was a lucky find. One day, the man walked into my shop and said he would work for free if I let him spread his lord's word. I think he must be a priest or minister of some kind.

It was Mephistopheles' idea to make the black pies with a red five-pointed star for the Sheriff. Unfortunately, he makes the black food coloring and special sugar topping at home and won't share the recipe. However, the Gothic crowd loves them too, and they're becoming one of our best sellers.

My idea of multicolored herb-topped or sugar-topped pizza has caught on. The other day, some fellow asked me to make him a tie-dyed pizza with extra herbs and sugar topping. He was wearing a shirt that said "Grateful Dead" on it. How could someone be grateful that they were dead? Besides, he looked alive to me.

I think I need to have my eyes checked, though. The young man made all these weird motions with his arms and hands and shook his head while waiting for his order. I asked him if he was feeling okay, and he said, "Yeah, I'm just playing my air guitar." I couldn't see anything, but I could hear the music. I think it might have been the noise from his earbuds, though.

Today two older women with blue hair came into the shop. They asked if I could make them a double-wide thick-crust pie shaped like a bingo board. The topping they wanted was horny goat weed shaped like numbers. One of the women said it was bingo night and their turn to provide the snacks. That's a two-hundred-dollar pie right there.

I guess in the new normal, normality doesn't cut it anymore. But who cares? I'm making money hand over fist, and I don't have to push a broom anymore.

Oh, I almost forgot. The name of my shop is "Regurgitated Ragu." So why don't you and the missus stop by one day? We can talk about that franchise, and I'll introduce you to Mephistopheles. Your first pizza is on me.

Your buddy,
Pascale, the pizza purveyor

Helen Obermeier is an engineer and part-time writer from Germany. Her favorite writing topics include bloody battles, space and time, and sometimes even her day-to-day corporate job. Her works have been published in several short story anthologies.

•   •   •

This story is a work of fiction. Any resemblance to real persons is purely coincidental. But it's also based on real events, and if you're one of my co-workers and reading this right now — you probably remember that day.

THE GREAT IT CRISIS OF 2021

HELEN OBERMEIER

I T WAS HALF PAST NINE on a Thursday morning, and Patrick was already having a very bad working day. He smoothed down the single button-down shirt he owned and watched the elevator doors open to the fourth floor. *General management, IT.* His face mask — which he was certainly free to wear even if nobody else did, right? — itched. His hand tightened around his notebook bag as he started out towards the office, for the first time in almost six months.

The latest update seems not to have cooperated with your company's local software, the anonymous, androgynous voice in the software supplier's support hotline had told him — he had imagined the person behind it strolling through an airy office in a fifteen-stories skyscraper. He had tried to argue with them from the safety of his one-bedroom apartment, where he had spent every workday since the beginning of the Plague. But the voice hadn't been in the mood for a discussion. So he had given up and listened.

Erin, his supervisor, hadn't liked the solution. Well, what should he have done? Argue with some smooth-voiced support machine? He was just a junior IT manager. His job was administrating user databases, resetting passwords, and telling people to switch it off and on again.

Yet here he was.

The carpet swallowed his steps as he made his way through the vacant office. The empty desks looked like a vacant assembly line, cables hanging idly. He frowned at the little fragrance sticks distributed on some of the surfaces, the ones that would smell like incense or herbs. Erin's little glass cube sat in a corner of the room. She seemed to have some kind of special lighting going on in there, several orange dots shining through the glass.

He saw her looking up, motioning him in with her hand. She had called him first thing in the morning. My notebook isn't working. Turned out she wasn't the only one. Turned out that he, Patrick, had to take care of this. He, of all people.

Then, just as they had been about to hang up: *Things have changed over here, Patrick.* Well, the fragrance sticks were new. He opened the door.

The sharp smell hit him like a wall. He was glad about the mask. The orange lights were candles, distributed more or less evenly on the desk, the shelf, a vacant old chair. Scented candles. He wondered about the designated flavor: ammonia?

"Took your time to get here." Erin's voice was different. Higher, and therefore somehow less assuring. More ... sharp. Just like the smell attacking his nostrils. "Would you close the door?"

He did. They stared at each other. This was the third time he had met her in person. The picture that used to pop up on his screen in her calls was full of energy, happy to serve the company. Here, in the office, her eyelids were hanging heavy over her dark eyes, and her skin — as far as he could see, with her wearing a black face mask — had a grayish hue.

"Uh, Patrick? Would you ..." She gestured to her notebook.

"Yeah. Sorry."

He put his bag on a free seat and pulled out the USB drive with the Help Kit, a simple exe. Erin's notebook was a corpse in his hands, the only dubious sign of life the faintly glowing power light. He slipped the drive into the socket. The update kit had to be distributed manually. *On a USB drive, for example,* the hotline voice had suggested helpfully. *A detailed manual will be included.*

He had suggested to Erin that he could send the help kit to someone else. Someone who didn't have asthma running in the family. Someone who had actually been in the office at some point in the last five months and three days.

Erin had not reacted well. *It's your fucking job, Patrick.* So here he was. Solving this problem by trekking through the company with a USB drive.

"So the updates were corrupted?" Erin asked. The candle flame wavered silently next to her.

"They just ... didn't cooperate with our software."

"I see."

The screen lit up. Numbers ran down. He glanced at Erin. She looked behind him, to the door. Then back to him. And then the home screen appeared. "Seems to have done it," he said. And realized that her eyes kept slipping to the door, as if she expected someone. Not in a good way, even.

"Great," she said now, pulling the notebook across the desk. "Thanks so much." She started typing. "Well, I guess you have to go on with it, now? Make the round? I told the board you'd be there at half past noon."

"Okay." He ignored the spike of terror in his gut. A wave of dizziness washed over him. Had the smell gotten worse? He blinked, kept himself from rubbing his eyes.

"So far, their stuff seems to be working, but better be safe than sorry."

He realized that the candles emitted a faint wisp of smoke. It seemed to surround Erin behind her screen. "Okay."

"Wait," she said, just as he was about to turn around. "Take one of these." In her raised hand, he saw a fragrance stick.

"Uh ..."

She waved it impatiently in front of his face. The smoke dispersed around her moving hand. "Just take it, Patrick."

Well, she was his boss. He slipped the stick into the front pocket of his shirt and turned to the door.

•   •   •

One department after the other. Only, thank the heavens and the Plague, some thirty-odd people. The ten percent of staff who held on in the office, against all risks and recommendations, were emergency staffing.

The Finance department was first. He entered the hallway, his eyes still itching from the candles. His hand hovered in front of the door, painted dark gray like any other door in the building. His heart was racing.

Get it together. These are your co-workers. You're all family, just like the e-mails from the board love to remind you. They're just people.

He inhaled and exhaled, made a fist, and knocked on the door.

No answer.

He tried the next door. Nothing. The knot in his stomach loosened. Maybe he wouldn't have to talk to anyone at all. He turned away.

The loud, almost forgotten sound of the company ringtone echoed in the empty hallway.

He almost dropped his bag. The only calls he ever got were from Erin. The phone slipped out of his fingers in his attempt to pull it out of the bag. Unknown number.

"H-hello?"

"Are you from IT?" The voice was calm and cool, with a sophisticated accent. "Are you here to fix this ... annoyance?"

Patrick suppressed the urge to look back at the phone screen. "Yeah, uh ..."

"My computer doesn't start. It hasn't for the whole morning." The voice was now pissed. It made his stomach drop. "Why are you hovering in the hallway like Jehovah's Witness?"

His gaze slipped back to the door. "You are, uh —"

"Just get in here." The call was terminated.

Patrick stared a moment longer. Then he put his hand on the doorknob. It gave way.

A chilly gust of wind slapped him in the face. His exposed hands tingled. The air was cold, icy cold. He blinked. The office looked like his own, the same desks, the same carpet. No decorations. There seemed to be an extraordinary clarity to the light, a brightness —

"Close the door, *please!*" A head rose up from behind a screen in the corner.

He slammed the door shut behind him. The room was cold as a freezer, and there was a chilly draught — he felt it ruffle his hair. But the windows, sparkling clean, were closed. A film of ice crystals had assembled on empty desks, on the topside of unused screens.

"Come over here, would you?" Finance didn't wear a mask. Her straight hair, dark blonde streaked with light or maybe white, was bound up in a ponytail. Her face was almost too angular to be called good-looking.

"Hello," Patrick choked out. The frosty air burned the inside of his mouth. "I'm from IT."

"Fine, fine. Now would you ..." She stepped away from her desk. She was all in black, suit and shirt and all. A silk scarf was slung around her high neck. Behind her on the wall, a huge graph, fiery red like the company logo, staggered upwards, with considerable drops in between.

Patrick had never seen such a tidy desk before. Pencils were arranged in order of color; every shelf held the exact same amount of paper. No speck of dust on the wooden surface — but then, there was the ice. It covered everything, a fine whitish film. It reminded him of mildew.

There was a potted plant perched right on the edge of the desk, its broad leaves sprawling across the wood and covered in crystals. He didn't know much about plants, but this one didn't look happy.

Suppressing a shudder, he set to work. The program started up. Cold air wafted over his face. There was a low hum. He looked up, towards the ceiling. Air con?

"It is running at full speed." Finance stood next to the desk, one slender hand resting on the back of her chair. Her skin was pale, but she didn't hunch down in the cold, didn't have goosebumps break out on her hands, like he did. "I made them upgrade it. It's the best protection. Perfect ventilation, no spread. The temperature is too low for any germs and viruses."

"I see," Patrick said. "It's, uh. Interesting." As his fingers moved across the notebook's keyboard, he could hear his joints pop.

"You don't even need that mask. I haven't fallen ill in years."

"Thanks, but, um. It keeps me warm."

The notebook chose this second to wake from its own cryogenic sleep and display the home screen. He wanted to tell Finance that the device wasn't supposed to run at those temperatures, but his tongue felt frozen.

"Oh, you get used to it." Finance looked at the screen. "That was all? Well, thank you. I really don't want to be the person calculating all the company's losses from those idle hours, but here I am." There were tiny lines on the corners of her mouth, barely visible because her face moved so little.

"Alright." He felt a sticky resistance while blinking. Were there ice crystals in his eyelashes?

She gave him a glance. Her eyes were a light brown, washed-out. "Anything else?"

"How ..." He swallowed. "How did you know I was in front of the door?"

No reaction on her smooth face. "You're not a bright one, are you?"

"Are there *cameras*?" Now there was a spark of heat piercing the confusion and, on top, the freezing cold. "And how did you know me?"

She made a dismissive gesture. "Do you even know what the financial department does? We need to see everything. Every little cent and dollar. We need *transparency*. To know all your faces is a matter of course." She straightened up. "And the cold helps with keeping a level head."

He nodded. His gaze fell on the plant again, slowly dying in this abysmal place. Thriving life was what Finance didn't need, apparently.

Her sharp, all-seeing eyes had noticed his glance. "Oh, that. Do you want it? It restricts the air flow."

That was probably the reason why there weren't any decorations in here. He reached out and took the pot. It felt icy to the touch. The hanging leaves covered his whole hand.

When he left the office, Finance's head had already vanished behind her ice-covered screen. Traces of ice covered the rims of the windows. Someone had scraped them clean. For transparency reasons, he guessed.

•   •   •

The hallway was a furnace. Patrick opened the top button of his shirt with stiff, prickling fingers. Maybe Finance was right. Maybe you did get used to it.

He continued down the stairs, sweat prickling on his forehead. The hallway was identical, except for the huge posters of the company's product in different renderings and situations — the product perched on a pedestal, people smiling with the product, black outlines of people holding the product into a sunny sky. This was Marketing. He had never been here before. Would he even get in? He pressed the button next to the glass door.

It swung up.

No people in sight. His breathing calmed. No rows of desks either, since they had been pushed together to form little isles. The group to his left had been painted a washed-out blue. Dark red to his right. The walls matched in color.

"Hey! Over here! You're the cavalry, aren't you?"

He froze. In the back, on another four-desk arrangement displaying a light green color scheme, someone waved. Friendly, young — *couldn't have said that about Finance,* he thought. His legs had started to move before he knew it. Soft music drifted to his ears.

The caller was tall with chin-length dark hair. *You have to be a certain kind of guy to pull off that look,* Patrick thought. This one was that kind of guy. His gray jacket fit perfectly, the collar of his white shirt was just the right way of ruffled-but-not-shabby. He wore white sneakers.

"Hi. How come I've never seen you before? Oh, right. IT." His smile stretched over half his face. Then his gaze dropped down Patrick's torso. "Oh, are we curing computers with plant magic now?"

Patrick looked down. Finance's potted plant was still in his hand, leaves dripping wet. "I ... no." He reddened. "Going to throw it away."

"Shame, it's nice. If you're into things that look dead, I guess." Accompanied with that dazzling smile, a row of perfect teeth. "So, welcome to Marketing. You want a cup of coffee?"

"No, I ..." Patrick got distracted. That guy's face was too symmetrical. And how did he get those eyebrows done? "Thanks, but I have to get going. I need access to your device."

"All business. I like that." Had that been a wink?

Feet unsteady, he followed Marketing to his desk. Postcards with inspirational quotes covered the wall — *Positivity is a mindset!* — with some random photos mixed in, one of them a group of fashionable and beautiful people at a fancy event.

"There it is. Do your thing, IT."

Patrick put the drive into the slot. Why couldn't all of them be like that? Well, maybe they shouldn't all be that good-looking. The notebook booted up. "This, uh, can take a few minutes."

"I've got all the time in the world." Marketing had acquired a cup with a violet-orange sunrise printed on it — *Keep your face to the sun and you cannot see the shadows,* the lettering said — and took a sip. "You're still wearing your mask."

Patrick blinked. "Y...yes."

"I mean, it kind of emphasizes your eyes," Marketing said, with a raised eyebrow. Those perfect brows. "But I think it really gets in the way of intuitive communication, right?"

His head was empty. Next to him, the notebook's hard drive clicked, hard at work. "Right ..." And then he felt himself pulling the mask off. The air felt strange on his face. There was a heavy, sweet smell — aftershave?

Suddenly Marketing stepped up to him. Patrick leaned back, his hip scraping against the desk.

"You seem like a rational guy," he said, and his eyes dropped down Patrick's shoulders. "You IT people usually are. So." He raised his eyebrows again. "We both know there is no pandemic, right?"

Patrick felt light-headed. It was hard to focus around all that smell. And those eyes. "Uh ..."

"Well, I should know." He raised a hand and ran it through his dark, shining hair. "Marketing is about make-believe, right? And I just know when someone's trying to sell me something."

"W...what would they want to sell?"

"A product to keep the people in line." His eyes glittered. "Like masks."

Actually, I have asthma, he thought, but he couldn't get a single word across his lips. He couldn't even bring himself to put the mask back on. It would be embarrassing. And Marketing was still looking at him with those bright, glittering eyes.

Then, suddenly, Marketing wrinkled his beautiful nose. "What's that smell?"

"W-what?"

A soft sound of disgust. Marketing stepped back. "You smell like that office down on 4th. That ... incense."

The fragrance stick. Actually, Patrick could smell it now: sharp and fruity.

"This stuff makes my head hurt," Marketing said. "You got to get rid of it." His eyes still were very bright. They looked as if shining with fever.

All of a sudden, Patrick felt his skin crawl. He had touched that person's keyboard. Those fingers had lain on his shoulder. He turned to the notebook. As gingerly as he could, without touching anything, he pulled the drive out and turned away. "Gotta go now." He pulled the mask up while walking.

"Wait."

Patrick's eyes flitted to the office door.

Marketing held up his sunrise cup. His face was blank, his slight smile not looking real at all. "Would you mind putting that into the dishwasher on your way out? Kitchen's just next to the office."

No, he thought. "Okay," he said and took the cup with his fingertips. He was glad of the mask. He was pretty sure he was grimacing under there.

"Thank you so much." Voice flat and dead.

Behind him, as he left the office, Patrick heard a quiet sneeze.

•   •   •

"Marketing is about make-believe," he murmured as he marched down the hallway with a vengeance. "*Asshole.*" He would not put that cup into the dishwasher. It was a nice cup, if you ignored the cheesy quote. He would just keep it for himself. He would have to disinfect it ten times over, of course.

His phone rang. Again. Erin this time. "Are you done?"

"Not yet. There were ... complications."

"Complications."

Anger swept through him. "Did you know that I'd have to enter an actual freezer to put that update on? Or into a ... a downright hazard zone?"

158

"I told you things had changed."

He shook his head. "What's going around here … it's not normal behavior, is it?"

A sigh traveled through the line. "Well, it's everyone's individual freedom …" She trailed off. Erin wasn't a person who trailed off, usually.

"Okay." What else was there to say? "I'll get on with it now." And he cut the call.

He walked into Project Management with anger still sizzling in his veins, almost counteracting the ever-present panic. He had wrapped the sunrise mug in toilet paper and stuffed it into his bag, along with the dying plant. The leaves gushed out of the bag as if the plant was trying to assimilate it.

"Hi, I'm from IT. Where's your device, please?"

Project Management looked pretty normal, except for the restless mood in the office between milestone charts and cost-benefit analyses pinned up on the walls, that one gray-haired guy's eyes positively gleaming as he received his revived notebook. "It's going great, actually," he said, his eyes darting to his phone every so often. "All on schedule. We're a team, all of us. Working towards a common goal." Patrick hadn't seen him blink in the ten minutes he had been here. "We're a team, all of us, right?"

"Right," Patrick said. "We're a team." On his way to the door, he turned back once. The man had bent over his cluttered desk. It looked like he was snorting something off a company badge.

Legal was a small anteroom with an empty gray desk and gray couches between gray walls. He wasn't allowed to enter further. Two people, their dark blue suits splotches of color between all the monochromes, presented their notebooks to him. The suits were very polite, talking to him in calm, friendly voices. He suspected they were using simple speech with him.

Then he stood next to Purchasing's desk, thinking of not much at all, as they mentioned the possibility of leaving the USB drive in their capable hands. "I could put in a word with

HR, you know," Purchasing said, their smile invisible beneath a snow-white mask, their sharp eyes never leaving Patrick's face. "Or how about some cafeteria coupons?"

"But … why would you *want* it?"

"Oh, come on. It's just a basis for negotiations."

Patrick eyed the drive. Purchasing's manicured hand rested on the notebook. Can I outrun them? he asked himself, for the second time that day. His gaze dropped to his bag. All he had to offer was his own notebook, his phone, a few tissues, the plant, and the mug.

He bent down and retrieved the mug, careful to touch only the toilet paper. "How about this cup?"

The long-lashed eyes narrowed. "This is hideous."

"Yeah, but it's … I don't know … retro. In a very cheesy sort of way."

Purchasing made a noncommittal sound. Their face showed pure disinterest.

"I, uh, I should disclose the fact that it's technically not mine. It's from Marketing."

"Marketing," Purchasing repeated. "Well. Stolen goods? That will certainly drive down the price. Three coupons, then."

"Uh, I don't want anything, thanks."

"That would be corruption." Long fingers nudged the coupons. "Take them."

"O…okay."

He made it out of the office without further incidents.

·　　　·　　　·

PR / Social Media's assistant looked like a fluttery bird. Maybe it was the rapid movement of her hands as she talked, the way she made Patrick dizzy by just not staying still. Maybe it was the glittering face mask, shining lilac and green. And the matching green¬-glittery eye make-up. And the shimmering green feathers sticking out of her unruly hair. When he was finished, she did a little spin on her feet, like a ballerina. The glitter whirling in the air around her made his eyes itch again. "Thank you, thank you so much! I was lost without it! You're a magician!"

"I'm definitely not." He realized he hadn't really been thanked, in a real, heartfelt way, by anyone up to now.

She asked him where he was going next. "Uh. Product design."

"Oh." A pause. When he looked up from the notebook, she giggled. "They are a special lot, aren't they?"

You have peacock feathers in your hair, he thought. But she seemed to have forgotten about her question already, her unsteady gaze flitting across the floor. "Hey, are those flowers in your bag? Are they a gift?"

"Um. No." On a closer look, the plant's moist leaves seemed to hang sadder than before. "Do you want it?"

She giggled again. "Oh, it's beautiful. But I'm allergic to flowers." Her eyes narrowed. "I think it's an Amazon lily."

He wondered about that as he stepped into the elevator down to Product Design. She had probably just said the first thing coming to her feather-covered head. An Amazon plant should have died in that Finance freezer, right?

Not much left to do now. Product Design, then the board. He stared at his reflection in the elevator mirror. His eyes were glassy, matching the headache that had started in his forehead. He deserved a break, he thought, as he watched the elevator doors slide open.

The light in Product Design's cube farm was dim. Screens glowed in the half-dark, half hidden by huge, irregular shapes. The air on his forehead felt wet and heavy. He stepped out of the elevator. The shapes were plants, he realized. Jungle plants? A thick border of them had been erected a few feet away from the elevator, huge leaves hanging down on sideboards.

"Stay where you are."

He froze. From the dim darkness of the greenery, two eyes were looking straight at him. Two human eyes. The voice had been low and sharp in the silence of the room — but there was something else, a high, grating sound. Cicadas?

Then all thoughts were wiped from his brain. Between rustling leaves, a dark, angular shape appeared.

"What the fuck?" Patrick said. It came out as a choked whisper. He had never had a gun pointed at him. A big one, at that.

"Keep your distance, friend." The voice was probably male. Patrick could see teeth flash, but the face was either naturally dark or covered in paint. "We all know distancing is key, right? No contamination."

"I ... I got a mask." He wanted to point to his face, but his hands wouldn't obey. *That guy is pointing a gun at me!*

"Yeah, that will keep the viruses away," the guy with the gun agreed. "But not the mental contamination. The distraction. The annoyance."

He had to get out of here. This was crazy. But his feet were stuck to the tiled floor. His eyes gravitated back to the muzzle of that gun. No way this was real, he told himself. This had to violate a hundred laws. No way.

Not the craziest thing happening today, though, was it?

"We told them we needed to work in *quiet*. All this monitoring, all that talking. It kills the spirit. The inspiration."

"Nobody comes here now. They all write emails." Another, higher voice drifting out of the jungle. He saw movement in the corners of his eyes. Other people. For all he knew, they had their own guns. And they were many. It made his intestines coil.

"But it's important." His voice was hoarse. "Your devices." Every word seemed to be swallowed by the jungle. "They're contaminated ..."

A shot rang out. He jumped back. *They shot at me!* There was a dent in the metallic surface of the elevator door. Not a real bullet, maybe, maybe, but real enough to hurt. "Okay." His hands had shot up into the air, trembling. "I'll leave."

In the elevator, he pressed buttons blindly. The doors shut out that dim, humid, black-greenish hell. The floor moved. He sank against the wall, his breath coming shallow. He couldn't breathe. He ripped off the mask, for the second time that day, and gulped in air, sharp in his lungs. A cough hung in his throat. He let it out, coughed more.

He would not put up with this. He was just a junior IT manager. He had a *condition.* Everyone in here seemed to have gone off the rails, except for him. "Fuck them," he murmured between coughs. This was it. Let Erin deal with it.

The elevator *pinged.* He stared into the empty hallway, Erin's hallway. Maybe he could just call her. He felt around the bag for his phone, next to the velvety plant and the slippery surface of the cafeteria coupons.

His shirtsleeve glittered. Little golden specks — no, they were green. *You're a magician.*

He had been sent to do a job.

His finger pressed a button. His whole body felt jittery. When the doors opened again, he walked into the jungle room as if it was any other box office. Which it was. Just full of extravagant and, honestly, pretty stupid decor.

"You again?" The armed guy appeared on the same spot.

"Yes, me again," Patrick said. He couldn't quite get the hoarseness out of his voice. His raised arms hurt already. "I need to see your devices now."

The gun went up an inch. "We told you —"

"You want to work, right? You want to use your inspiration, and so on." His throat itched. He swallowed. "But your devices are dead. Right?"

"It's a ploy," a new voice from the left said. "Something to blackmail us. To bend to their rules."

"I really, really doubt that." He nodded his head towards the bag in his raised hand. "I've got an USB drive in here. It will repair all your stuff. Then you can go back to using your inspiration for something that matters. Not for whatever the fuck you're doing right now."

Silence. The cicadas clittered.

Then the second voice said: "What's that plant?"

"That is an Amazon lily." One of his hands held up the bag, the other the plant. It didn't look much like the huge ferns distributed around the desks, but it wouldn't be called Amazon for no reason, would it? "It's been through a lot." *Like me,* he thought.

"It's really pretty," the second voice said. "And it matches our theme. Gets the right vibes across."

"What, you want it?" Patrick made a show of looking thoughtfully at the little plant. "I don't know. It really gets the right vibes across, you know ..."

"Give us that and we can talk about your USB drive." The gun lowered. Just a bit.

"No." Maybe he had learned from Purchasing, after all. "I'll look at your devices now. Then you get the plant. And if someone tries anything —" he felt pretty good saying that, it sounded like right out of a movie — "I'll report you all to the board. I have an appointment there, you know. And I'm *definitely not* afraid to talk to them about *anything*."

The cicadas sang their endless song. Sweat had broken out on his face again. And there was this itch in his throat. His upheld arms trembled more.

The gun vanished.

•   •   •

There were nine people in total. He had to fight his way through undergrowth and hanging vines to get to them. The guy with the gun turned out to be dark-skinned and face-painted, topping his looks off with an old army helmet. The second voice accompanied him, a person with a mask and pilot glasses.

"Sorry for, you know." As his notebook lit up, the helmet guy's face did as well. "But there's no being careful enough."

"No worries." Patrick glanced at the guns. They still looked very real.

"So the updates were corrupted," Glasses said. An eerie echo of Erin's words.

"They didn't cooperate with our ..." Patrick shook his head. "Yeah, no, they were corrupted." He had known it all along. But then, what to do about it? And why would he care?

The helmet guy straightened up. "You need a gun, IT? We could give you one. Only one, though."

"No." He shook his head so violently that the headache flared up all anew. "I don't need it."

"Your loss." The guy took the notebook and turned away, probably to climb up a tree. Junk rattled around on the vacant desk: leaves, dead insects, paperclips, charging cables ... and something that gleamed, a little silvery-green object. Silver and green were the company colors. They reminded him of the peacock girl.

"What's that?" he asked.

The guy turned. "That badge? It's ages old. Don't even know why I kept it. It was some outstanding merit bullshit."

If it's bullshit, Patrick thought, *why did you keep it?* "Can I have it?"

"Sure, whatever. And now excuse me."

Patrick pinned the badge to the front pocket of his shirt. Glasses hovered silently next to them. He started to get a feeling that their invisible eyes were very inquisitive. "You don't look so good," they suddenly said.

"Comes with being threatened at gunpoint." Truth was that he didn't *feel* so good either. His legs were weak, his arms heavy, and another cough tickled the back of his throat.

Well, he would deal with that later.

He stepped back into the elevator. His finger hesitated for a second on the top floor button. Instead, he tapped on a number on his phone screen, hesitated. Finally, he pressed *Call.*

The very same smooth support voice greeted him. He waited until it had finished its well-honed introductory sentence before he said: "Your software was corrupted."

The answer came without any hesitation. "In case you are dissatisfied with your product, you are welcome to use our complaints hotline."

"You told me it was incompatibility or some other bullshit. But it was your software." He felt sweat break out on his face yet again. This time, it was from anger. "Can't you at least admit it?"

"In case you are dissatisfied with your product …"

He cut the line without saying goodbye and turned back to the elevator, pressed *10*. The elevator had barely started to move when his phone rang again. Could it be —

No. It was Erin. "Where are you? You have six minutes to get to the board."

"On my way."

"You are?" Surprise in her voice. The elevator pinged at level 10. Patrick stepped out, notebook bag in one hand, phone in the other, feeling like a real busy person for a moment.

"Look," Erin continued into his ear. "I thought about it and I think it's better if I do it."

It was his turn to be surprised. He leaned back against the wall. Leaning felt pretty good. His muscles ached.

"You don't like to be in there anyway, do you? I'm used to those guys, I can handle them."

"Well …" He stared at the mirroring door facing the elevator, at himself slumped on the wall.

"Just come to my office. I'll do the rest for you. Okay?"

This is your job, Erin's own words, earlier. He pushed himself upright. His legs were still wobbly. "I just repaired all the devices in this building." He didn't tell her how he had been threatened, shot at, contaminated by a biohazard, covered in glitter and bribed. She had been the one to warn him that things had changed, after all. "I'm not going to stop now."

"But, Patrick —"

"Erin? I'm in the elevator, there's no signal …" He pressed the red button.

The board's reception room was sparkling clean, carefully designed. It was hard to remember that it belonged to the building he knew, the world of colorless carpet floor and uniform desks. The desks in this room were glass, the computer screens of a delicate, mortally expensive silver breed. "I'm from IT," he said to the first assistant who rose from their desk. "I'm here to repair the damaged devices."

"You're the expert?" the first assistant asked mildly, combined with a quick once-over. The two had turned away from their screens and looked at him, a carefully assorted combination of skin tones and hairstyles. Their expressions were identical — contempt so gentle and full of pity, it could have been mistaken for friendliness.

He found he had no fucks left to give. "Don't they expect me? Are their devices working or aren't they?"

"They are using their secondary devices right now." The assistant's voice was so sweet Patrick felt as if his ears were stuffed with honey. "I'll accompany you."

He followed the assistant into the next room, which turned out to be a hallway, as pristine as the office. In passing, he noticed the room numbers — 7, 8, 9. *Room 104.* How long was this hallway going to be? He looked back. The entrance looked a mile away, the walls twisting towards it.

"Well, whatever," he said aloud. The assistant didn't answer. But sure enough, the following number was a 50, then a 60. Door 104 was grey, nondescript. The assistant knocked. A narrow gap between door and frame appeared, black as night. The assistant spoke soft words into the darkness.

The door opened wider. The assistant gestured. Patrick's stomach jolted. He very much didn't want to go in there.

But he had thought that before, hadn't he? He made his legs work.

The door closed behind him and the darkness was total — for a few long seconds, until his eyes adjusted. In the shimmer of a few weak lights distributed around the room, shapes moved. Their faces were unrecognizable, their shapes vaguely human.

One of them was pretty close to him. "There is no mask mandate here, young man." The calm voice seemed to vibrate through his bones.

He had to force the words out of his throat. "I'll keep it, thanks."

A chill ran through the room. Heads turned. He gritted his teeth. Then another voice said: "I understand you could repair this? How long will it take?"

"Just a few minutes."

His hand found the USB slots without looking. The faint glow was coming from the phones on a long, U-shaped table, around which they were sitting and standing. The phones were on the lowest brightness setting he had ever seen. They talked above him in low murmurs while he worked. He could have understood the words, if his head didn't feel like it was stuffed with cotton.

He finished the last one and stepped back. "Is that all?" the person next to him asked. "Thank you very much."

Patrick narrowed his eyes into the darkness, trying to make out the speaker's face. He would probably never see them up close again. This was his one chance to ask. *What the fuck is going on with this company?*

"*A few minutes* are over, I think," the voice reminded him gently.

"Just one thing," Patrick said quickly. "Can I say one thing? I'm not going to take long."

The only part of the person's face he could clearly see was the shine of their eyes, their gaze dropping down. Were they looking at the badge pinned on his shirt, *exceptional merit?* Would they think he had earned it? Well, maybe he had, with the day he had been having.

"Twenty seconds." Still mild, but Patrick heard the iron beneath.

He took a breath. "The software update was corrupted." His voice trembled slightly, but maybe they wouldn't pick up on it. You should take it up with the supplier. They say they aren't responsible, but that's not possible. That problem cost the company a lot of money. Ask Finance ..." He trailed off.

"I see." No way to see in this light how the face reacted to this. "Thank you for being mindful."

He knew a dismissal when he heard one. He picked up his USB drive — spent now, having worked its magic on every device in the building — and left the room.

•   •   •

The hallway outside the dark room was doing this warping thing again. Then it started to spin around him. He stumbled, reached out to steady himself against a doorframe. He felt sweaty and cold at the same time.

A sneeze shook him, and another one.

No wonder. All those temperature changes — the freezer, the jungle. No wonder he had caught a cold. But he had done the job. He had done it all alone. Through the pounding in his head, it was hard to remember why this was even important. He made it to the reception room, passed the assistants without a word, pressed buttons on the elevator. His hand touched his forehead. Well, this was a temperature if he'd ever had one.

A temperature. He whipped out his phone, googled symptoms.

Fuck.

"That asshole," he murmured. Marketing, with his beautiful eyes gleaming in fever. He should have left his mask on. He'd never heard of the Plague setting on that quickly — but then, he'd never heard of what he had seen today in the office, either.

He called Erin, careful to keep his mask tight against his skin. The downward movement of the elevator made his stomach roll.

"How was the board?" She sounded calm, professional — with a certain note of snappiness.

"Good." His voice was starting to go. He cleared his throat. It hurt.

"How ..." She hesitated. "How were they?"

"Strange," he said truthfully. "Erin, I'm going to go home now. I think I've caught it."

"Oh, shit. Get well soon." A pause. "Oh, *shit*. You were all over the company today!"

"I wore my mask. Not thanks to anyone in here, though."

"Oh. Well." She sounded apologetic. "You did a good job. Overall."

"Yeah. Thanks." He was almost at the entrance. "And, Erin — I'll come back into the office. I've got some canteen coupons to redeem. If this Plague doesn't kill me, that is." And he ended the call. For the second time in just a day, he had cut her off.

He suppressed a cough and leaned on the company building's glass door with his elbow.

For an eternal moment it seemed like it wouldn't budge.

Alex Grehy spent a lifetime writing technical non-fiction in the corporate world before breaking free in her late fifties, when she discovered a gift for writing on the dark side of fiction. Her work has been published worldwide and she is a regular contributor to *The Sirens Call* and the *Ladies of Horror Flash Project*. Her essays on her experiences as a "Lady of Horror" have been published in the *Horror Writers Association Newsletter* and *The Horror Tree* blog. Her sweet life is filled with narrowboating, rescue greyhounds, singing and chocolate. Yet her vivid prose, thought-provoking poetry and original view of the world has led to her best friend to say, "For someone so lovely, you're very twisted!"

•   •   •

This piece was so much fun to write — but I hope it doesn't give the real corporate world any nefarious ideas.

DEMON EXPRESS DISTRIBUTION

A CORPORATE MARKETING STRATEGY

ALEX GREHY

YOUR WORSHIPFUL EVILNESSES,

Thank you for giving Inferno Marketing Consultancy the opportunity to present this great strategy for the new millennium.

I'm here today to offer you an unparalleled opportunity to grab a share of the global distribution market in partnership with our manufacturing arm, Mass Exploitation Manufacturing (Unlimited, Ununionized). You need the souls, we need the cash — it's a win-win, I'm sure you'll agree.

It's your time to clean up. Or maybe that should be dirty up, it's the other side that does the clean right? Just my little joke. Right — moving on with the PowerPoint.

Let's first define the problem, ahem, not that Hellfire Inc. has problems, only challenges.

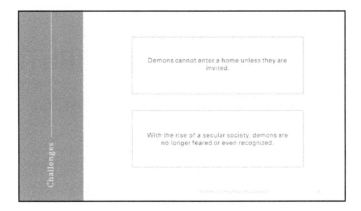

Our market research suggests that your soul revenue is levelling out. This is bad news — I know souls last for eternity, but you need new stock to keep your imps and devils motivated and to stoke the eternal fires. The earth is warming up, and I hear that hell is freezing over, metaphorically, but it's not too late for you!

We've used the good old 1970s Boston Consulting Group matrix to define your markets — you can't beat the boomers when it comes to capitalism.

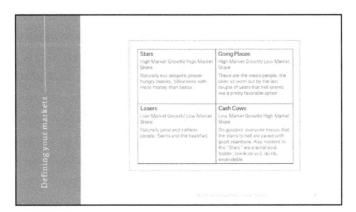

Let's give you a run-down on our proposed strategy *vis-à-vis* your client markets:

- Your "Cash Cows" are reliable mass market souls. There seems to be an endless self-generating supply of do-gooders and mindless goons, so you don't need to do anything to maintain your core business.

- Your "Losers" are literally a lost cause. They're so holy they're going straight upstairs to heaven. Sure, it's fun to turn a few around but it'll never be a mass market.

- The "Stars" are few in number, but their souls are juicy with evil. But they're an easy market — these guys are heading your way regardless.

- That leaves the "Going Places" quadrant. That is what our proposal is all about. We want to catch the billions of souls that have tiptoed into 2022, exhausted and too frightened to hope in case the bogeyman comes to get them. Not forgetting rising costs and falling wages — these people are in no position to turn down a bargain. If you follow our, if I may say so, genius, strategy, they're yours for the taking!

Now we're getting to the interesting bit — how to grab a share of this rising soul market.

I can see you smoking at the ears, your Worshipful Evilnesses, but stick with me.

With respect, your long-standing strategy of undercutting the value of the human soul, and your slogan, *we buy any soul*, well, it's cheap, it doesn't play to our influencers. If you want 5-star reviews, you need a 5-star offering. You need to up your branding, get on trend.

Let's look at your USP — that's "Unique Selling Points", not "Unquiet Souls Purgatory". Sorry about that, but there are only so many 3-letter acronyms to go around.

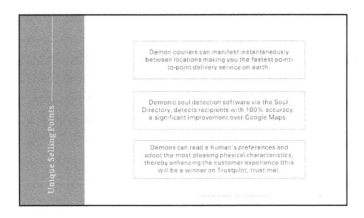

Speed and accuracy, it's what every customer wants; factory floor to consumer in no time at all, well, you might want to take an hour, say, or people will get suspicious. Demons don't need any pay, so you can undercut your rivals, but not by too much — again, people love a bargain but "something for nothing" just looks like a scam.

Now let's look at brand names — our exclusive online focus group gave the following feedback:

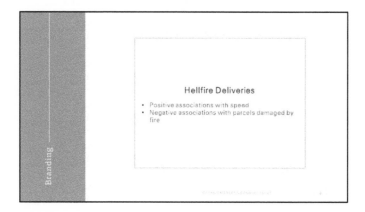

I'm delighted to announce that "Demon Express" won the vote, our influencers love it and can't wait to get the word out — especially with your new slogan — are you ready? Ta-Dah!

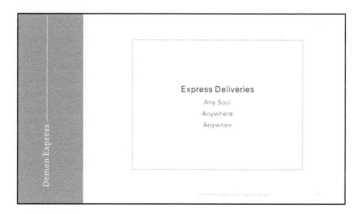

With my company's existing corporate infrastructure, we can get you ready to launch as soon as you sign on the dotted line, but don't wait too long,

People are travelling again, they need new barbecues, garden furniture, bikinis — then it'll be Halloween, Christmas. Valentine's Day — If they want it, you can deliver it!

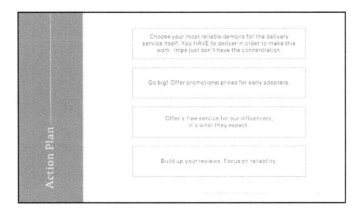

Action Plan

Choose your most reliable demons for the delivery service itself. You HAVE to deliver in order to make this work. Imps just don't have the concentration.

Go big! Offer promotional prices for early adopters.

Offer a free service for our influencers; it's what they expect.

Build up your reviews. Focus on reliability.

We'll give it a few months to get established then we'll run a promotional offer. This is the best bit!

Here goes — You send out free adult coloring books with every order!

Look, Mephistopheles, I know that crayons melt in your hot paws, but stay with me here.

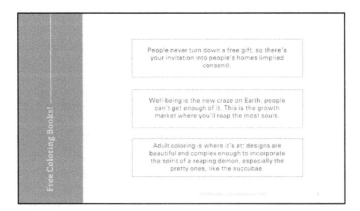

Free Coloring Books!

People never turn down a free gift, so there's your invitation into people's homes (implied consent).

Well-being is the new craze on Earth; people can't get enough of it. This is the growth market where you'll reap the most souls.

Adult coloring is where it's at: designs are beautiful and complex enough to incorporate the spirit of a reaping demon, especially the pretty ones, like the succubae.

So once your reaping demons, hidden in the coloring books, have been accepted into human homes, well the world's your oyster. This is the fun bit — You get to choose the demon's trigger and the level of havoc unleashed. Of course, we wouldn't presume to tell you how to torture the souls once you get then into Hell, But I think you'll like "tempt into sin" options that our focus groups came up with:

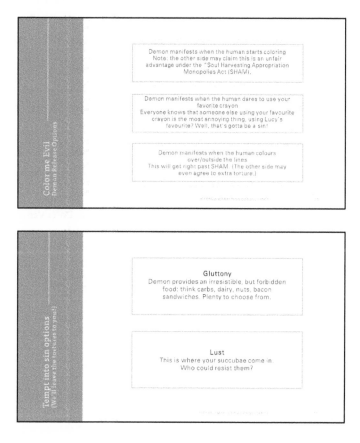

So there you have it, a business that literally delivers what every human wants in exchange for everything they've got. Like I said, win-win!

Ok, so if you sign the contract today, we'll launch the courier business this month. I've got a vial of blood here, can't risk staining the cuffs of my best shirt, right?

That's the easy bit, but the coloring books are going to be BIG — like, the demon apocalypse, so you need to consider a date of significance.

Frankly Hellfire Inc.'s procurement process has let you down. You missed a great opportunity with the Mayan doomsday in 2012 and you've missed a perfect ambigram in 2021 — 12-02-2021. The next one's in 2080 — Do you really want to wait that long?

Then you missed another doozy on 20-02-2022, But hey, two is not the number of the beast, so I guess it's understandable that your in-house marketing missed it.

But that doesn't mean 2022 can't be your year, the year of catastrophe, the end of days — no sirree! Humans are tired, more tired than they've ever been, and they've been looking over their shoulders for Doomsday for the last two years.

We think you should launch on 22-11-22 — a palindrome in the Gregorian (cursed be his name) calendar and just when everyone's breathing easy because the world didn't end on Halloween.

To conclude our presentation — Demon Express is the service that the world has been waiting for — It's the apocalypse, wholesale!

• • •

Terms & Conditions apply: As cash is not valid currency in Hell, Inferno will collect and retain all cash payments arising from provision of the courier service. The "love of money is the sin" clause exempts all billionaire directors of Inferno Consulting from instant entry to Hell. Hellfire Inc. receives all souls. Inferno accepts no responsibility for accidental incineration of packages delivered by demons.

William Shaw is a writer from Sheffield, currently living in the USA. His writing has appeared in *Strange Horizons*, *Daily Science Fiction*, and *Doctor Who Magazine*. You can find his blog at *williamshawwriter.wordpress.com* and his Twitter *@Will_S_7*.

•   •   •

I love comic books. I do not love the way comic book creators are treated. This story was inspired by that basic indignity, and by the feeling I think we all had at some point in the pandemic, that the most disturbing things in our fiction were springing to life around us.

WHY BE AN ARTIST?

WILLIAM SHAW

W E DO IT FOR LOVE. We certainly don't do it for money. No matter how many blockbuster movies get made from our work, no matter how many toys get sold based on our designs, none of that ocean of cash ever trickles down to us. We certainly don't do it for our health. I've had carpal tunnel syndrome for the last three years, and when my wrists aren't killing me it's my back; all this time hunched over a desk, making galactic battles and dinosaur adventures happen on my Wacom tablet before they get printed on glossy paper. We certainly don't do it to advance our careers. Once you've reached my level, where the big publishers come to you for a handful of ongoing titles, you're pretty much maxed out. Working round the clock for a worse hourly rate than the men who take the garbage away, overflowing with cigarette ends and instant noodle boxes.

It's a dirty job, being a comic book artist. No-one's got to do it, per se, but if you ever stop or even slow down, there's a million eager kids waiting to take your place, all of them better and less worn out than you. It has its perks, but even those come with downsides these days. Being adored by fans used to be cool, it was a lovely little ego boost; now it just means weirdoes who go outside even less than you will scream bloody murder if you draw a teenage girl's tits too small for their liking. Getting free comics in the mail used to be nice — all part of the research, don't you know — but nowadays the complimentary product is a weekly tranche of PDFs on a screen you already stare at way too much. And working from home was a precious luxury when I was fresh out of art school all those years ago. But then ... well. You know what happened then.

What you may not know is that the comics industry was hit pretty hard by all that. Comic shops closed, distribution was put on hold, sales numbers took a dive. Work was even harder to find than before, but the deadlines only seemed to get shorter. I was going out of my mind, staring at my screen three hours a day trying to find out what the hell was going on, then another ten hours making sure Captain Fantastic's cape flowed just right. You remember. It was a crazy time. So crazy, in fact, that when Captain Fantastic literally leapt off the page and started talking to me, it took me a minute to realize something weird had happened.

"Come again?" I asked.

"I said, greetings citizen! You look like you're in need of some help! I am Captain Fantastic!"

He actually was, you know. Tall, handsome, muscular without being beefcake-y, a purple and red jumpsuit with a big yellow cape. Captain Fantastic. Exactly as I'd drawn him that morning.

"Erm," I said. "Where did you come from?"

"My home planet is Sirius VII, but I came to Earth as a teenager, and since then I have vowed to protect the vulnerable by fighting crime wherever I find it!"

Yep, that was the official backstory alright. It was written at the bottom of every issue's title page. But it didn't explain how this exile from Sirius VII came to be standing in my bedroom/home office. I glanced back at my computer screen, and realized that the splash page I'd been working on all morning was missing a costumed crime-fighter.

"Did you ... come out of my comic book?"

"That's right!" Captain Fantastic smiled. His teeth were so white, it was like looking at the sun. "In times of great distress, heroes like me can cross dimensions to aid the downtrodden! I sensed your anguish from across the void, sir, and I have come to offer my assistance!"

Well, well, well. Either I was going mad, or the help I desperately needed had finally arrived. Alright, most likely I was going mad, but no point looking a gift horse in the mouth.

"Right. Well. You see, there's this pandemic ..."

Captain Fantastic's face fell. "I'm sorry, citizen. I have no medical knowledge, so I am unable to cure what ails your world."

"Ah. Can you do anything for my bad back?"

"No."

"Can you help me draw my comics faster?"

"No."

"Can you help me get better wages?"

"No."

A fat lot of use this guy was. "Oh, never mind then. Thanks for dropping by, anyway."

With that, Captain Fantastic gave me a somber salute and took off out of my open window. I was disappointed. I'd thought hallucinations were meant to be more fun than this.

I sighed, and went back to work.

•   •   •

I'd almost managed to convince myself it was a dream. Comic book heroes can't actually come to life, after all. I was completely stressed out. Everyone was. I just needed to get outside more. Go for the government-prescribed daily walk. Get away from work for a bit. As soon as I'd finished this month's edition of *Western Action*.

I was three pages in, and the white-hatted hero was riding his noble stallion into town. I had just finished shading the flicky-flacky doors of the local saloon when that same white-hatted hero rode his noble stallion straight into my home work space. He jumped down from his horse and looked around, obviously baffled.

"Howdy," I said, before I could stop myself.

"Howdy," he responded automatically. "Erm ... I think I'm a little lost. Can you direct me to the Last Chance Saloon?"

The Last Chance Saloon? Blimey, the script I was working from was clichéd. "I'm afraid not, partner," I said. "But don't you worry ... we take kindly to strangers in these parts."

The cowboy looked around dubiously. "And what parts might they be? The Wild West?"

"No. Middlesbrough."

"I see." He clearly didn't, but he was trying, bless him. "What can I do for you today?"

"Ah. Well, I'm having issues with my bosses."

"Your bosses?"

"Yes. They said they'd pay me last week, but I haven't seen a penny yet. Plus they're giving me a bunch of extra work, which would be fine except I'm already up to my eyes and I haven't left the house in three days."

It was actually four days, but no need to worry him.

The cowboy looked concerned. "Your bosses treat you like that? An honest, hardworking employee?"

"Well. An honest, hardworking freelancer. No overtime or benefits."

"Well that just ain't right. I've half a mind to ride over there and give them a piece of my mind." He drew his pistol and cocked it menacingly.

"Ah, I wouldn't do that,' I said hastily.

"Why not?"

"I'd get in trouble. It would be intimidation."

The cowboy looked crestfallen. He slowly put his gun back in its holster.

"Well, I'm awful sorry, but it doesn't look like I can help you, partner. Now if there's nothing else I can do, I'd best be on my way."

"Thanks anyway,' I said. "It was very decent of you to offer."

"Don't mention it," said the cowboy. He got on his horse, which slowly trotted out of the front door, though not before taking a big steaming dump on my hall carpet.

If I hadn't believed before, I definitely did now. Hallucinations like that didn't happen twice, and the smell of horse manure was strong enough to convince anyone.

●　　　●　　　●

It was a few days later and I was working on a strip for *Detection Weekly* when it happened again. One minute I was drawing a hard-bitten cop booting his way into a scuzzy bar room, the next that same hard-bitten cop was booting his way into my bedroom. The door flew off its hinges and crashed to the floor.

"Now what have we here?" growled the cop. "Where were you on the night of the 31st of March?"

"The same place I am every night," I told him. "Sitting here, drawing comics."

The cop looked confused, so I pressed my advantage.

"Listen," I said. "You're the best detective on the planet, so maybe you can help me out with a little problem I'm having."

I explained about what happened with Captain Fantastic, with the cowboy and the horse shit, and now with him. Either I was going mad, or I was somehow bringing comic book characters to life. What on earth was going on? And what could it mean?

The cop looked thoughtful, scratching at his square, stubbly chin. Finally, he said: "And this only started happening recently? After this ... what did you call it? Global panini?"

"Pandemic," I said. "And yes. It started last month."

The cop grunted. "People do weird things in a crisis. I've seen it on the streets. Maybe you've always had this in you, and it's taken all this stress to wake it up. Maybe something's changed about your environment. Either way, looks like you've got this power now. The power to bring things into your world."

"But it's not helping," I said. "The people I bring here can't actually fix anything. Unless you've got a vaccine up your sleeve?"

"Sorry, kid. Only a spare handgun and some ammo."

"Well then. Why aren't the people I bring through any use?"

The cop considered. "Seems to me the people you've brought through so far ain't exactly skilled physicians or labor negotiators. But you're not paid to draw skilled physicians or labor negotiators. You're paid to draw fictional characters. We come from you. If you don't know how to cure diseases or boost your paycheck, then neither do we."

I just sat there, stunned, while the cop stood, drawing up the collar of his trench coat. "See you around, kid," he said. "Good luck saving the world."

•   •   •

The cop was right. I was actively trying to bring things through now, but nothing I did was any use. I tried drawing a group of scientists, and ended up with a bunch of male models in white coats. I tried drawing a vaccine, but all I got was a needle full of water. Getting desperate, I tried drawing a pile of cash. But when it appeared in my room it was all just flimsy paper, blank on one side; Monopoly money.

I was also starting to get in trouble, work-wise. I'd now handed in three comics where the main character vanished halfway through, and while a few pretentious critics hailed them as postmodern masterpieces, my editors were pissed off that I hadn't stuck to the script. I was in danger of losing my reputation in the business, and with it the few scraps of financial stability I had. I was reading the news. There was no chance of me getting a job elsewhere, with half the economy shut down and a deadly disease still running rampant.

I doubled over in my chair, head in my hands, defeated. What the hell was I going to do? Then I had a thought. An awful, awful thought. But I was exhausted and out of ideas, and the more I turned it over in my head, the more it made sense. After all, here was a character I knew all about. Who didn't use complex technical or scientific methods to do what he did. Who you could always make a deal with.

I pulled the tablet towards me and started to draw. A classic design. Two horns. Dark eyes. A goatee. That wide, terrible grin. A shadow fell across my desk, and the room was suddenly filled with the smell of sulfur.

And as my ears rang with that awful, mocking laughter, all I could think was, finally. I'm getting something done.

Not for me, you understand. I've read plenty of horror comics, I know how these things go down. I'm definitely going to hell for this. But I, for one, was sick of living in the end times, and I was pretty sure everyone else was too. If I could get things back to normal, then my soul was a small price to pay.

I didn't do it for me. I did it for you. All of you, around the world, going about your lives in peace and happiness thanks to my sacrifice. No, don't thank me. I didn't do this for thanks. I didn't do it for money, or for fame, or to advance my own career.

I did it for love. For a comic book artist, what other reason is there?

Derek Des Anges has been telling stories to people since he wa seven and no one has been able to make him stop yet. He has published several novels, a couple of poetry collections, and a smattering of short stories under a variety of aliases, to prevent the fiction cops from catching onto just how disparate the genres and subjects are.

• • •

This particular piece of magical realism was a game with myself to see if I could bring together the idea of a haunted mirror, and the observable effect that during the Covid lockdowns, quite a lot of people had enough time to think about aspects of their lives they'd been deliberately avoiding until then - resulting in a whole slew of close friends coming out as trans. Sometimes self-knowledge can be almost as intimidating as being stalked by an otherworldly creature.

THE TRUTH

DEREK DES ANGES

G RAHAM O'NEILL HAD SEEMED LIKE a healthy, functional, and decent man until lockdown.

He'd seemed a moderately functional, reasonably healthy, and overwhelmingly decent man for the duration, as functional as might be expected, and about as mentally and physically healthy as anyone was managing to be while the gyms were closed and their social lives were limited to zoom quizzes. He'd even resisted buying a lockdown puppy to abandon as soon as everyone was let out again, and thanks to living with his parents, albeit in the 'studio flat' at the bottom of the garden that was very definitely a *shed*, hadn't succumbed to the Pandemic Baby Boom either.

Unfortunately he had, just as things started looking up again and the shops reopened, followed by the pubs and bars, found himself afflicted with truly catastrophic insomnia.

Which was why, as he saw it, he was sitting in the attic.

The attic was shared with the house next door; not so much a quirk of design as an acknowledgement that what was now two semi-detached houses in the suburbs had been, a hundred or so years ago, one detached house with space for *domestics* and a stable block, now sadly demolished and replaced by a very ordinary garage. When Graham was a kid, he'd often imagined there were ghosts of horses standing in the garage next to his parents' car.

Perhaps it was the memory of the ghost horses that had driven him to explore the remainder of the house while his parents were taking their first overnight stay in eighteen months. Perhaps it was just that his melatonin supply had run out and the replacements had yet to arrive. Perhaps he'd been trying to find signal that wasn't as awful on his mobile as it was in the studio shed.

He couldn't really remember. All that really mattered was that he had a bandana over his mouth and nose for reasons other than potential plague-infection for once — the attic was supremely dusty — and there was junk up here he didn't remember ever having seen before in his life.

For example, he was pretty sure neither he nor his sister, who was currently perfectly happy doing something valuable with elephants in Tanzania, nor his parents, who probably wished they were in Tanzania visiting Louise instead of wandering around the Highlands in the rain, had bought the rocking horse. It looked like it had been up here since the dawn of time, and probably preceded the division of the houses. The wicker chair, too, looked as if it had been made back when gramophones were a thing. The pearlescent dressing-table, behind them, glimmered even under the dust, catching the moonlight that snuck in between a cracked tile on the neighbor's side of the house.

Graham made a mental note to mention the tile to his dad when they got back.

The dressing-table looked far too expensive and grand to be anything that belonged to *his* family. When they'd moved over to England in the Seventies, his Mum was fond of telling him they'd had next to nothing apart from Granny's old saucepans and a wheelbarrow full of carpets. This dressing-table looked like the kind of thing people *inherited*.

Graham squeezed past the rocking-horse. Even with the bandanna over his nose and mouth he could feel the dust beginning to prickle his nostrils.

The moon traced a silver-white streak across the dusty table-top; under the grey cloak it was exquisite, the kind of mother-of-pearl you expected a statue of Aphrodite to be rising out of in a museum.

Graham leaned on the horse. This was, he decided, the kind of dressing table that movie stars and fairy-tale princesses sat at when they were inconsolable over some misunderstanding with their beloved boyfriend. Or their faithful hound had croaked. Something momentous and expansive.

The two angled mirrors at either side of the central oval had, surprisingly, been removed. One was replaced with a sheet of yellowed newspaper and the other a collage of pictures of ponies, cut from children's books and magazines. But the central mirror was untouched, and untarnished. It reflected an identical darkened attic, a rocking-horse's face, and a similar shaft of moonlight.

"Go on then," Graham said to an audience of no one, "how tired do I look *now*?"

As he leaned around the edge of the frame, its worn gilt painted over mouldings of leaves and flowers, still twinkling with one or two probably-fake pearls, he had a sudden twist of misgiving in the pit of his stomach, as if he'd had too many coffees and was about to need the bathroom very abruptly, or he was back in the office and had just spied the head of the division coming around the corner. The part of him that had never fully gotten over a single horror movie he'd seen in his life whispered that if he looked now he'd find his entire face melted off, or a monster standing behind him.

Don't be an eejit, he told himself, unscrewing his eyes from their cowardly wrinkles in the middle of his face.

Graham put his hand over his mouth.

There was no melted face in the mirror. There was no monster behind him. There wasn't even a vampiric absence, a void through which the back of the attic could continue to be seen.

Instead, there was an entirely different person opposite him.

Spirals of dyed-red hair in loose-curls hung down to her chin. She wore small, round glasses, the complete opposite of the sharp rectangular ones he'd jammed up against his eyebrows, the ones which were supposed to balance out his face and didn't. Her hands had a pair of small silver rings, one on the forefinger of each, and she, like him, was wearing joggers and presumably pajamas, although hers looked considerably better on her.

In fact, the enumeration of small details couldn't hide the first thing Graham had noticed — guilty at his own response, as always — which was that she was utterly, incontrovertibly, entirely, and incomparably beautiful. *Perfect*, from the slightly off-center dark eyebrows to the point at which her legs vanished out of sight in the frame of the mirror.

Barely even realizing that he had, Graham put his forefinger side-on to his mouth and bit it in awed frustration, and fell in love on the spot.

She raised a hand in an awkward wave.

"Oh *right*, you can see me as well," Graham said, apparently operating on exactly the level of intelligence that had seen him have to re-sit at least two A-levels. "Hi."

She could see him, but as he quickly discovered, they couldn't hear each other: her mouth moved, and no sound reached him. Graham felt a little better about just puking out whatever idiocy popped into his head, although not much better.

She said something that looked like a hello, and waved slightly less awkwardly.

"Hi," Graham repeated, waving again.

She looked sad, he thought. He wasn't quite sure why someone who looked like that would have anything to be sad about — if he'd been able to command that kind of glorious pile of red hair and look that put-together in a set of teal joggers that were nominally marketed at Nanas, he'd have been hard-pressed to be sad about anything short of a direct asteroid hit, but perhaps she wasn't so devastatingly easily pleased. Or she had to look at him, which would constitute a tragedy for most people; Graham had to do it to shave most mornings and he knew he'd rather not see what was going on in the mirror.

Or, he thought, brushing habitual self-pity under the carpet in case it made him look like even more of a sad-sack and pushed her to depart into whatever magical world she inhabited, she was just tired. After all, it was the middle of the night. She probably had insomnia too.

"Can't sleep?" he asked, immediately feeling like kicking himself.

She nodded. He didn't quite catch what she said, but she put her fingertips to the mirror, pressing them against the inside of the glass until the tips turned white, as if she was trying to push her way through, and mouthed something like, "I've been waiting a long time."

Ah, Graham thought, disappointed. *It must be a dream.*

Still, just because it was a dream didn't mean he couldn't enjoy himself, did it? In fact, it being a dream meant he could probably enjoy himself *more* than in real life, where something like this would probably mean that he'd completely lost his mind as a result of that much-famed Lockdown Stress everyone was suffering from and which, barring the complete failure to get his hair cut, he thought he'd escaped from relatively unscathed.

"Is ... is that why you look so sad?" he asked, trying his best to make his mouth shapes distinct, and wondering if she could actually hear *him* even though he couldn't hear her. Probably not. Mirrors only showed light, after all. Then again, mirrors didn't usually show things that weren't there in the room you were in. Unless they were magic.

She nodded. Her pretty red curls brushed her cheeks, and she pressed her palm flat against the glass. There was a kind of desperation in her movements that made him uneasy.

Let me out, she said.

Graham blinked.

Let me out, she repeated. *Please.*

There was no mistaking what she'd said. His lip-reading might not be up to all that, but accompanied with the pleading expression and the way she had plastered her hand against the glass it was as clear as the mirror's surface itself.

The beam of moonlight that fell between him and the mirror looked like a shaft of light falling between prison bars.

Graham's uneasy feeling began to crawl up his spine on cold feet, like a spider made of ice. He shivered, watching the girl on the other side of the mirror, and a sensation of *imminence* came over him, that dream-like feeling of something about to happen, the kind of prickling in the skin one got before the start of a storm or — a thought that sat badly with the current situation — like the moment before one dived in for a kiss.

He made the mistake of wondering why she was stuck in the mirror in the first place.

People — things — get imprisoned in mirrors when they're dangerous, he thought, remembering some long-forgotten fairytale that had come with him in his blood, probably, over the Irish Sea along with Granny's saucepans and that wheelbarrow.

Inside the glass, the girl's hand curled into a fist against the mirror's silvered surface.

I know you need me. Please let me out.

"I'm sorry," Graham blurted, stumbling backwards, "I don't even know how I'd do that."

•   •   •

It would be wrong to say that Graham woke up sweating with this on his mind, because although the sofa in the living room, where he was sleeping until his parents came back, was warmer than his shed, it was still not really warm enough to make him sweat.

It would also be wrong to suggest that he immediately went to sleep and didn't in fact go to bed around dawn after drinking two unnecessary coffees, just so that he could be certain he hadn't been dreaming after all.

Most of all it would have been inaccurate to say that Graham O'Neill was woken by anything other than a phone call from his parents, causing him to panic that something was terribly wrong until they explained that they'd run into a friend of his dad's from his previous job and were going to extend their stay a little longer. While his mood of impending doom *might* have been related to his possible-dream, it was also just the O'Neill family's habit to begin every phone call with a rambling litany of disasters which always sounded as if it was about to culminate in "and then she was taken into police custody and now the car's on fire".

Once he was awake, however, the grim light of day sluiced away some of the otherworldliness of the previous night and set him wondering if his coffee-drinking, too, had been a dream.

"Oh, a Zoom meeting," Graham noted, once he'd checked his calendar. "Oh, cancelled," he said in a somewhat happier tone, when he'd checked his emails.

He picked up a bowl of dry cereal, and made his way up to the attic.

By the time he got to the attic stairs he'd finished the cereal; he left the bowl on the bookshelf in the hallway, and hesitated with his hand on the trapdoor.

"And if this turns out not to be a dream, and I'm actually insane," Graham asked the spider that was dangling by the trap-door's edge. "What do I do about it?"

The spider, rather than supplying a helpful but definitive answer by speaking, just ran off.

Think, Graham thought, pushing the trap-door open. *If you met a girl like that somewhere that wasn't your attic mirror, what would you do?*

Panic, probably. Panic, text someone that he was in love, have a lot of weird and uncomfortable feelings he didn't entirely understand, fail to get her number, stalk her on social media, send her a friend request, regret it, and *maybe*, if she took the first step, go on a date and say something weird or stupid and be treated like a leper.

"And the non-catastrophic version of that?" he asked the attic beams, closing the trap-door slowly behind him.

Talk to her, probably.

The light was coming from a different direction now. Instead of falling in an ominous beam across the attic from a broken tile, it was falling in a continuous kind of diffuse nothing-ness from every single gap, no defined source, just a general lightness that came from everywhere and nowhere all at once.

There was the rocking-horse. There was a patch of moss under one of the bits where the roof had leaked. There was — distressingly — a patch of black fuzz by the uppermost end of the roof beams, where the beams met the ridgepole of the house, which Graham was almost certain were some sleeping bats.

And there was the dressing-table, still, with its mirrors blacked out by a collage on one side and newspaper on the other, only the central mirror looking back at him.

It seemed less spooky by daylight, as these things often did, but his heart thumped nonetheless as he stepped carefully from slat to slat and over the endless junk his family and the long-gone neighbors had accumulated over the years.

The daylight showed an indistinct shape in dark teal clothes moving towards him in the mirror, and when he stopped with his arse pressed against the rocking-horse, there she was: the same as last night, reflected in the identical attic, her captivating red curls and intelligent eyes.

"Hello again," Graham said somewhat awkwardly, raising his hand.

She raised hers in return. *Hello, Graham. Have you come to let me out?*

Graham bit his lip.

She bit hers.

"Uh. How do you know my name?"

She tapped the side of her nose. It should have been a playful gesture, but she looked almost pitying, as if he'd disappointed her.

Graham felt queasy.

He leaned harder on the rocking-horse. "Look, if I ask you what you want — apart from me to let you out, which I don't know how to do — am I going to regret it?"

I can't answer that, but I think you know the answer to what I want, she said, still looking slightly sad. In the mirror, the girl was also leaning against the rocking-horse, but she had her palm pressed flat against her heart, between her boobs, as if what he was saying hurt her.

"... What *are* you?" Graham asked, and stopped himself. He rubbed the stubble on his face, and wished like hell he'd shaved better. Or that it didn't grow at all. He hated shaving anyway, but he hated the way he looked with facial hair more, and somehow the presence of a beautiful girl on the other side of the glass made him more conscious of it than ever. Of everything about himself. "I mean, you don't really live inside a mirror. No one does that. Unless you're a ghost or something."

You know what I am, she said, with a tight smile. *You know what I am and who I am, and you know you need me, and you need to stop lying to yourself about that, or I can never come out of here.*

The conversation really wasn't going the way he'd hoped, Graham thought, but it also wasn't going the way he'd feared, exactly, and he wasn't sure what to do about it besides clutch the rocking-horse's polished surface and write the whole experience off as one of those dreams that one has after a false awakening, the kind of dream which always feels like a swindle because you're just in your own house doing normal things but it still isn't *real*.

"I ..." he couldn't find an answer for this. He couldn't find an answer for why he'd come back, really, either: other than to look at a face that made his heart flutter and sink at the same time, and to assure himself he hadn't been dreaming, and he couldn't even manage the latter. "More research," he said, slowly. "I think."

•   •   •

The afternoon's work was so interminably dull that he drifted over to Reddit, and found himself trawling through a subreddit that was mostly dedicated to people who quite sincerely believed that there were mystical entities, ranging from folkloric cryptids to demons to Pokemon, living in the real world. People whom, until very recently, he'd have dismissed as complete nutjobs.

Now he skimmed through their posts looking for something that reflected his own experience, caught himself thinking the word *reflected*, and winced. A cup of tea sat cooling, utterly forgotten, beside him.

Two people were redirected to other subreddits: "That sounds like repressed trauma, dude" and "mate, I think you're having one of those gender diaspora things"; but most were taken with either mind-bending levels of sincerity or a very good approximation of it.

> *I think there's a Bigfoot in the woods behind my house*
> *I summoned a demon and it won't stop eating my cat's food, help*
> *Being haunted?*

Although the latter did turn out to be carbon monoxide poisoning, Graham felt there was enough sympathetic response to the unsolved and probably insane that it wouldn't hurt him to make a post under an anonymous account, and maybe see if anyone knew what he was talking about.

He was about to start writing one when the next post in the feed came up, entitled, *How to summon a succubus?*

"A what now?" Graham muttered, hitting his tea with his elbow. It sloshed lukewarm pale brown onto the tabletop, but nothing got too wet.

He opened a Wikipedia tab and read through it while mopping up the tea.

> *A succubus may take a form of a beautiful young girl, but closer inspection may reveal deformities of her body, such as bird-like claws or serpentine tails.*

Graham scratched the underside of his chin and slurped half-cold tea. He didn't recall the girl in the mirror having any deformities. She was — not perfect, necessarily, she had blemishes and unevenness like all people, like him — she was just. Normal and heartbreakingly lovely.

"What if I'm under a spell already?" he asked the empty room, and the phrase sounded perfectly ridiculous to his ears.

He finished his tea.

"There's no such thing as succubuses," he informed the laptop, closing the tab.

●   ●   ●

The thought that haunted him all afternoon was: *There's also no such thing as magic mirrors, and yet here you are.*

When he logged out of work for the day, Graham gave in to the urge to post to the subreddit.

> *There's a very beautiful woman in the mirror in my parents' attic. Not in any other mirrors in the house. She says she wants me to let her out. I'm not really sure how I would go about doing that, but do you think I should try?*

No one answered him until well after dinner. He was well into a repeated episode of a sitcom he hadn't liked in the first place — the third in a row — when his phone finally made a noise to let him know he'd got a notification.

> *No. You have no idea what that could be. It might be a demon. Lots of things take on the form of pretty girls to trick men.*

Well, that seemed pretty conclusive. Graham was relieved, and went back to the sitcom, but a nagging feeling remained in the back of his head: he was relieved, obviously. He didn't want to be the idiot that let a demon roam free around the countryside. His parents would never forgive him. Everyone would think he was an arse. He was relieved to have someone agree with him that this was a bad idea. Obviously.

The nagging feeling continued to nag at him.

She was really sad. Not about being in the mirror, but *for him*, somehow. He'd forgotten to mention that part. They'd only ask him how he knew that, and he didn't *know* how he knew that, only that the look on her face was so pitying, so sympathetic, that he felt like she knew about every miserable moment he'd had in his life, and *knew the answer.*

There was another bing: a different person had a different opinion.

> *Never let out anything you see in a mirror! It's in there for a reason!*

Graham wasn't sure he could argue with that one, but the rational remnants of his mind said: *A mirror can only reflect what's already there.*

He put the phone face-down on the arm of the sofa, but it binged at him indignantly as if he'd personally offended its mother.

> *Have you seen her anywhere before?*

He hadn't been expecting that one.

His instinct was to say no, of course not. If he'd seen a woman like that in real life, he'd have remembered her. If he'd seen her on TV, he'd have written down the actress's name and probably followed her on Twitter. If he'd dreamed about her, he'd never have insomnia.

And yet.

She looked so familiar. Like he knew her as well as she knew him.

The responses kept coming now:

> *Dangerous!*
> *No, no, no. Never. You can't trust things like that.*
> *My brother let one out and we never saw him again.*
> *Not even worth it to bang, dude.*
> *Are you insane? Do you want to be murdered? Because that's how you get murdered.*

Eventually, he turned the sound on his phone off. Everyone seemed to be in agreement: better to forget this entire episode had happened, and not do anything stupid, or mad. Just go to sleep, forget the entire business.

•　　•　　•

Of course, he didn't. Despite lying down and turning off the light and trying really hard to convince himself that the two paracetamol he'd taken for his headache were in fact sleeping pills, his brain remained unconvinced by the charade and had him staring at the ceiling for over an hour.

He heard the church bell down the street strike midnight, which didn't even make sense because he was pretty sure that it was already past that when he went to sleep, and that there wasn't a church bell there anymore anyway, but he accepted that the situation was just going to continue being weird until he did something about it.

Graham got off the sofa, put on his trainers, debated with himself whether he should have put on some trousers with his trainers, and when impatience had won out, he traipsed up the stairs to the attic landing.

There was no spider waiting by the trapdoor this time: he'd evidently scared the poor thing away by asking it existential questions earlier in the day. Spiders didn't like them any more than people did, it seemed.

In the attic all was still, calm, quiet, and dark. Either the moon was clouded, or just at the wrong angle, but there was not a single spot of light anywhere.

Recalling the bats he'd seen huddled up at the beams during the day, Graham was highly tempted to go back. He reminded himself that bats tended to be outside at night, looking for ... whatever it was they ate. Blood, possibly. All he had to worry about were big spiders and the fact that he'd either gone mad or was being haunted by his imaginary childhood best friend, the one he used to dress up as sometimes before his sister grassed him up for nicking her skirt.

"It's probably fine," Graham said, out loud. He put his phone on torch mode, surreptitiously swept away all the notifications for more Reddit replies which might conceivably have a different opinion of the situation, and informed the empty attic, "This is probably fine, right?"

He bumped into the rocking-horse, let out a little squeak of shock, and nearly blinded himself by accidentally shining the phone's light directly into the mirror.

"Ow."

He set the phone on the dresser table and peered into the dusty glass.

"Hello?"

It was harder to see her with the phone mostly spotlighting some hitherto unregarded spot on the attic's ceiling — really the underside of the roof — but all the salient features were there, and the feeling was there. The feeling convinced him, more than anything else, that he was right. Fear, deep embarrassment verging on shame, sure — but also a longing that cut through the fear like a knife, like homesickness cuts through hundreds of miles.

Graham gave her an awkward wave. She returned the wave exactly.

Are you ready now? She asked, and there was a flicker of hope in her eyes that glinted even in the shadows cast by the misaligned phone light.

"I need to know your name," Graham said, pressing the palms of his hands against the dresser table. There were two good reasons for asking, he thought, and one of them was because someone on Reddit had said if something gives you its true name, it's in your power. The other reason ...

You have to give me that, she said, pressing her palms against the mirror table and gazing at him just as intently as he gazed at her. *Are you ready?*

"I'm ... scared, actually," Graham admitted, looking down at his fingers as he spread them over the dusty surface.

When he looked up, she said, *Everything worth doing is scary.*

Graham wasn't sure that always held true, but he admitted he didn't necessarily *know*, on account of avoiding things that freaked him out as much as this did.

"Wh-what do you want?" he said, instead. "I mean, what are you going to *do* if I let you out?"

I want the same thing you want, she said, reaching towards the glass without him moving a muscle. *I want to live. Don't you think it's time?*

Graham nodded. His head felt like it weighed a ton and a half, and the nodding felt like it was going to break his neck.

He lowered his head, and closed his eyes.

"I'm ready now," he said, as if he was announcing it to the world instead of only to her reflection. "I'm coming out now."

Kelly O'Neill opened her eyes in the attic room of her parents' house and for the first time saw herself in the mirror as she really, really was.

"Oh," she said, in soft recognition, as her heart cried out in joy, "*here* I am."

Frank Sawielijew is a Russo-German author with Bulgarian roots whose stories are heavily inspired by the pulp classics and often mix elements of fantasy and science fiction into a flavorful blend. He writes in both English and German and had a handful of short stories appear in various anthologies since 2015. With a background in ancient and medieval history, he regularly draws inspiration from mankind's most ancient tales and cultures, from bronze age Mesopotamia to high medieval Europe. He has also contributed his writing and level design to computer games developed by small independent companies.

•   •   •

The lockdown allowed many people to experience the peace and quiet of working from home for the first time, free from all the annoyances of modern office culture. For companies that managed to shift to home offices completely, productivity even saw an increase! Despite that, employees were forced to return once the lockdowns lifted. What should have been a relief often wasn't. Tech companies that like to provide "recreation" and a "family-like" atmosphere demand more from their workers than mere work: they demand time and dedication to the company culture. My story shows the exaggerated extremes to which this can go, and why, perhaps, the home office is the better solution after all.

COMPANY CULTURE

FRANK SAWIELIJEW

W ITH A SIGH, LILY REMOVED THE STICKER from her webcam. Another useless meeting of empty corporate speeches and technical problems awaited. While the upper half of her body was dressed in a fancy blouse, her legs wore sweatpants and her feet were bare. Her coffee mug was filled with whisky, not coffee; the last time she tried that in a live meeting, her boss smelled it.

For all their shortcomings, online meetings had some undeniable benefits.

"Hello everyone!" came the overly cheerful greeting from Miss Smithers, Lily's boss. Too much makeup made her face look like a chemical testing facility. "I'm so happy to see you all on this bright and beautiful day. We've made a *lot* of progress on our projects, and I have some wonderful news for the coming week."

Lily took a large sip from her mug and prepared for the worst. She already knew what was coming. The anticipation filled her with existential dread.

"As you all know, the lockdowns are over and life has returned to normal. That means we can finally return to the office and work together in a friendly and productive environment. I'm sure you all missed interacting with your coworkers. Starting next week, I expect to see you all back in the office again. Aren't you excited?"

Lily's earphones bombarded her with a cacophony of compliant *yes*es and *of course*s. It had been her deepest, darkest fear since the lifting of the lockdowns. The tranquility of her home office, a soothing reality just moments ago, was now a fading memory.

Clinging to a last, desperate sliver of hope, she dared to ask her question: "Uh, Miss Smithers? Would it be fine if I continued working from home? I have highly optimized my workflow here and been really productive, so ..."

Miss Smithers dismissed Lily's request with a wave of her hand and a shake of her head. "Your productivity is highly appreciated, Miss Harley, but I am sure it will soar even higher within the friendly and open environment of our office! Besides, all employees are expected to participate in our company culture. That includes you, and me, and everyone else in this chatroom today. After all, we are more than just a company. We are family!"

Lily gulped down half her mug's content to cope with her new reality. It barely helped.

"So," she asked, "we all have to come in on Monday?"

The boss nodded with way too much enthusiasm. "Yes! I expect to see everyone in the office on Monday. Spend the day with your co-workers! Enjoy the wonderful benefits of our friendly company culture! And remember, we have monthly dress code themes: this month it's asymmetry, so please get creative with it! Since we'll be seeing each other in person soon, I will end this meeting early. Goodbye, everyone!"

She waved into the camera and put on a fake corporate smile. Whenever Miss Smithers attempted to express happiness, Lily had to think of radioactive fuel rods: yes, they glowed, but if you stared at them too long they made your eyes melt.

Everyone else smiled back with the same artificial expressions of pretend happiness. Lily concealed her frown behind the rim of her cup. Only one man on her screen kept his expression neutral; there even seemed to be a touch of annoyance in the set of his jaw. *Kevin*, said the name tag at the bottom of his picture.

Their moment of bonding was not to be. Miss Smithers closed the chatroom and Lily found herself staring at the black void of a dead connection. Her own reflection stared back at her. Its eyes were vacant orbs devoid of hope.

"I'm being overly dramatic. It's not that bad." She took another sip of whisky. Slowly but surely, it was getting to her head, dulling the pain. "It's not that bad."

She took off her blouse and tossed it into a corner, revealing the old, worn-out t-shirt underneath. Her comfortable clothes would have to stay at home. They were too plain to be in line with the office dress code.

Not too casual, but too plain. The office dress code demanded cheerful. Bright. Quirky. Because it was a happy office for happy people. An office filled with diversions to keep up morale. An office that had a dozen rooms for leisure, but only one for work.

Lily abhorred offices like that. But her job at Apate Advertising paid too well to quit over something this trivial. Whether she liked it or not, she would have to endure.

She finished her mug of whisky and quickly refilled it.

A last farewell to her home office's simple comforts.

•　　•　　•

The weekend had come and gone, and now it was Monday. Every fiber of Lily's body protested when she pulled herself out of bed, but it had to be. Attendance in the office was required. Participation in the company culture was mandatory.

The dress code was bright and asymmetrical. She put on a green t-shirt underneath a long-sleeved red crop top, and a violet skirt that went to her knees. Her right foot was clad in a long blue sock, while her left was bare within her turquoise oxford.

She thought she looked like a peacock, but peacocks were exactly what the workplace rules asked for.

She filled a thermos with regular coffee — no whisky this time — and left her beloved apartment, the home office that had treated her so well.

Her car's engine sounded angry when she turned it on, as if complaining about the early hour. Usually, it was only awoken in the late afternoon, to drive to the store or the gym, sometimes the pub.

Today, it had to enter rush hour and fight its way through traffic jams and reckless drivers rushing to work.

"I know how you feel, old boy," she said to her car. "I don't want to do it, either. But we have no other choice."

Traffic was a nightmare to navigate, but deep down, Lily was glad for each and every delay. Every red light, every snail's pace stop-and-go jam gave her a couple more minutes before she had to face the dreaded office with its enforced cheerfulness and group activities that had nothing to do with her job at all.

Coming from the highway, she turned right into 2nd Street, then left into River Road where the office building loomed before her like a concrete giant. Its bright blue coat of paint did little to mask the hideous brutalism of its shell.

The parking lot was populated by cars with too many stickers on the bumpers. Lily hadn't interacted with her colleagues beyond work emails and online meetings, but already knew by the appearance of their cars that she wouldn't like them.

She rode the elevator up to the second floor and exited into a hallway adorned with garishly patterned wallpaper. The way to the office led past more rec rooms than a company of this size could ever need. A billiards room, a movie lounge, a snack bar, even a hall for playing table tennis.

Only one room was designed for actual work. A large open plan office without an inch of privacy, computers arranged painfully close to each other and not a single wall to hide behind. A man in a teal Hawaiian shirt speckled with prints of palm trees and exotic fowl greeted her.

"Hey! Wanna join our gaming group? I've arranged an oldschool Quake deathmatch for after lunch. All the employees are taking part. We're allowed to use our computers for gaming — isn't that cool?"

Lily sighed. "Thanks, but I'd rather use mine for working. So ... which one's my workspace?"

He shrugged. "Just pick any and put up a name tag. Like this, see." He pointed to a piece of paper next to his keyboard, folded to stand upright. It said Charlie. The last time Lily had seen a name tag like this was in elementary school.

"Great. Thanks."

She picked a place as far away from Charlie as she could and sat down. The computer booted up quickly. At least the hardware was good. As was the software. It had the newest edition of Photoshop installed, which took her a while to get used to; at home, she had used an older version. Pirated, but nobody had to know that.

Despite Miss Smithers' promises, the vibrant office culture did not cause Lily's productivity to soar. The din of a dozen conversations kept intruding through her ears, robbing her of her focus. From the few snippets she could make out, none of the conversations seemed to be work-related.

She missed the peace and quiet of her home office already.

Whenever she glanced at the screens of the people around her, she saw games and chat windows instead of business applications. Nothing about this office culture was conducive towards productivity in any way. Everyone indulged in distractions, and the open layout of the office offered Lily no reprieve. Whether she wanted to or not, her coworkers' distractions distracted her just the same.

Apart from herself, only one man tried to concentrate on his work, gaze fixed on his screen and teeth clenched. Lily recognized his neatly trimmed beard and slicked-back hair, and admired his decision to violate the office dress code. A pale blue button-up shirt, black jeans, brown loafers. Not a single splotch of garish color in sight, and perfectly symmetrical.

"Hey. Kevin?"

"Please," he said with a sigh. "I just want to work."

"So do I. But I can't concentrate with all this noise."

He turned his head and looked at her. "Hey. I remember you from last call. You were the only one who didn't smile like an idiot." His eyes wandered down, scrutinizing her from head to toe. "Your outfit is terrible."

She laughed. "Office regulations. Unlike you, I wasn't brave enough to defy them."

He shrugged. "I don't care about any of that crap. You know why I got this job? To work and make money. Not to participate in some stupid company culture. We're supposed to finish that advertisement for Burger Palace by Wednesday, but nobody else seems to care."

"Wait ... so you're writing the text for that ad? I've been working on the graphics for a week. Looks like we're the only ones putting any work into the project."

"Huh. So you do graphic design? Which other ads did you work on?"

"The video for the Lucky Ladies casino. I edited the footage and added visual effects."

"I wrote the script for that and was on site with the actors when they filmed it."

"The Super Socks logo. I designed that."

"I came up with the tagline. *Life rocks with our socks.*"

"What about the movie poster for Galactic Conflict VI: Tarth's Revenge? I painted the likenesses of the actors as their characters, and the big spaceship battle in the background."

"I did the layouting and added the title."

"If we did all these on our own ... what is everyone else doing?"

Kevin waved his arm in a sweeping gesture. "Isn't it obvious? They participate in the company culture! Unlike us."

Lily's eyes roamed through the room. Everyone in the office was involved in a conversation, and through the door she could spot some people playing table tennis in one of the rec rooms. "Right. They've had these optional activities even during the lockdown. I guess some of these were online? I never joined in."

"Me neither. But hey, at least we're getting some actual work done."

Miss Smithers burst into the room with a loud *hello folks*, interrupting their conversation. She greeted every employee personally and got way too close with some of them, giving them hugs and kissing their cheeks. Her outfit was beyond questionable. Each arm of her jacket had a different color, as had each leg of her pants. The blouse that could be glimpsed underneath her jacket looked like it was lifted from an abstract art exhibition, dappled with dizzying patterns that boggled the mind.

When she came to Lily and Kevin, she raised an accusing finger.

"Mr. Conall, your clothes are terribly dull. Aren't you aware of the office dress code? Please wear something more colorful tomorrow. You may consider this an *informal* warning, by the way. Miss Harley, yours are quite lovely. Wearing only one sock is a nice way to break the symmetry, but I'd like to see some more patterns on your clothes. It's all flat colors right now. There's a lot of room left for improvement!"

Lily cleared her throat. "With all respect, Miss Smithers, but I don't see how our clothes have anything to do with the job. Can't we just wear what we want?"

Miss Smithers looked down at her with a patronizing smile. "It's all about the company culture, Miss Harley. We are a young company with a bright and cheerful image, and we want every single employee to embody those values. Happy workers are efficient workers! Do it like your colleagues and display your happiness for all to see!"

Lily didn't see much efficiency from her all-too-happy colleagues, but she swallowed the comment. As long as she got paid on time, she couldn't care less what the others did.

"Now, what kind of pizza would you like to have?" Miss Smithers asked. "It's the first day we're all together in the office, so I'm ordering pizza to celebrate the occasion."

Lily shook her head. "Nothing for me. I brought my own sandwich for lunch."

There was the accusing finger again, wagging back and forth like a dog's tail. "Must I remind you that everyone is expected to participate in the company culture? That includes you two. I never saw either of you at any of our lovely team-building events, but now that we're all back at the office you can no longer evade your responsibilities. What do you want on your pizza, Miss Harley?"

Lily sighed inwardly, careful not to display her frustration. After all, Miss Smithers wanted to see *happy* employees. She put on a cheerful voice and answered, "Pepperoni, mushrooms, prosciutto, olives."

"Same for me," said Kevin. He hadn't even paid attention to her ingredient list.

"Lovely." Miss Smithers clapped her hands and curled up her lips in a sickly sweet smile. "We'll have so much fun eating pizza together, you'll see! Now get up off your chairs and mingle. We're a family here, and family work together. Come on! I want to see more participation from you two."

Miss Smithers went into her office — the only private office room in the entire building — and Lily thought she could get back to work now. But every so often, Miss Smithers poked her head through the door just to glare at the two diligent workers for not wasting enough time with non-work activities.

Lily accepted her fate with a sigh. "She keeps staring at us. I guess we should get up and have some *fun*."

"Great. I miss my home office already."

"Tell me about it."

They got up and mingled, projecting the cheerful mood Miss Smithers expected them to display.

It cost them way more effort than their actual work ever required.

•   •   •

They spent two hours exploring the office building's many rooms and interacting with their colleagues. If she hadn't known better, Lily would have thought it a holiday center rather than an office. People enjoyed themselves with games, sports, films, books, snacks — but not one of them worked.

"How does this company get any work done with a culture like this?"

"We get the work done." Kevin took a sip of his coffee and shrugged. "At least, we usually do. When we're not forced to *participate*."

When the pizza arrived, they were all expected to gather in the snack bar. The room was much too small to hold everyone, making it uncomfortably crowded. Miss Smithers pushed her way through the crowd and engaged everyone in conversation. Lily just wanted to eat in peace, but there was no way to escape.

The conversations were as dull as they came. And none of them were in any way related to work. Not even Miss Smithers talked about the jobs everyone was supposed to do. It was as if she didn't care. As if the only thing that mattered to her was the vibrant company culture, and a veneer of happiness on her employees' faces.

Lily was glad when it was finally over and she could return to the office. As much as she hated its open layout, compared to the cramped bar it was paradise. She didn't even manage to enjoy her pizza in this oppressive atmosphere.

"Alright, back to work," said Miss Smithers, "but don't forget: we're having our daily mindfulness session in three hours. Everyone is expected to attend, even our two little recluses!"

A wave of laughter went through the crowd, and Lily felt a dozen eyes stare at her. She pushed her way through the suffocating mass of bodies and fled back to the office. Kevin was right behind her.

The others trickled in slowly, one by one, in no rush to return to their computers — many of which weren't even powered on yet, even though it was far past noon.

Lily released a deep sigh of relief when the din of conversations finally subsided. It still wasn't as quiet as her home office, but quiet enough to concentrate on her work. She was almost finished with the new Burger Palace logo due on Thursday. Still plenty of time to polish its look and come up with a handful of alternative designs. The clients usually picked her original design, but she liked to offer them a choice.

But the moment of peace was only temporary. Soon, the sound of gunshots and loud grunts pounded against her eardrums, blasting her concentration to bits.

She glanced at the other screens. Instead of working, people faced off against each other in a Quake deathmatch. Most of them didn't use headphones, so the office was drowned in a cacophony of *hop*s and *argh*s and *bang*s and *brrrt*s. It was impossible to work like that.

"Hey Kev," she asked, "wanna go grab another coffee?"

He ran a hand over his face and nodded.

They retreated to the snack bar, now a haven of peace within this noisome hellhole.

"At this rate, I'll have to do all my work at home after hours."

"Uh-huh. At least the pay makes it all worth it."

Lily filled her cup to the brim. No milk, no sugar, but she wished she had some rum or whisky. "Does it really? I feel like the so-called office culture is going to wreck my mental health in the long run. Also, how long do you think this company will survive with so many slackers on the payroll?"

Kevin shrugged. "Guess you're right. Might be a good idea to look for alternatives soon. I haven't felt this tired in years, and the day's not even over."

"Almost makes you wish for another lockdown, huh?"

He offered her a smile. "Not quite. I do enjoy sharing a coffee with my only sane coworker."

She chuckled and looked down at her cup, cheeks flushing red. "So do I."

•   •   •

Lily had barely settled down in her chair again when Miss Smithers burst into the room and called for everyone's attention.

"Alright everyone, it's time for our daily mindfulness session. Most of you already took part in some of the optional sessions we organized during the home office period, but now that we're all back at the office, attendance is mandatory for all employees. Please follow me to the meditation room."

A dozen mouths responded simultaneously, "Yes, Miss Smithers."

Kevin raised an eyebrow. "That was weird."

"Uh-huh. Reminds me of a cult more than a company. Creepy."

But there was no escaping Miss Smithers' urging stare. She accepted no excuses. If they wanted to keep their jobs, they had to participate.

And right now, Lily still wanted to keep her job. Her bills didn't pay themselves.

Reluctantly, she got up and followed the others into the meditation room.

The room was spacious but dark, with no windows in its walls. The only source of illumination was a row of candles lined up at the back of the room, behind a marble statue of a woman with smooth ivory skin. It looked ancient Greek in origin, or perhaps Roman.

Everyone slipped out of their shoes, and Lily followed suit. She had to grin when she saw the bright green socks on Kevin's feet. He did add a little bit of color to his outfit, after all.

Miss Smithers closed the door behind them, locking out any light from the outside. She told her employees to assume positions, and they knelt down before the statue in a semicircular formation.

Lily looked at Kevin for reassurance, who only shook his head. Neither of them liked the look of this.

"Miss Harley, Mr. Conall. You are expected to participate in the company culture," Miss Smithers reminded them. "Please assume your positions."

Lily bit her lip and acquiesced. It was only a silly ritual to strengthen the team spirit, she told herself. There was nothing to worry about. Nothing to worry about at all.

She found an empty spot between two employees and knelt down, as did Kevin. Three other people sat between them. She wished he were closer.

Miss Smithers pulled out a sharp knife from underneath her suit jacket. Its blade gleamed silver in the candlelight.

"Let us give our blood to Apate so she may bless our company with good fortune."

"Praise Apate," chanted the employees, "we shall rejoice in your blessings."

She cut into her palm and let a few drops of blood go into a golden chalice, where they intermingled with crystal clear water. Both knife and chalice were handed down to the rightmost employee, who added his blood to the mix. He gave them to the one on his left, and so knife and chalice traveled from employee to employee.

When they reached Lily, she pretended to cut herself by wiping the flat of the blade across her palm, then held her hand over the chalice as if dripping her blood into it. The water was already stained red as wine, and the coppery smell of freshly spilled blood crawled into her nostrils. It almost made her gag.

She gave knife and chalice to the one kneeling to her left and took a deep breath. Her heart pounded rapidly within her chest. This was more than just company culture. This was a straight-up company cult.

Once every employee had added their blood to the chalice, Miss Smithers picked it up and poured the concoction into a small hole within the statue's mouth. It must have been a mere trick of the light, but Lily thought she saw a change in the statue's expression.

But then, its marble arms moved as if they were flesh, and an accusing finger was pointed at her. The other pointed at Kevin.

"Blasphemers!" Miss Smithers called them out, the feigned friendliness gone from her voice. "You did not give Apate your blood! Your refusal offends our goddess! Seize them!"

Lily jumped to her feet and ran to the door, dodging past a dozen hands that reached for her.

It was locked.

She pulled at the door's handle, punched the door, kicked it, hit it with her knee until it hurt, threw her hips against it — all to no avail. It didn't budge.

A hand grabbed her by the shoulder, another by the thigh, another closed around her wrist. They pulled her back from the door and dragged her to the floor.

"Let me out of here! I don't wanna give my blood to anyone! I quit! Miss Smithers, I quit!"

"I'm sorry, Miss Harley," said Miss Smithers, her formerly sweet voice now cold as ice. "Your contract only allows you to quit with two weeks' notice. And as long as you are an employee at Apate Advertising ... you are expected to participate in the company culture."

Lily screamed and cried and begged, but her coworkers did not loosen their grips upon her arms and legs. She could feel the touch of a knife against her left palm — but before it could bite, it dropped from its wielder's hand.

Kevin pummeled the coworkers with his fists, drawing their attention to him. Two tried to tackle him, but he downed one with a knee to the groin and the other with a punch to the jugular. The ones still holding down Lily were dispatched with a few quick jabs of his elbows.

The others kept their distance, wary of his flying fists.

"Thanks," said Lily as she sat up, rubbing her shoulder. Her coworkers' rough handling had left her with a couple of painful bruises.

"I knew those martial arts lessons would come in handy one day," he replied. "Door's locked?"

She got to her feet and nodded. "We need something heavier than fists to bust it open."

"You'll come to regret your defiance," Miss Smithers shouted. "Apate demands her sacrifice, and she will have it!"

The statue began to move. Its smooth legs bent forward and its shapely marble feet stepped off their dais and down onto the soft carpeted floor, leaving a deep impression in their wake. Made from hard, solid stone, its limbs moved nevertheless as smoothly as a being of flesh.

It approached Lily and Kevin with fluid motions, but all its grace couldn't hide its immense weight. Each step of its marble feet echoed through the windowless room and made the ground tremble underneath their impact.

Kevin lowered his fists, unsure how to meet such an opponent. Against its body of solid stone, he would only break his knuckles.

The statue rushed forward and jumped at Lily in an attempt to tackle her. Kevin grabbed her by the arm and pulled her down. They tumbled to the floor while the statue crashed into the door, smashing it open under the impact of its solid marble body.

Kevin got to his feet quickly and pulled Lily up with him. "Run!"

He didn't have to tell her twice. She ran as fast as her legs could push her, jumping through the broken door. The statue's hand reached for her as she passed it by, and its fingers managed to snatch the tip of her sock. She fell down again, but quickly yanked herself free. A big chunk of cloth tore out of her sock, and the statue screamed. It was like the sound of nails scraping against a chalkboard.

The other employees poured through the open door. They were upon her before she could get back on her feet.

"Kevin! Help!"

Kevin yanked a computer screen from a nearby desk, ripping out its cables with a swift motion. He swung it against his coworkers and hit one over the head. The screen exploded in a shower of sparks. The others recoiled, giving Lily enough time to pull away and pick up speed again.

They ran straight for the exit, vaulting over desks and chairs. A lot of hardware clattered to the ground in their wake. The other employees pursued them like a horde of zombies, stumbling over the debris on the ground.

Lily kept glancing over her shoulder, panting and sweating as she ran through the corridor leading towards the elevator. Their pursuers were far behind, but the statue was among them now. Its heavy steps made the entire building shake under their impact.

To their luck, the elevator door opened right away and they slid inside. Kevin pushed the button for the first floor and breathed out in relief.

"We made it. I didn't see any stairs on my way in, so I don't think they can follow us without waiting for the elevator to come back."

"I'm never going to work a job that advertises its friendly office culture again." Lily looked down at her body to assess the damage. Apart from a handful of bruises and a ripped sock, she had come away unscathed.

That loathsome statue hadn't gotten a single drop of her blood.

With a *ding*, the elevator arrived at the ground floor. They stepped out and headed for the exit.

Upstairs, something was pounding heavily. Cracks appeared in the ceiling and flakes of white plaster rained down upon them. Lily barely managed to jump away before a big chunk of ceiling broke off and crumbled down. It hit Kevin in the back, making him stumble forward and dazing him for a moment.

The statue jumped through the newly created hole, and this time Lily had to grab Kevin and pull him out of its way. It swung at them with its marble fists, hitting a wall. More plaster rained down from above and a large crack appeared in the wall.

The statue's shape was elegant and feminine, but its fists hit harder than a truck.

Lily and Kevin scrambled for the exit, the irate statue at their heels.

The front door was a flimsy thing of glass. Kevin leapt right through it, shattering it into a thousand pieces. Lily followed right behind, shielding her face with her arms as she dove through the shower of shards.

She headed straight for her car, only to realize that she left her purse in the office.

"I don't have my keys! Where's your car? Quick, before the statue gets us!"

Kevin grabbed her by the arm and pulled her along while his other hand fished the keys from his jeans pocket. He unlocked his car, a green Renault Twingo, and climbed inside. His hand pushed the key into the ignition and started up the engine.

Lily looked into the rear view mirror. The statue was almost upon them.

"It's almost here!"

Kevin set the gear to reverse and said, "Here goes nothing."

His left foot slowly released the clutch while his right went down on the gas pedal with full force. The car's little engine roared, and Lily was almost thrown from her seat when it jumped backward at high speed. The backside bumper folded inward with a loud crunch as it collided with the statue. The marble goddess hadn't expected this sudden reverse and lost her balance, falling onto the hard pavement with her back. Her right arm broke off at the shoulder and rolled away, and her left leg fractured at the knee.

Kevin switched gears and drove away, leaving the bloodthirsty statue broken at the parking lot.

He rummaged through the side pocket in his door and fished out a pack of cigarettes.

"Smoke?"

She hesitated for a moment, but then grabbed one. "I don't usually, but yeah. Thanks."

He gave her a lighter, and she lit up. She watched tendrils of white smoke travel up to the car's ceiling, where they lingered for a while before they dispersed.

"So ... what do you think of going independent? Freelance. We've been doing all the work on those ads ourselves, anyway."

He kept his eyes on the road, focused on traffic. After a while, he replied with a shrug. "Sure, why not. Found our own little company." He grinned. "A company where all the employees are like a family."

She took a drag of her cigarette and smirked. "Well," she said, "I wouldn't mind having *you* as part of my family. Besides, a shared home office would cut down on rent."

"Yeah. I think for now, I'll just invite you over for a coffee. I don't want to hear the word *office* ever again."

He drove onward, heading towards his apartment, and Lily felt the tension leave her body with every mile of distance they brought between themselves and Apate Advertising's offices.

She put her hand on Kevin's while he worked the stick shift and smiled. Freelancing together was a wonderful idea.

She never wanted to see the inside of an office again in her life.

Steven D. Brewer teaches scientific writing at the University of Massachusetts Amherst. His fantasy story "Revin's Heart" has been serialized by Water Dragon Publishing. As an author, Brewer identifies diverse obsessions that underlie his writing: deep interests in natural history, life science, and environmentalism; an abiding passion for languages; a fascination with Japanese culture; and a mania for information technology and the Internet. Brewer lives in Amherst, Massachusetts with his extended family.

●　　　●　　　●

It is said you cannot make things foolproof because fools are so ingenious. So our protagonist discovers in this short tale of the dog who chases the car and CATCHES IT. Now what? In Fantasia's "The Sorcerer's Apprentice", the Sorcerer cleans up the mess, just giving Mickey a little swat on the behind for his trouble. But stories of this type have been told back to the time of the ancient Greeks. What's going to happen this time?

THE RIGHT MOTIVATION

STEVEN D. BREWER

A<small>FTER DINNER, MADISON CHECKED HIS PHONE.</small> He found a curt response to the thread of messages he'd been exchanging with a potential employer.

"We regret that we are unable to hire you as you have indicated you do not have a motivator," it said. "We apologize that we did not make this requirement clear in the application materials as our new HR director believed it went without saying. We will revise the template we use for future job postings and wish you success in your job search."

"Blah, blah, blah," Madison said.

He went back to his computer, returned to the job boards, and spent half an hour looking for anything else worth applying for, but there was nothing. You basically had to have a motivator for an employer to even consider you anymore.

Masaka motivators were small implants that interfaced with the brain and enabled people to focus and work on tasks without getting bored or distracted. According to Masaka, motivators made people excellent students and employees who worked tirelessly while on the clock. Motivators had quickly become extremely popular and now nearly everyone had one.

Madison's parents had thought motivators were a bad idea, so they refused to have one implanted when Madison was little. Most children these days got a motivator installed before they began school. Children with motivators consistently got better grades, had higher academic achievement, and had an easier time getting employed. At least, that was how it had been, originally. Now, you practically couldn't get a job without one.

When he was younger, Madison had bought into his parent's thinking and took pride in struggling to stay focused while the other kids just did their work. But now he was more conflicted and sometimes secretly wished he had one too, since it would make things so much easier. But would it really? He snorted.

"Motivators are a joke," he thought. *"You just write the task for the motivator and the person doesn't even have to think about it."*

On a whim, he drafted a joke social media post to tell people to send him a dollar and reshare the post. He cast it in pretend "motivator speak" — the highly stylized language for tasks used to invoke the motivator that you'd see regularly in movies and dramas. And he used a bunch of their buzzwords. Plus, as the *coup de grace*, he included the images of a couple of the motivator "activation codes" — obscure symbols that communicated directly to the motivator. Then he clicked Submit. And then, he went to bed.

His phone pinged as he was turning out the light and so he checked his notifications. Someone had deposited a dollar in his Paystir account. He chuckled and then silenced the phone, rolled over, and went to sleep.

The next morning, he got up, made coffee, and checked messages. His social media post had gone viral. No. More than viral. It was literally the only thing being shared. He scrolled and scrolled and scrolled but, other than advertisements, there were literally no other posts.

He went to check his Paystir account and got an error: the account didn't exist. Puzzled, he checked his mail and found a helpful message from Paystir explaining that the number of transactions had exceeded the capacity of his account category and so his account had been automatically upgraded, with the fees charged to his new account. He checked the balance and his eyes goggled: the balance had 8 digits above the decimal place. And money was still pouring in. He sat back, bemused.

"Is this a good thing? Or a bad thing?" he wondered. "Or a very bad thing ..."

He wandered into the kitchen and poured himself a cup of coffee. But when he checked the fridge, he was out of cream. Grumbling, he pulled his shoes on and headed out to visit Konbinis, the convenience store down the street.

Walking at a leisurely pace, he noticed someone had put up flyers on the telephone poles with a print out of his post. He quickened his pace and went into Konbinis. He found the cream in the refrigerator case. Next, while he was there, he poured himself a fresh cup of coffee with cream and took it to the counter to pay.

The man behind the counter was doing something on his smartphone. Madison tapped a bell on the counter when the man didn't immediately turn to help him. The man, with a glazed and irritated look, put down his phone and quickly tapped on the point-of-sale terminal and it displayed a total. Madison tapped his phone on the paypoint and it pinged confirming the transaction. As the man snatched up his own phone again, Madison could see that it was displaying his social media post. The man returned to robotically tapping the screen, completely ignoring Madison.

"You're welcome," Madison said.

Walking back, Madison noticed that the streets were unusually quiet. He hadn't noticed initially because it was often quiet on a Sunday morning. But it wasn't Sunday, he realized: It was Thursday and normally the street would be jammed with traffic. But it was not.

At the cross street, Madison looked left and saw the billboard by the highway and realized that it too was displaying his ad. He picked up his pace again.

When he was nearly home, he saw a man sitting on the ground leaning up against the wall next to a stack of handbills that were fluttering in the breeze. Madison could see that he'd been putting them up every two or three feet on the whole street, but had finally run out of energy and was asleep — or unconscious.

At this point, Madison finally and unequivocally understood, without any possible prevarication, that his joke ad posted to social media, was going to lead to — indeed had already led to — serious, serious trouble. Madison tiptoed past and went to go into his building.

"Mr. Dali?" someone said. Madison turned and saw a woman wearing a black trench coat with dark glasses and a coiled wire leading to a small earpiece.

"Really?" Madison said. "Isn't that outfit a bit cliché?"

"They had a special on trench coats at the coat factory the other day," she said without inflection. "They're terribly comfortable. I think everyone in the future is going to be wearing them."

"Really?"

"No, Mr. Dali," the woman sighed. "I'm sorry. I'm Special Agent Misty McGee. I'll need to ask you to come downtown with me."

"Do I have any choice?"

"I can put handcuffs on you, if that would make you feel better."

Madison considered trying to dash to his apartment, but a similarly dressed man appeared on the steps between him and his apartment. So, he reluctantly relented and allowed himself to be escorted to a dark SUV where he was directed to sit in the back — where there were no handles inside — and the two agents got in the front and drove him downtown.

"Is your name really Madison Dali?" McGee asked.

"Thank my parents," Madison said. "That's exactly the kind of sense of humor they had."

They entered an underground parking garage. A gate raised automatically as they entered and they drove down and down until they reached the lowest level. The door to the SUV was opened for him and he was escorted to a door into the building that opened when Agent McGee pressed her badge against a sensor. They led him through a maze of corridors to a room with a table and a couple of chairs and shut him inside.

"Can I get you anything? A cup of coffee or tea?" McGee asked. Madison raised his coffee cup as if toasting her and she left without further comment. Madison took a sip. Thanks to the insulated cup, it was still hot.

"*Coffee is good*," Madison thought. "*Creamy.*"

After a few minutes, McGee came back in. She sat down in the chair and then leaned forward.

"Do you have any idea how much trouble you're in?" she asked.

"Bullshit," Madison said. "All I did was post a message on social media."

"But you do understand that the disruption you're causing has national security implications," McGee continued.

"I didn't manufacture defective motivators and make people install them," Madison countered.

"I'm sure we could get a conviction for reckless endangerment."

"If you can find a judge without a motivator."

McGee sighed.

"Look," she said. "What we really need is to figure out how to fix this. My colleague and I are the only two left in the organization. The capital markets are starting to seize up because a significant part of the global money supply is already in your account."

"Maybe you should try asking me," Madison said.

"Will you help us fix this?"

"Try asking nicely."

"Will you *please* help us fix this," McGee said.

"That's more like it," Madison said, rubbing his hands. "Have you tried contacting the company?"

"Everyone at Masaka has a motivator installed," McGee said. "It's a condition of employment. They don't even answer the phone anymore."

"Surely, you've been able to find someone who knows this stuff ..."

"Nope. You're it, kid. How did you figure out how to hack the motivator system?"

"I didn't," Madison said "Well, not really. Look. I was just angry because I can't find a job because I don't have a motivator, and no-one will hire you without one. When I wrote the post, I was just shitposting — making fun of the way motivator tasks are written. I just made up some shit and copied and pasted some of the graphics."

"So we're screwed then," McGee said.

"Not necessarily," Madison said. "Hang on. There was one thing I noticed. Look here." He brought up a picture on his phone.

"In a real motivator task, as I understand it, you use this graphic *or* that graphic. You never use them both together. I put both in because I thought it would be funny. Maybe that's it?"

"How does that help us?"

"Let's try making a new task that asks people to delete or remove all of the copies of the other task."

"But won't that just end up reaching a steady state where one does it and another undoes it forever?"

"Not if one task takes less time. Since we're not going to ask for money, this time, the undo task will be faster and will eventually win. And once the first one is totally gone, it shouldn't happen again."

Madison first deleted his original post. Then he spent a few minutes crafting a new task and revised it several times to make it as concise and simple as possible. He added the two graphics and clicked submit.

"Is that it?" McGee asked.

"Well, it's submitted. I don't know how long it will take before we start to see results. Let me check my account balance." He brought up the Paystir screen on his phone. The balance was now, he had to count, 13 digits long and still increasing. He reloaded the screen and identified change in the 10th digit. He waited a little while longer and reloaded again and this time noticed change only below the 9th digit.

"It looks like it's slowing down," he said. "It'll probably take a few hours or days."

"You do understand you'll have to give all the money back," McGee said.

"That's fine," Madison said. "I wasn't serious about the money. It was just meant to be a joke anyway. But how are you going to figure out how to give all the money back?"

"I'm not going to," McGee said. "You are. I mean, you said you were looking for a job ..."

After retiring from Abbott Laboratories, Steve Soult has pursued his lifelong interests in art, photography, and writing full time. He enjoys writing about ordinary people involved in extraordinary situations. His three grown children are all engineers in Silicon Valley. He lives in Morgan Hill, California with his wife, Susanne, and his dog, Snowy.

•   •   •

"Human Relations" is largely based upon my personal experience, where an adversarial relationship between Manufacturing and the R&D Engineers "in the ivory tower" frequently existed. The device introduced in this story will later be used in my story, "Reduction in Force", which was published in the first "Corporate Catharsis" anthology.

HUMAN RELATIONS

STEVE SOULT

AFTER THE PANDEMIC HIT SILICON VALLEY, NeuroTech Medical Devices established a site policy that all non-manufacturing personnel should work from home. To do this, I set up a makeshift home office in one corner of our spare bedroom in our small two-bedroom apartment. I chose the right-hand corner near the bedroom window primarily for its light. However, it also enabled me to look out the window and watch the day go by.

My office consisted of a well-worn walnut six-foot folding table with a scratched top for a desk, a used mesh office chair in fairly good condition, and two side-by-side computer monitors. On the left side of my computer monitors, I had a brand new LED desk lamp and some small office items.

On the right side of my monitors I had a collection of pens and pencils stowed in a black 14k gold-trimmed NextGen coffee cup. I got the NextGen coffee cup at one of the

Advanced R&D Team significant milestone celebrations. They were developing a highly-advanced memory erasure device, unlike anything else on the marketplace. If all went well and according to plan, the device would enter its clinical trials early next year.

Also strewn across my desk were stacks of loose papers, organized according to category. On the left side of my monitors, I had the state-of-the-art cell phone issued to me by the Company.

Under my desk were my computer workstation and some cardboard storage boxes containing work-related files and papers. The rest of the bedroom was filled with stuff including several moving boxes stacked against the bedroom walls. My wife, Paige, and I never seemed to have enough spare time to unpack the boxes from our move from Boston a few years ago.

Looking at the stuff surrounding my office, I thought, *we had better do something about clearing out this junk. The baby is due in six months and it will need a nursery.* I sighed. *The problem is that we don't have anywhere to put all of this stuff. Maybe I should bite the bullet and rent a storage space.*

I decided to get a cup of coffee. I got out of my chair and walked into the apartment's living/dining area where Paige's home office was located. She was focused on her workstation monitor and Henri Le Pooch, our black poodle mix, was curled up right next to her bare feet.

She looked up from her monitor and smiled. "You look tired, Pierre. How's it going?"

"Okay, I guess. The quarterly reviews are due by the end of the month, so it's a very busy time for me and my staff."

"Don't worry, it'll be alright. Just go through them one at a time and, before you know it, it'll get done."

"I suppose." I shrugged and continued, "With almost all of the exempt employees working from home nowadays, the first-line managers are finding it very difficult to write their appraisals. The appraisal form was never designed for employees who are working from home."

"As the site's Human Relations Director, why don't you just change the form? You know, have a work-from-home version."

"Actually, that's a pretty good idea. I'll bring it up at our next executive staff Zoom call on Monday morning. But I'm not sure that Boston will go along with it."

Paige chuckled and replied, "Then it will be *their* loss."

"That's for sure!" I grinned and gave her thumbs up.

• • •

I returned to my desk with a nice hot cup of coffee and sat down. I wiggled my mouse to wake up my workstation and entered my password. Just as I opened an employee's appraisal that had been forwarded to me for review, the Company's cell phone rang. It was the Site Director, Hassim Rashid.

"Hi, Hassim, what's up?"

"Pierre, there has been a possible OSHA reportable event on the Manufacturing Pilot Line. I need to have you look into it ASAP."

"Okay. Do you know what happened?"

"Two employees had an altercation. Something about the site's masking policy. During the altercation, one of them fell and was injured."

A knot formed in my stomach. "That's really bad."

"It sure is. Any sort of physical conflict at work is against Company policies."

"I know ..." I nervously ran my fingers through my hair. "Not only that, it's a violation of the Company's conditions of employment."

"That's right. Do whatever is necessary to resolve this situation. If you have to fire them, then fire them. But move quickly. We can't afford to let this situation get out of hand."

"Okay, I'm on it."

"Good! Let me know as soon as you find out anything. Oh, and by the way, Jackson will be calling you this afternoon. You had better go into the office to receive her call."

Oh no, I thought. *Dr. Rita Jackson was an Associate Vice President in Boston who was secretly called 'The Butcher' within the Company. She was known for carving up pieces of the Company and getting rid of their assets and personnel. Jackson was the last person that I wanted to talk to right now.*

"Okay, I'll head on over to my office shortly. Thanks, bye." I hung up and placed my cell back on my desk.

•　　•　　•

Dr. Rita Jackson had scheduled a Zoom call with me at 2:00 PM from her office in Boston. I joined the call about 5 minutes early and waited for her to start the call. She started the call right on time.

Rita was a large heavy-set woman. She had short black hair and wore black round wire-rimmed glasses that complemented her round face and magnified her eyes. She glared at me with a penetrating gaze and scowled. "Corporate wants *you* to resolve this situation on the Manufacturing Pilot Line ASAP," she said.

"All right," I replied. "But a proper solution will not necessarily be quick or easy."

"We don't need a *proper* solution," she said gruffly. "We need to nip it in the bud right now, before the situation gets out of hand!"

"But, we are dealing with *real* people here, Dr. Jackson."

"That is irrelevant. Just fire both parties involved. End of story."

"Laying them off will only exacerbate the problem."

She shifted to a more erect position in her chair. The chair complained with a loud squeak. She slapped the palms of her hands on her desk and said gravely, "Perhaps, Mr. Arneau, you do not fully understand the gravity of the situation here. If this incident gets widely known within the Company, it could have a divisive effect between our employees. Worst of all, if news of it ever gets leaked to the press, that would be a public relations disaster for the Company."

I sighed and replied, "I understand that. I will talk to both parties and ask them to not discuss the incident with anyone either inside or outside of the Company."

"They had better not!" she said angrily. "If they do, it will be grounds for their immediate dismissal."

"I don't think that that will be necessary," I replied. "Of course, on the other hand, a lot depends upon how we handle the situation."

Rita furrowed her brow and asked, "What, then, do you propose?"

"I believe that the best approach is to address the situation with counseling and an in-service training program."

"How long will that take?"

"If we do it in-house, it should take about four weeks."

"That's completely unacceptable!"

I shrugged and said, "All right, another alternative would be to hire an outside consulting firm. They could get started as soon as their contract and non-disclosure agreement are signed. However, that would be much more expensive."

"How expensive?"

"I don't know precisely. But, based upon my previous experience, they will probably charge between $250 and $350 per hour."

"Can they resolve the situation quickly?"

"Most likely it will not take as long as if we were to do it ourselves."

Rita's upper lip twitched slightly. "All right, let's do it. Be sure to spare no expense."

"Okay, I'll get started on it right away."

"Send me a status report every afternoon at 4:30 PM, my time. We want to resolve this situation ASAP and I need to appraise Corporate each day on our progress."

"Okay, I understand perfectly," I replied.

"Good! I'll look forward to receiving your first status report tomorrow." She ended the Zoom call.

•   •   •

I had just finished my daily progress report for Jackson. Although I had called the top three consulting firms on the Company's Approved Vendor List, none of them had anyone immediately available to help.

Jackson is going to be pretty disappointed with my status today. What am I going to do now? I muttered under my breath, "I could really use some help here."

Suddenly, there was a loud *rat-a-tat* on my door. It sounded like someone was hitting the door with some sort of hard object. Startled, I jumped, caught my breath, and said in a loud voice, "Come in."

The door opened slowly and an elderly man stepped into my office leaning heavily on an old black cane for support. Smiling, he took off his brown tweed hat and held it in his hand. He was nearly bald but had neatly combed white hair on each side of his head. The color of his neatly trimmed beard matched his hair.

The color and pattern of his tweed suit matched his hat. It was way out of fashion and looked like it could have been purchased at a neighborhood Goodwill store. Tied loosely around the neck of his white shirt was a bright red tie with a golden paisley pattern. He wore brown wing-tip leather shoes, which were dusty and needed to be shined.

The old man placed his hat on the hat-rack near the door, bowed slightly, and said, "Bernie Bidwell at your service, sir."

I was amazed. *Who is this guy? He looks a little like Dr. John Hammond from "Jurassic Park". He's not even wearing a mask!*

I pulled a purple N95 mask, with the NeuroTech logo on it, out of my desk drawer. As I put it on I considered offering one to him as well. "Um ... do you have an appointment, Mr. Bidwell?"

"I certainly do! It's at 4:42 PM today and I believe that I am right on time." He thumped his cane lightly on the floor. "Please check your calendar and I am sure that you will find it there."

"All right, let me do that. But, by the way, do you have a mask? We are all required to wear them on site and to maintain social distancing."

"I do." Bernie pulled a red bandanna from the left pocket of his pants, folded it, and looped it under his chin. The bandanna had a golden paisley pattern on it, which matched the golden paisley pattern on his red tie.

While he was fumbling with tying the bandanna behind his head, I thought, *I never schedule appointments this late in the day. I wonder if this is some sort of prank by my staff. Well, in any event, maybe I should go along with it for now.*

I brought up my calendar on my computer and was surprised to find that I did have an appointment with a B. Bidwell at 4:42 PM this afternoon. I didn't remember seeing this appointment when I checked my calendar earlier in the day.

"Ah ... um, well, you are absolutely right, Mr. Bidwell. I do have an appointment with you this afternoon." I nodded to him. "I am pleased to meet you."

"The pleasure is entirely mine, Mr. Arneau. But, please call me Bernie." He finished tying the bandanna and pulled it up to cover his nose.

"All right, ah, Bernie. Please have a seat."

"Thank you." Bernie leaned heavily on his cane as he ambled slowly over to the chair in front of my desk. With a satisfied grunt, he plopped down in it. "Ah, it certainly feels good to get off my feet."

"Where are you from, may I ask?"

"Oh, I travel quite a bit. Most recently, I was up North."

When he did not volunteer any additional information, I asked, "And, what did you want to see me about?"

"I'm here to help *you*, of course. Didn't you ask for help?"

While it was true that I needed help with the situation, I didn't recall asking anyone for help yet.

"While I may need some help with a situation here, I was planning to hire a HR consultant from one of the top firms in Silicon Valley. Corporate has offered to pay for it."

"Ah ... *them*," he scoffed. "You don't need to do that. I will help you and I will do it *gratis!*"

"Um, I'm not sure that I can accept your gift of free services. It is against Company policies. Besides, you don't know what the situation is."

"Of course I do," he replied. He then proceeded to describe the incident in detail. He knew when it occurred, the names of the employees involved, my conversation with Dr. Rita Jackson, and what I had done so far.

How could he possibly know all of this?

At this point, I was convinced that I had fallen asleep at my desk and was having a very strange dream. I pinched myself to see if I was awake.

Bernie chuckled and said, "Don't worry, you're awake."

•   •   •

As I walked down the hallway towards my office the next morning, I noticed that my office door was open. *What is going on here!* I thought. *This is a breach of security. I hope that I didn't leave my door unlocked yesterday evening.*

I quickly strode the rest of the way to my office door and looked inside. Bernie was sitting in the chair in front of my desk. He was softly humming a festive tune.

What is he doing here? How did he get into my office without my being present?

Bernie turned around, looked at me, and smiled. "Oh, there you are, Pierre. I wanted to be here early this morning to prepare for our employee interviews."

"Um, that's fine, but how did you get into my office?"

"I arrived early, so I just let myself in."

"Wasn't my door locked? Entering my office without proper authorization is a breach of security."

Bernie waved his hands, chuckled, and smiled broadly. "Oh, don't worry about *that*. According to our contract, which you agreed to yesterday, I *am* a properly authorized person." Then, he added in a cheerful voice, "Let's get to work. I'll help you review the employee's files and prepare for their interviews. The questions that we ask and how we ask them will be of the utmost importance."

I sighed and agreed, "All right. Pull your chair around so that you can see my screen more easily." I rotated my computer screen slightly so that we could both see it.

We spent the rest of the morning reviewing the employee's personnel files in great detail. Bernie seemed to be far more interested in the employee's personal information, rather than in their work history. Up until the incident occurred, both of them had sterling reputations within the Company. They had received numerous informal rewards from their fellow employees. In addition, they had both received formal Company awards from Boston.

"I don't see anything in their files that would explain why the incident occurred," I concluded.

"Yes, but you must look beyond what is in their files," Bernie replied. "I am sure that there must have been some mitigating circumstances."

"Like what, for example?"

"That is what we will discover during the interviews."

At lunch time, we went downstairs to the site cafeteria. The special for the day was Lasagna with a tossed green salad with Italian dressing on the side. I ordered it. It didn't appeal to Bernie so he ordered a cheeseburger with fries from the grill. After our orders were ready, I paid for them, and, after Bernie got some condiments for his lunch, we sat down at a table next to the window facing the neatly landscaped grounds outside.

After Bernie put ketchup on his fries, he opened his hamburger bun and assembled his cheeseburger. He put lettuce, tomato, pickle, ketchup, mustard, and a large gob of mayonnaise on it. He then squeezed the bun back together and gave a contented sigh as some of the sauce oozed out from its sides.

He took a large bite out of the cheeseburger and held it to one side as he said, "This is one of the best things about being a consultant." He had some sauce smeared on the corner of his mouth.

"What? Lunch."

Bernie wiped his mouth with a paper napkin and replied, "That's right. They say that 'There is no such thing as a free lunch', but I'm not sure about that." He raised the cheeseburger triumphantly. "In any event, I do want to thank you for lunch, Pierre. It's really great!"

Although I tried to learn more about Bernie's background and work experience during lunch, he either sidestepped each question or changed the subject. After lunch, I knew no more about him than when we started.

After our lunch, it was time for us to interview the two individuals involved in the incident.

• • •

Our first interview that afternoon was scheduled for 1:00 PM. It was with Duane Finley, who was a Senior Mechanical Engineer with the Company. He arrived right on time for his interview.

Duane was a large man with blue eyes and graying auburn hair. His grizzled beard and ruddy complexion suggested his Irish heritage. He was breathing heavily and there were beads of perspiration on his brow. He wasn't wearing a mask.

I gave him a fist bump and motioned for him to sit down in the chair in front of my desk. "Please take a seat, Duane. Can I get you anything to drink; a bottle of water perhaps."

"A water bottle would be great." Pulling a handkerchief from his pocket, he wiped off the beads of perspiration on his brow. Then he coughed.

I wonder if he has COVID. If so, he shouldn't even be here.

I pulled a cold water bottle from my mini-fridge and handed it to him. He unscrewed the top and took a swig. Then, he nodded and said, "Thanks."

"Duane, let me introduce you to Bernie Bidwell, who will be participating in our interview today. Bernie is an outside

HR consultant who has been hired by the Company. He has many years of experience in these types of matters."

Duane said, "I am pleased to meet you Mr. Bidwell."

"The pleasure is entirely mine, Duane. Please call me Bernie."

"All right, Bernie. Thanks."

"Well then, let's get started." I smiled and looked at Bernie. "Bernie, I believe that you have some questions for Duane."

"I do, thank you." Bernie asked him, "Duane, I notice that you are not wearing a mask. Why is that?"

"Um, it affects my breathing. It is difficult for me to breathe with a mask on."

"Why is that?"

"I have acute asthma." Duane reached into his pocket and pulled out an inhaler. "When I have an attack, I have to use this. It was prescribed by my doctor."

"Oh, did your doctor also give you a note excusing you from masking?"

"Yeah, I have a copy of it here." Duane pulled out his wallet and removed a tightly folded piece of paper. It was stained and well-worn. After he carefully unfolded it, he handed it to Bernie.

Bernie took it and said, "Thank you." After he read the note, Bernie asked, "Did you give Medical a copy of this note for your personnel file? It's quite important."

Duane put his inhaler back in his pocket. Then, he covered his mouth with the back of his hand and coughed again. "No, I suppose that I should have."

I asked, "So your cough is a symptom of your asthma?"

"Yeah, that's right."

I raised my eyebrows and looked at Bernie. He nodded slightly in return and asked, "So, when you went down to the Manufacturing Pilot Line to meet Will, you did not wear a mask because it would have affected your breathing?"

"That's right."

"Did you explain to Will the reason for not wearing a mask?"

"He didn't give me a chance to. He yelled at me to put a mask on, came right up to me, and poked me in the ribs with his finger."

"I see ... How did that make you feel?

"It made me really angry."

"What happened next?"

"He yelled at me again and when he tried to poke me again, I put my hands up to block it. When I put my hands up, he stepped back, tripped, fell, and hit his head on the Pilot Line roller conveyor. He got a nasty cut on his forehead."

"Did you push Will?"

"No, I didn't."

"All right, that's good. What happened next?"

"They called the site's Emergency Response Team. The ERT got there within a few minutes and treated Will. I tried to explain to them what happened, but no one would listen to me."

"What did you do next?"

"I went back to my cubicle. I was really upset and didn't really get anything done for the rest of the day."

"All right, thank you." Bernie looked at me and asked, "Pierre, do you have any additional questions?"

"I just have a couple of questions," I replied. "When you got back to your cubicle, did you tell your manager what happened?"

Duane coughed and frowned. "No, I was really upset and needed some time to settle my nerves."

"All right, have you talked to anyone else about the incident?"

"No ... not really."

"Please don't. It is important that you not talk to anyone about it right now."

"Okay."

"Good. I think that we are done. Is that right, Bernie?"

Bernie nodded and replied, "I'm done."

"Good. Do you have any questions for either of us, Duane?"

"Am I going to lose my job over this?"

246

The directness of his question caught me by surprise. "Um … we're not sure yet. We have to talk to Will to get his side of the story and then we have to talk to both of you together. We will do that tomorrow morning."

The color drained from Duane's face and he started coughing. He quickly pulled his inhaler from his pocket and took some deep breaths through it. After his asthma attack subsided, he said, "Sorry about that."

"That's perfectly alright. When you feel up to it, you are free to go now," I replied.

• • •

Our second interview that afternoon was at 2:30 PM. It was with Will Wainwright, who was the Manufacturing Pilot Line Supervisor. Will arrived a little early. He had a large white gauze bandage taped to his brow.

I gave Will a fist bump and said, "Will, please let me introduce Bernie Bidwell to you. He will be helping with our interview today. Bernie is an outside HR consultant who has been hired by the Company. He has many years of experience and this should prove to be very helpful."

Bernie stood up and gave Will a quick fist bump.

Will said, "I am very pleased to meet you Mr. Bidwell."

"I am very pleased to meet you too, Will. Please call me Bernie." Bernie replied.

"Okay, Bernie. Thanks."

"Well then, let's get started." I looked at Bernie and said, "Bernie, I believe that you have some questions for Will."

"Yes I do," Bernie replied with a twinkle in his eyes. "When Duane entered manufacturing without a mask on, what did you think?"

"I thought that it was a violation of our site's policy. Every employee on our site must wear a mask. This is posted on every door of the facility."

"What did you do when Duane approached you at the Manufacturing Pilot Line?"

"I went up to him and told him that he had to wear a mask."

"Did you poke him with your forefinger when you said this?"

"Um, well, I was very upset and I poked him lightly in his chest to get his attention and to make sure that he was listening to me." Will dropped his head slightly and said in a low voice, "I probably shouldn't have done that. It made him angry."

"What happened next?"

"I told him again to put on a mask and tried to give him another little poke for emphasis. He quickly raised his hands to block my finger. I was afraid that he was going to push me and I stepped backwards. When I stepped back, I tripped, and hit my head on the conveyor. It gave me quite a cut." He pointed to the bandage on his brow.

Bernie nodded and asked, "Why were you so upset about Duane not wearing a mask?"

"Um, that's sort of personal."

"Don't worry too much about that. We just want to understand what was going through your mind at the time."

"Well ... All right, my Mom, who is living in an assisted living facility, was just diagnosed with COVID. The facility has been locked down for months and several of the residents have died from COVID infections."

"So, you were worried about the members of your team getting infected?"

"That's right. Duane had a cough and I was afraid that he had COVID."

"I understand completely. Thank you for sharing that." Bernie turned to me and asked, "Pierre, do you have any other questions?"

"I only have one other question. Have you spoken to anyone else about the incident?"

"Only the Director of Manufacturing. We had to decide if it was an OSHA reportable event. Because I was not severely injured, we did not have to file an OSHA Reportable Event Report."

"That's fine. But it is quite important that you do not talk to anyone else about it."

"All right."

"Good. I think that we are done. Do you agree, Bernie?"

"I agree," Bernie replied with a nod.

"Good. Do you have any questions for us, Will?"

"I would like to know what happens next."

"We will talk to both of you together tomorrow morning. We will discuss our findings with both of you and ensure that we described what happened during the incident accurately."

"All right, that sounds good."

"Do you have any other questions?"

"No, not at this time."

"Good, you are free to go now," I said as I motioned towards the door. "We shall look forward to seeing you tomorrow morning."

•   •   •

The next morning, we met with Duane and Will. They both arrived on time for our meeting.

Bernie said, "Gentlemen, we have met with you individually and now have a much greater understanding of what actually happened on the Manufacturing Pilot Line."

Bernie described our understanding of the incident. After he was done, both Duane and Will agreed that our understanding was correct. They seemed relieved.

At the end of the meeting, Will and Duane apologized to one another and agreed to work together to make NextGen a superior product.

The meeting had gone quite well.

Bernie helped me draft my status report, which documented the final resolution of the incident. When we were satisfied with it, I sent it to Jackson.

Jackson called me almost immediately. "Pierre, I have read your status report and it is completely unacceptable."

"Why is that?"

"When Wainwright jabbed Finley in the ribs, this constituted a physical blow. This is a direct violation of NeuroTech's policy that states that employees may not hit or strike one another under any circumstances. If they do, then it is a violation of their conditions of employment."

"With all due respect, Dr. Jackson, a slight poke with one's forefinger does not constitute a physical blow. In this case, it was intended by Will to emphasize the importance of Duane wearing a mask in Manufacturing. Therefore, NeuroTech's policy does not apply in this situation."

"I absolutely do not agree and I insist that Wainwright be fired," she said angrily. "In addition, the threatening gesture that Finley made towards Wainwright constitutes a psychological attack that made him fear for his safety. Therefore, Finley should be fired too."

"Dr. Jackson, I strongly disagree with you. Holding up one's hands with outfacing palms is a defensive gesture. There is absolutely no way that it could be construed as an *attack*."

"Arneau, if you don't follow through with this, I will take punitive actions against you for insubordination. At a bare minimum, I will submit a Letter of Reprimand to your file. Then, if you continue your insubordinate behavior, I will personally ensure that you are fired on grounds of insubordination."

I was astonished by her outburst. Not knowing quite how to respond to it, I said, "Fine." I hung up.

Well, so much for my career, I thought.

Bernie looked into my eyes and said, "Pierre, please don't worry too much about Jackson. She is a very troubled person."

"She may be troubled, but she has the authority to fire me."

Bernie shrugged and replied, "Perhaps, but what is most important here is that you do the right thing. Trust me. If you do the right thing, everything will turn out all right."

"I would certainly like to believe that."

"That's good." Bernie rose from his chair and grabbed his cane. As he walked towards the door, he said, "Well,

Pierre, my work here is done and it is time for me to leave. Please give my regards to Paige and, of course, to Henri Le Pooch. They will be very happy to see you when you get home this evening."

Bernie opened the door, walked through it, and softly closed it. After he left, I leaned back in my chair, sighed sadly, and rocked slightly back and forth. Then, I noticed that he had forgotten his hat. I rushed over to the hat stand, grabbed it, and opened the door to call to him. When I looked up and down the hallway, he was nowhere in sight.

•   •   •

I found it difficult to get to sleep that night. Rather than disturbing Paige and Henri Le Pooch too much with my tossing and turning, I moved to the sofa bed in the apartment's living room. At around 5:00 AM, I decided to just get up, have a cup of coffee, watch TV, and wait for Paige and Henri to join me.

I had decided to submit my resignation. After Paige and Henri got up, I took my time and drafted my resignation letter being careful to be concise and to the point. I asked Paige to review it before I submitted it. She had some helpful suggestions that I incorporated into the final draft.

We had lunch together and I took Henri for a short walk. Although he was delighted with our walk, he seemed to sense that something was up with me.

After our walk, Henri followed me into my office and lay down next to me while I signed in. I finished the draft of my email to Jackson announcing my resignation and attached my letter to it. Everything was ready.

Just as I was going to click on the send button, Henri sat up and nudged me with his wet nose. I moved my hands away from my keyboard to scratch behind his ears. Henri partially closed his eyes and made soft contented growls.

"All right, let's do this," I said to myself as I patted Henri on his head.

I moved my hands back to my keyboard.

Suddenly, my cell phone rang. The call was from Boston.

"Hello," I answered.

"Pierre, its Anna Kesler from Boston. How are you today?" Anna was the CEO of NeuroTech Medical Devices.

I wonder why the CEO is calling me. This is really amazing.

"I'm fine, thank you."

"That's great. I wanted to let you know in advance that Dr. Rita Jackson has resigned from the Company to pursue other opportunities."

I was completely flabbergasted. Trying to mask the excitement in my voice, I replied, "Oh, I really didn't expect that."

"We didn't expect it either. But I have some good news for you."

"What is that?"

"Do you happen to know a Dr. Bernard Bidwell?"

"Yes, I worked with him to resolve an HR incident that we had here recently. But I didn't know that Bernie had a PhD."

"In fact, he does. Dr. Bidwell is one of NeuroTech's primary angel investors. However, although he is entitled to a position on our Board of Directors, he has remained an enigma. In fact, no one that I know either within or outside of the Company has actually met him in person."

"That's really interesting. He didn't seem to want to share any of his personal details with me. I had no idea ..."

"Well, I wanted to tell you that Dr. Bidwell has recommended that you assume Dr. Rita Jackson's position as an Associate Vice President here in Boston. Unfortunately, that means that you will have to move to the Boston area near our Corporate Headquarters."

I tried to suppress my excitement as I said, "That's no problem. In fact, that would be wonderful!"

"Great! We will be in touch with you later to discuss the details."

"Thank you so much!"

"You're very welcome. Your promotion was well deserved. Have a great day!" She said as she ended the call.

Alexa Kellow has worked for local and national newspapers, has a PhD in Politics and currently works as a freelance grants manager in the charity sector. She has written two children's chapter books for Purple Mash, and has had several short stories published. She lives in Cambridgeshire in the UK with her husband, two children and cats who must be mentioned otherwise the children will have words.

●   ●   ●

I really did find writing "Home Help?" cathartic. The beginning of the story was an exact moment that happened to me in March 2020. My husband was ill with Covid, isolating at home, and I was juggling home schooling and multiple video calls — and then I got ill too. Luckily he was never hospitalized, and I count us amongst the lucky ones. It was a very stressful time for so many people for so many reasons — be it loneliness, illness, overwhelm or loss. Now it feels like such a surreal time, but one that has changed the world permanently.

HOME HELP?

ALEXA KELLOW

T HIS IS THE MOMENT it gets real for me. I'm on an external-facing video call with a client. My husband is quarantining in the master bedroom. The kids are well into their umpteenth hour of screen time. And I am starting to feel a little hot. A headache begins pounding behind my left eye.

"Oh no," I surreptitiously text my assistant Becky, also on the call. "I think I've got it."

She sends back, "Oh no! Don't tell Dominic!" She's right, our boss is highly suspicious of malingering, and he won't let a mere global pandemic persuade him otherwise.

It's an important and long call with Talamore, a big funder. On the irritatingly named "comfort break" I turn off my camera, throw some snacks at the kids and wash down two Tylenol with cold coffee. Two and a half more hours to go, guiding the client through the proposal. My headache grows worse than any other in my life, but I keep up the

"Great question" and the "Let"s put a pin in that". No one knew, except Becky. I'm a pro.

Eventually it's over, and I stagger to the sofa and throw an arm across my eyes. Everything is too light, too loud. The attention-starved kids climb on me, elbowing me with abandon and settle in for some quality time. James seizes my face with sticky hands and demands more snacks. But I can't face moving my head even a fraction, so I play for time by saying "Mommy doesn't feel so great."

On the call, I had momentarily considered quarantining myself from them. But honestly, how would that work? Sure, their Dad can recover in peace, but we could hardly both lock ourselves away from a four- and six-year-old.

I am eventually forced to leave the sofa when Merri demands a drink. I get up slowly, but standing brings on fresh waves of pain. Once I've topped them up with snacks and water, I test my temperature in the bathroom. The screen flashes a red sad face — a high temperature. Oh god. I shut the bathroom cabinet and cross to the window and stare out at the street. I wish I could open it, but none of the windows in this apartment open.

Its eerily quiet for midday. There are a few single pedestrians. Way fewer cars, but more ambulances. Our apartment is in the old hospital building, around the corner from the big new medical center. This means that sirens are a permanent feature of living here to the extent that they don't really register any more. Well until now. I watch one flash past, before slowing enough to take the corner. I feel a plummet of anxiety.

But hey, I'm in my thirties (just). Thank goodness that younger people and especially kids are not bearing the brunt of this. Then I guiltily think of my Mom and Dad. When I watched the first press conferences, hastily called, experts with an air of wild-eyed panic in their smart suits, I felt certain I would never see them again. But the practicalities of kids being home, entertaining them around work and then Scott being sick had pushed them out of my mind.

I pull my cell from the pocket of my slouchy cardigan, thinking I should text Mom to check in. I won't mention I think I have it, I haven't told her about Scott either. She'll panic and want to help. But she's nearly a thousand miles away, sheltering in place just like us. Besides I wouldn't want her to get it at 71.

But hey, maybe Scott will be better soon, and I can take a turn in the master bedroom while he juggles kids and deadlines.

Before I can text Mom, I see a message from Scott. I have been leaving him plates of food outside the bedroom door and collecting the empties for a few days. We've stayed in touch by text — him sending requests for more water, his charger, and so on.

But this message is different:

Sweets Im struggling here might need to see someone

My stomach plummets again. Ignoring the pounding of my head I dash from the bathroom, through the open space living area to the bedroom master bedroom. For the first time in four days, I open the door and go in.

I hear a wheeze immediately. The air feels like pallor. It's dark, and I swipe for the light switch.

Startled by the light Scott turns his face towards the pillow. I go to him, he's a little too warm, he's clammy, and his skin looks grey.

"Marie?" he croaks, making him cough immediately, then he sucks in some air with difficulty. "I can't ..." More coughing. I don't let him finish, I'm on the phone calling for help.

Later, once he's been strapped to a chair and wheeled into the elevator, I lay on the floor of the kids' bedroom. They were terrified of the masked EMTs and even more terrified of seeing their Dad leaving with an oxygen mask over his face.

They had a lot of questions and I dug deep and pulled out my twinkliest brisk Mom act, jollying them through the rest of the day like Mary Poppins. When I put them to bed, they wobbled again, so I stay with them, laying on the floor between their beds long after they've fallen asleep. I'm exhausted but my brain is racing. I try not to think about the images of Chinese and then Italian hospitals that have horrified us all. I try not to think about the sirens going past the apartment. I try not to think about the weird feeling in my lungs, a little bit crispy. My pounding head.

That night I sleep fitfully, in and out of weird dreams. I'm way too hot, and then far too cold because of the breeze from the window. In the small hours of the morning, I think I am awake and I see that Scott is at the foot of my bed, bending over something. But then remember — and reality crashes back into my consciousness — he's not here, he's sick. I check the time, it's 4 a.m. — the official hour of dread. I lay and worry, monitoring the weird sensation in my chest, breathing in deeply now and then to check I still can. What if I get too sick to look after the kids? What then? I doze in and out of sleeping, thinking over and over that there is someone at the foot of my bed, maybe the kids need something, but then realizing whoever it is is too tall to be either of the kids, before the next wave of sleep takes me deeper.

The next morning, I text Scott, asking for an update. After a couple of hours of fretfully checking the phone every few minutes when I'm meant to be working, I call the ward. They sound busy and harassed. I am told he is the same — no better, no worse. Sleeping. I don't know whether to feel comforted or not.

The rest of the day passes in a drudge of making do. I fix the kids snacky food now and then, but the TV and iPads take the parenting load while I sit at my laptop in the same room, trying to focus on prep for more work calls tomorrow. Becky texts me at lunchtime, tells me to rest and she'll try to cover for me. *"I'll rest when I'm dead,"* I think, besides, she has a three-year-old to wrangle. I message her, "I'm fine, it's such a busy time." The truth is I am pretty sure Dominic is looking to furlough working parents as soon as he can, and we need this money — especially with Scott out of action. I try to persuade myself that I am feeling a little better, but by four o'clock I am bone tired, the headache has gone but I feel as if I could sleep where I fall.

The kids are cranky and fractious from infinite screen time and a lack of outside, exercise and routine. When they get into a fight about some inconsequential bullshit I find myself yelling at them, bringing on a coughing fit that scares them both. Once it starts to subside, Merri says, "Are they going to take you away like Daddy?" I promise "No, of course not sweetheart!" But once they are distracted with being allowed to watch funny animals on YouTube, I go to the kitchen and lean on the side. I slide down the work units to a crumpled heap on the floor and cry.

After a reasonable time of feeling sorry for myself I stand up and prep the kids a crappy meal, feeling guilty, but too tired to stand in the kitchen too long. By the time they are asleep I drag myself to my bedroom and curl up, falling into a deep sleep immediately. Again, it is a bad night. The woman in the bed beside mine is moaning softly all night. I wake around four in the morning again and test my breathing. My inhalation makes a troubling wheezing sound, and I can feel that crispy sensation again. When I breathe, I am aware of the little branches of my lungs.

When I wake in the morning it is to the sound of a persistent alarm. I can't place it. I sit up and swipe for my phone. It's Dominic, my boss. I stare at the screen, then decide not to answer. Then he texts me "Marie, we need the figures for the Talamore contract asap." He has been finessing this project for a long time but I'm the one to actually plan and write it. I thought we were nearly done, but an email also from Dominic confirms that more detailed figures are needed. I don't get dressed, I just get up, give the kids some breakfast — they whinge that their favorite cereal has run out — and swig some coffee and painkillers. Then I get right onto the figures. They would take most of a day even if I was in tip-top shape and not also fielding seven zillion requests from the kids, but this is Covid times and as such it takes me past the kids' bedtime to get most of it done.

Once they are down for the night I eat some chips and a bit of cheese, all the time fully aware that this is not the food that's going to support my immune system. So I eat a couple of the kids' vitamin gummies. I go to the window and look out for a brief break, drinking yet another coffee to try to stay awake. No one on foot at all. An ambulance. Another. Other than them, the world is quiet even in the heart of this massive city.

I go back to the work, just a few more things to finalize and then I can send it to Domimic. But before I do that, I fall asleep at my laptop.

I wake in the dead of night, in bed but unclear how I got here. The woman in the next bed is fighting for each breath. A nurse appears and bends over her, turning the woman to face towards me and I see that she is young, in her twenties. Our eyes meet and I feel paused in a universal moment, a shared experience. Her red hair is fanned around her head on the pillow and covering one eye, but I can see how sad she looks. The nurse walks between us, her long skirts blocking my view. Once she moves, I look again for the woman. There is a form on the bed next to mine, covered in a white sheet.

I wake once again at four in the morning with a start. If I have been taken to hospital, who has the kids? I push myself up then, fast despite my feeble arms. "Merri? James?" I yell hoarsely, bringing on a coughing fit. The nurse appears next to me, I can't see a single detail of her face under her white cap. She firmly pushes me back onto the bed and places a cold cloth over my eyes. My eyes are hot and my limbs ache. Each breath feels like a deliberate and painful action. Eventually, I drift off.

I awake in the apartment. Something feels off. I grab my phone and see it's nearly 11 a.m. WTF. I'm a mother with two young kids, I haven't set an alarm in the best part of a decade.

In a flash of panic, I struggle from the bed and limp through to the living area. James and Merri are both dressed. There are plates with the remnants of chocolate spread on them stacked on the kitchen worktop. They are playing a board game. Merri"s hair is tightly braided and has a bow in it.

Jesus, I must be hallucinating.

"Guys, what ..." I start.

They dash over and hug me, smelling of clean clothes and toothpaste. "Hey, you got yourselves up! Great job!"

I'm amazed. They have got themselves up before, but that usually extends as far as eating dry cereal from a bowl, wearing a onesie and hunching over a tablet each. "How did you do your hair like that Merri? And guys — did you cook your own pancakes?"

They share a glance.

"I'm not crazy about you cooking without a grownup," I say.

"We didn't!" James pipes up, before being silenced by an elbow from Merri.

I'm suddenly exhausted and decide to let them off. I set Merri up on her homeschooling tasks and hand James his tablet. Then I steel myself to open my work laptop, and incur the wrath of Dominic for not submitting the Talamore figures last night.

I find an urgent email with the title "Where ARE you Marie?", a voicemail on my phone, and a Teams message on my laptop from two hours ago that says, "Marie we need you on this call today".

But underneath, I see with absolute astonished horror, is a reply sent from me that says:

SIR I HAVE INFLUENZA STOP GRAVELY ILL STOP PLEASE CEASE MRS THORNTON

What the actual hell. I'm not even married. Thornton is Scott's surname.

"Merri, James? Did you play on my computer?"

But I already know that they didn't. And neither did I. Then a message from Dominic arrives underneath:

Ok, message received. Let me know when you're back on board.

I frown at it. What is happening? Why don't I remember getting the kids up? Making pancakes? Did I really write this message in a fit of delirium? I guess I must have ... But hey I guess it doesn't matter. I can rest up.

I snuggle up with the kids on the couch — we watch a movie together and I listen to them both read. They are puppylike in their attentiveness, and I feel a keen bittersweet love for their loyalty, their joyfulness in my company despite days of basically ignoring them. I try to ignore the sense of unease that I have forgotten a large chunk of the day — maybe that's just a symptom.

Mindful of them needing exercise, I set them some challenges from my nest of blankets on the couch. They have to find things in the apartment and run back to me — find something triangle shaped, find something beginning with the letter "B", something that will fit inside an egg cup. Once they have their finds, we play the memory game — I take one thing out and they have to figure out what is missing. On the last round I chose to take out a necklace James had found — a tarnished silver locket which must have been pilfered from their grandma's dress up collection. But then the phone rings, and I start, fearful it is Dominic, but it's the hospital, which surely should have been my first thought.

I leave the kids playing and take the call in the kitchen. The man on the other end identifies himself as the nurse who has been caring for Scott. He gives me an update — still not much change. I thank him profusely, and wish him well. He sounds beyond exhausted.

Once the kids are asleep, I force myself to eat some healthy food and stay away from work. I even turn off my phone and go to bed early. The day of rest has helped a lot but as the evening approaches the familiar sensation returns to my chest. Again, I keep checking I can breathe in as fully as normal — I can't, not entirely. I lay awake worrying about Scott, about what happens if I take a turn for the worse like he did.

Finally, I have a good, restful sleep. No more dreams of the hospital ward. When I wake it is late again — nearly midday. Once again, I am totally confused. Again, the kids are dressed, and say they've had bagels and fruit. Some plates are washed up on the draining board. We never do this — they go in the dishwasher. I also see a sharp knife.

"Guys, did you use that knife to cut the grapes?" I asked, wondering if it is better they chanced cutting themselves in the name of not choking on a grape.

The kids share a glance. Merri shakes her head.

"*We* didn't," James says. Merri pokes him with her foot, and her eyes go big.

"Did I?" I ask. God, this can't be good can it.

"What? No, it was Mrs O'Sullivan", James says. Time seems to hold steady a moment. He's just looking back at me, face open. Then he looks to Merri, who is just staring at me.

I cross to James and hold him by the shoulders. "Mommy's not cross, but I need to understand what is happening." James looks at Merri, and then looks away. "Did you let someone in here?"

"No, of course not," Merri says. "She's been here all along."

I'm cold, suddenly chilled like a finger has just been run up the back of my neck.

"What do you mean?"

They don't answer, just glance at each other.

"What did she look like?" I try to sound light-hearted.

"She had a long dress", Merri says.

"And red hair," James says shyly, "On top of her head."

I want to ask more, to interrogate them, but a Mom's job is to absorb the horrors for their children, in that precious period when they still can. I go into bustle mode, get them busy in the kitchen making banana bread, and try not to think about anything.

Later that night, when they are both asleep and the apartment is dark and quiet, I retreat back to my bed with my laptop. I google "St Lucians hospital history". I find out it was built in 1915 and just a few years later was crowded with people infected with Spanish flu. I look around the bedroom and all too easily can see the beds laid out, and feel the vast suffering and loss concentrated in the building we now call home. I read "The Spanish influenza epidemic had the highest impact on adults aged 20-40. From 1918 to 1920 an estimated 50 million people worldwide died, creating many orphans."

The woman in the bed. What happened to her children? *She's been here all along.* Could she really have interacted with my children or am I having some sort of delusion and dragging the kids along with me?

I feel a wave of grief and sadness and start to weep uncontrollably — all the days of fear and tension about Scott, me, the whole world. I cry for the woman in the bed, and I feel the guilt of my privileged life. I cry until I fall asleep.

When I wake early, the morning sunshine, the mundane chatter on the radio, the kids bickering over who sits where, makes the conversation with the kids seems absurd. Thoughts of ghosts are banished to the night. Surely it is much more likely I simply woke up in a feverish state and made them pancakes and cut-up grapes, and looked after them for long chunks of time without remembering. They are kids, their imaginations are wild I tell myself. How easily we lie to ourselves to keep our beliefs intact. I feel I have turned a corner — mentally and physically. I am ok, we are going to be alright.

And when Scott comes home two days later — mostly recovered but weak and easily tired — I focus on him, on managing the kids' sudden shyness with him, on cooking nutritious meals for us all, and of course, working. And I forget about a very strange week.

•   •   •

Completely forget about it, until today. It's Fall 2022 and I'm clearing up the kids' room. They are back at school, Scott is out of the house at the actual physical office. Sure, you still see people with masks on, and Covid is still an issue, but it feels like for most people, the pandemic is over. I have taken some leave to sort stuff at home, because we are getting ready to move out. And behind James' bed I find a necklace — a tarnished silver oval locket. It looks familiar, but I can't think why. Curious, I pry it open and find inside a black and white photo of two small children, a boy and a girl. I carefully pull out the thick, yellowed photo. On the back is written "James and Mary O'Sullivan, 1917".

Richard Zaric was born in Winnipeg, Manitoba, Canada and has lived in various cities in North America before settling back in his hometown. He earned a Bachelor of Commerce (Honours) from the University of Manitoba and has been in the marketing research industry for over 30 years. His first book, *Hiding Scars*, is a historical fiction novel and was published in 2018. He is presently pitching his second book, a young adult novel entitled *Stealing Amazing Fantasy #15*. He also enjoys writing short fiction and likes to experiment with different voices. He is just as likely to read the latest hot literary novel as he is to flip through an old comic book.

•   •   •

The idea for "Little Free Library" came from literally doing exactly what the main character did: walk around the neighborhood during the height of COVID. Gyms were closed and it was the only way I could get exercise. I began to notice these little libraries sprouting up, sometimes in front of houses, sometimes in front of churches. I added a dash of urban fantasy. I found the COVID period to be contemplative. I thought about my past, the hits and misses. It led me to believe that everyone has had ups and downs, but ultimately we need to be happy and content with who we are. Life is good. Enjoy the here and now.

LITTLE FREE LIBRARY

RICHARD ZARIC

B EATRICE PULLED HER LAVENDER MASK UP HIGHER. She hated it when it slipped down to the tip of her nose. She stopped and fiddled with the adjustable straps around her ears. If her mask was on too tight her ears would look folded and distressed. Sometimes they would hurt. Maybe she should buy some new masks?

Most of all, it grated on Beatrice when her glasses fogged up, which was all the time now that the season had changed and the leaves were gone. She noticed that even after entering a store that her glasses would remain foggy far longer than she'd have expected. What would it be like in the dead of winter?

Still, the crisp morning air felt refreshing. As much as she dreaded going out for a walk each day, after a block or two, regardless of the weather, she felt better at the end of the walk. At least she accomplished something.

It helped to vary the routes. She had some standard routes when she couldn't make a decision, but still liked to mix it up. She never felt bored and sometimes walked past some of the same faces every few days. The gentle "Hellos" or even the slightest nod of the head felt that there was some civility, some friendliness left in the world.

The Code Red lockdown had been in place for about a month, but many months before that Beatrice was working from home. If you could call it that. With the economy ground to a halt, it seemed the entire world was on pause. Waiting. Usually she had one or two video calls on Zoom or Teams, but there clearly wasn't that much work. She was frequently finished her tasks by 2:00 or 3:00. Hardly a full day. Sometimes she had a queasy feeling in her stomach. *I should be doing more. Maybe I'll get laid off like some of the others.* It was best not to dwell on it.

Someone from work told Beatrice that she and her husband "commuted" to work every day. They worked at home, but each work day after breakfast they would go for a half hour walk around the neighborhood before they logged on their computers. Their regular commute before COVID was a half hour, so instead of being in a car, they decided to incorporate walks "to work" as a regular routine. At the end of the day, they would do the same, walk for 30 minutes "back home."

Beatrice decided to do the same thing. Her regular commute was 40 minutes, so she went for a 40-minute walk before and after her work day. She rented the bottom floor of a large home in the Oak Meadows part of town. She loved the quaint feel of the neighborhood coupled with the relatively close distance to downtown. The mature trees and century-old homes oozed character.

The sun had still not poked its head up by the time she stepped out of her suite. She liked to be out of the house by 6:00. She wasn't usually concerned about safety in the mornings. In the evening walks, sometimes she had to pass by some unsavory-looking men. Unshaven with sloppy clothes.

The tip off was the shoes. Men that walked around in worn, poor-quality shoes usually had souls that were of poor quality. That was what Beatrice's mother used to say. If a man can't take care of his shoes, how is he going to take care of you? She stopped going for post-work walks after a week.

Then again, mother always was old fashioned. Mom grew up on a farm. Went to church every Sunday. She ended up marrying when she was just 19 years old. Beatrice was now 28 and couldn't imagine being married. When Beatrice was 19, she was too busy rebelling.

Beatrice did a double take when she first saw the little library in front of a house. It was right beside a large, overgrown spruce tree. She was near her turn-around point, or 20 minutes into her walk. Today's route ended in the middle of Cache Bay. She'd been to the bay before. How could she not have noticed the library, especially earlier in the year in the late spring or summer when the sun was out at that time of the morning? She stopped in front of the box. The way the box was nestled near the large spruce, it would be easy to miss coming from the other direction unless you turned your head quickly. But not the direction Beatrice usually came. She should have noticed it months ago. Then again, it was painted a dark color. From the street light a few houses over it looked to be a deep green. It was mounted on a brown six-by-six post. Perfect camouflage against the background of the evergreen it stood beside. Wasn't a little library supposed to stand out so it would be more noticeable? It wasn't going to get much traffic if it was quasi-hidden.

After looking both ways, Beatrice approached the little library. Not that it mattered because no one was ever around at that time of the morning. Come to think of it, she never really saw anyone during the day.

This little library featured two doors that opened once you took off the simple hook latch. There were two shelves. Most of the books on the top shelf stood upright. The light was too dim to see the titles along the spines. The bottom shelf looked to be dominated by children's books, all thin and colorful. When she pulled out a book, she had to angle it in the light of the full moon. *Smelly Socks* by Robert Munch. She put it back and pulled out another. *The Magic School Bus Inside a Beehive*. She activated the flashlight on her phone. Adult books were on the top shelf. There were two from the *Twilight* series. Several bodice-busting romance novels. Some non-fiction including books about Nelson Mandela, astronomy, and butterflies found in Minnesota. She didn't recognize most of the dog-eared fiction books. They looked like the type of books you'd see rotting away in a cabin beside a lake. But the last book, the one on the very left of the top shelf intrigued her. *Black Beauty*.

Beatrice had to take off her foggy glasses to better examine the cover. She had always wanted to read the book, but never got around to it. She cried when she watched the movie at Pam's house when she was eleven. She always liked horses. Always wanted a horse. But Mom and Dad weren't horse people. Dad wasn't prepared to build a separate structure because there wasn't any room in the barn with all the cows they had. She pleaded. Horses and cows got along. She would take full care and responsibility. No chance, her parents wouldn't consider it.

She started to put the book back into the little library, but stopped. When was the next time she'd ever have an opportunity to read *Black Beauty*? Sure, she could order a copy from Amazon in 10 seconds. She could find a copy through any book store. But would she actually do that? It almost seemed like fate that *Black Beauty* happened to be in that particular free little library. She slipped the book into her pocket.

Over the next three days, Beatrice devoured the book. When she finished it, she put it on the small table beside the blue chair in her living room. The book felt a little old-fashioned, but that made sense seeing as it was written well over a hundred years ago. The poor horse, after a carefree childhood, faced hardship through most of its life, never being able to do what it wanted.

Beatrice took a deep breath and stared outside her living room window. Five o'clock and already pitch black.

She felt old-fashioned. Her name was old fashioned. Leave it to Mom to name her Beatrice. When was that name popular? 1852? The first thing anyone thinks when they hear Beatrice is someone's grandmother, not a young woman. Her middle name was worse: Clarabelle. She thought about changing her name when she was of age and could make those decisions, but never got around to it. She couldn't imagine what Mom would say if she did.

When she was a little girl Mom would dress her in flowery full-length dresses. The black shoes she made Beatrice wear on each first day of school always hurt. All the other girls got to go on sleepovers much earlier than Beatrice. She never went on one until she was 16 and, even then, it was at a cousin's house a few sections over. She wasn't allowed to wear make-up until around then as well.

Thank God Aunt Darla spoke to Mother. "Things are a little different than when you grew up. Girls are a little more independent and like to look good. You have to relax with Beatrice or she'll end up a bitter old maid."

Mother begrudgingly accepted this, but it took time. Usually Mom looked the other way, shaking her head. Maybe it was because Beatrice was an only child? Perhaps it was because Mom never knew any life other than living on a farm, being a wife and a mother. She never saw any other path and expected the same for Beatrice.

The next morning, she took the same route to the little free library on Cache Bay. She hadn't been there since she'd picked up *Black Beauty*. The line-up of books looked about the same. It had only been a few days, so she didn't expect there to be that much turn-over. She had *Black Beauty* with her, but also *Vision in White*, a Nora Roberts romance novel. Might as well contribute to the library.

As she went to place the two books in the same area where she had found *Black Beauty*, she noticed a thin book that wasn't in the library before: *Animal Farm*.

George Orwell. She'd heard so many good things about the book, but had never gotten around to reading it. Such a small book. More a novella, really. She took *1984* in school, but the other English class got to review *Animal Farm*. Her friend Becky told her all about how farm animals rebelled against a lazy farmer and took over the farm. The animals set up a system but very soon the pigs assumed control and ended up manipulating and taking advantage of the other animals. The entire story is an allegory for the Russian Revolution and the growth of Communism, but was presented in a way that could be enjoyed by adults or children. It sounded more interesting than *1984*, which Beatrice found depressing. She took the book out of the library and put it in her pocket.

It took her only two days to read *Animal Farm*. She probably could have done it in one night if she wanted to stay up late. She loved it. Such an imaginative story dripping with sarcasm.

It reminded her of the time she rebelled against her parents. They made all the rules, just like the pigs in *Animal Farm*. She was 18 years old and wanted to go to university. She'd worked at the Co-op store in town since she was in Grade 10 and was saving her money. She never got to go anywhere and so never had an opportunity to spend it. She wanted to take plant science to learn better ways to grow crops. Mom thought it was a waste of time. Dad was too busy tending to the cows to care, although he'd rather have her help out around the farm than waste her time in a university.

Mother would always point out particular boys in Beatrice's yearbook, the ones she felt she should be meeting. The boys from good families. Mom didn't hide that she'd much prefer Beatrice to stay close to home.

That was the last thing Beatrice wanted. She got good marks in high school. Why throw that away only because Mother wanted her to hurry up and get married? Did she have to live the exact same life as Mom? Married young and pregnant right after.

Beatrice would see Mom's expression while looking at family pictures from her five siblings. They each had several children. Sometimes Beatrice would lose track of her cousins' names. Mom and Dad tried for more children, but couldn't have any. Mother never did say why they couldn't, if it was something with her or Dad. Maybe Mother thought that if she couldn't have too many children, maybe Beatrice would make up for it with children of her own? And if Beatrice lived close to home, the better the chance to see grandkids.

But why should Beatrice follow Mother's wishes? Shouldn't she be the one to decide how to live her own life?

The day that Beatrice hugged Mom and Dad goodbye in the back step before she left to live in residence was tearful. Beatrice remembered the hollow feeling she felt in her heart. She was leaving the safety of home for the great unknown, but she knew she was making the right decision. Mother's lips were pressed together. "If things don't work out, you come right on home. There will always be a room for you."

Beatrice came back home the first two summers, but in the third year she found a waitressing job in the city and moved into Crystal's apartment. Crystal's old roommate left to live with her boyfriend, so the opportunity presented itself. Beatrice had moved away for good.

On a blustery morning a few days after reading *Animal Farm*, Beatrice walked the Little Free Library Route, as she called it. About two centimeters of snow had fallen overnight. She adjusted her glasses so they sat lower on her nose and were less likely to fog. One good thing about a face mask was that it acted like a second scarf. Although the air had a sharp winter's bite, in keeping with late November, the freshly fallen thin carpet of snow radiated rebirth and innocence. Why did so many people not appreciate winter?

She brushed off the snow around the little library so none would drift inside when she opened the tiny doors. She took *Animal Farm* from her pocket and placed it in the same place on the top shelf where she'd found it, the very left of the top shelf.

A book caught her eye that she hadn't noticed before. *The Sisterhood of Traveling Pants*. Definitely young adult, but something that she'd always wanted to read. One of those coming of age novels. Beatrice used to love reading those types of novels when she was younger. They felt empowering and allowed her to believe in her dreams. They helped her become independent.

She took the book and carefully shut the door to the little library.

On the way back home, Beatrice walked past a couple holding hands. She gave them both a wide berth as neither was wearing a mask. The cooing and giggles gave away the freshness of their relationship. Beatrice missed that. Being alone at home during the pandemic felt like living in a posh prison. She could do whatever she wanted within her place. Eat or drink whatever she wanted. She could even smoke drugs if she wanted to, not that she would. A quiet solitude. Her sentence had no known end date. Like a hostage.

But that intimate touch. Being right beside someone. A hug. A kiss. Feeling someone's naked body against her own. Those were sensations she hadn't felt for a long time and wondered if she would ever feel again.

Video calls were not the same. She texted back and forth with friends on occasion. But how many more Hallmark movies could she watch? Beatrice found herself crying at the littlest things, even heart-felt TV commercials.

While reading *Traveling Pants* she recalled some of the shenanigans she'd gotten into with Crystal. When they went to a bar, they would play First Drink. The one who was able to predict the closest to when they'd get a drink offered to them wouldn't have to take the garbage out for a week. Crystal usually won.

Mother would say that Crystal was a bad influence. Although Mom never outright said that Crystal was a tramp, Beatrice could feel it from the long silent stretches during phone calls back home. "You shouldn't be in bars all the time. A lot of seedy characters that are only interested in one thing."

Beatrice couldn't tell Mother that one thing was something that Crystal liked. Until Beatrice met Leonard, she certainly didn't mind the one thing as well. If anything, Crystal taught Beatrice to be street smart, something she would never have learned if she had stayed at home and settled in town. Crystal liked to have fun and lived a little on the edge. They were in their early twenties. What else were they supposed to do? She knew she had a true friend that time when they hosted a get-together around St. Patrick's Day. Beatrice drank too much green punch. Coupled with some grasshopper shooters, around midnight everything hit her like a ton of bricks. While Beatrice was vomiting the alcohol and all the sushi she had for dinner, a friend of Crystal's was getting too friendly. He put his arm around Beatrice, as if to help her, but really he was trying to feel her up. Crystal noticed and kicked that jerk out and told everyone the party was over. Later, she held Beatrice's ponytail while Beatrice emptied out the last bits of sushi and grasshopper shooters.

Beatrice liked to remember them as her wild years. It was a time when she felt liberated from the shackles of her parents' backward sensibilities. Everything seemed black and white. Right or wrong. No middle ground. She was young, vital and at the very top of her game.

Or so she thought. Once she met Leonard in her soil science class, her world changed. Beatrice had never before felt those hard feelings in the pit of her stomach. Leo was kind and gentle, but had a fiery streak if you got him going. He liked to have fun and played beer league hockey every Thursday. They dated hard for two years. It was her first real relationship. Mom and Dad liked him when she brought him home for Christmas.

Just when Beatrice thought that Leo would be the one, she caught him sleeping with Louise, a co-worker of his from the Safeway where he worked stocking shelves. She was the cute girl working check-out. Beatrice immediately broke up with Leo. That first night Crystal got a pizza, ice cream and chips and they watched *The Sisterhood of Travelling Pants.*

Work kept Beatrice busy and she couldn't finish *Sisterhood* for a week. She was curled up on the couch when she completed the novel. It made her think about Crystal. She hadn't talked to her in a few years since Crystal moved to Toronto. She picked up her phone and they chatted for an hour. It felt like they picked up right where they left off. Beatrice promised to visit once it was safe.

The next morning Beatrice trekked to Cache Bay. It was early December and the temperature had dropped about 15 degrees to hover around -25°C, not including the wind chill. Along the way she could hear her footfalls squeak against the packed snow and ice of the residential road. On this morning she put her hood up to block some of the icy north wind. Beatrice's glasses fogged over to such a degree that she had to pull them down to see over them. It made for an uncomfortable walk.

It had snowed overnight and her steps were the first at the library. Before taking *Traveling Pants* out of her pocket and opening the doors to the little library, Beatrice paused and looked down. Even before the previous night's snowfall she did not recall seeing any other footsteps near the library other than her own. She had walked the same route yesterday morning. Was she the only one using the library? That couldn't be possible because each time she went she saw at least one other book that had not been in the library the prior visit.

But someone must have been adding books. She didn't notice *Traveling Pants* or *Animal Farm* the first time she looked in the library. Maybe she didn't look hard enough? Besides, it wasn't like she was at the library every day. It was only the days when she needed to return a book. Even then, it was dark, so it would be easy to miss something.

Beatrice took out her phone and activated the flashlight. She felt like an archeologist who had just discovered a tiny porthole in an unexplored section of a pyramid. Thankfully the wind prevented the vapor from her breath from obscuring her view although she didn't know how long she could hold her phone with her bare hand outside of her mitt.

The books on the bottom shelf were still exclusively children's picture books. The titles of the adult books on the top shelf looked to be the same as every other visit, from what she could recall. All except the book farthest to the left: *Hunger Games*. Another book she'd always wanted to read after seeing the movies. How could she not have noticed it before? She exchanged it for *Traveling Pants* and turned off the flashlight function on her phone. Someone had to have been visiting the little library. And why was it that neither *Animal Farm* nor *Black Beauty* were in the library any longer?

Before pocketing her phone, Beatrice tried to take a picture of the books, but just before she could press the button, her phone died. Not a surprise seeing as how cold it was. It seemed odd because her phone still had quite a bit of juice in it before she started on the walk.

Back home she splashed warm water on her red cheeks and put her glasses on the counter to defrost. After pouring a cup of coffee, she flipped through *Hunger Games*. It looked like another fast read. All those young adult books didn't take that long.

Beatrice wished she was as brave as Katniss. Strong and resilient. Overcoming the odds. Not that long ago, perhaps five or six years ago, she might have felt like that. Young. Brash. But she didn't feel like that any more.

She never did meet anyone like Leo again. She dated a few others even to the point of having sex with some of them, but they all seemed temporary. Transitory. Each suffered from at least one fatal flaw. Grant drank too much. Morris lacked ambition, happy to work as a gas jockey. Akeem's family made Beatrice feel uncomfortable, an outsider after which Akeem called off the relationship. Drew would rather watch football on TV.

And now COVID-19.

Would she ever meet anyone to share her life?

The *Hunger Games* book followed the movie fairly closely, but it was a few years now since she saw the film. Six? Seven? There was a time when each year seemed to take forever. Now the years seemed to melt by. She remembered Father used to complain about the passage of time. Was she destined to do that as well?

Like everyone else has said, this year couldn't end soon enough. COVID. The silliness of the election. Wildfires. Racial tensions. And each new year seems worse than the previous one. What will the new year bring? Beatrice shuddered.

But, just like Katniss from the novel, she will have to find the inner resolve to continue. She was still young, not even 30. She had food and shelter. Working at home was safe. Boring, but safe. Going grocery shopping was her most dangerous act.

Hunger Games was also a quick read. She wondered if the rest of the trilogy was in the strange tiny little library?

The morning after she finished the book, she visited the tiny library in Cache Bay during her morning walk. It was calm and clear. She could see the stars. The cloudless night meant colder temperatures, especially at the time Beatrice ventured out, well before 6:00 am.

It hadn't snowed since the last time she visited the little library. Her heart dropped when she noticed that there was only one clear set of footprints going to and leaving the library: her own from a few days ago. She bit her lip and approached the library, taking *Hunger Games* out from her pocket. It looked like there would only be a return this time.

She opened the doors to the library and put the book in the exact same space in the shelf as before, the very left of the top shelf. Just before closing the doors, she took out her phone and turned on the flashlight. Why not?

Everything looked the same as she'd left it several days ago. She screwed her eyes to where she'd just placed *Hunger Games*. Beside it there was a paperback she hadn't seen before. *Fahrenheit 451*. Yet another book she'd always wanted to read. How could that be? She was certain she had carefully scanned all the titles, especially those on the left portion of the top shelf.

She looked down at her feet. The footprints were only hers. How could anyone place *Fahrenheit 451* in the exact same place on the shelf?

Beatrice looked around at the dead street. A shiver rolled down her spine, She felt vulnerable. Exposed. Someone must have been playing tricks with her. But how would they know which books she wanted to read?

She turned off the light on her phone and pocketed the book, her mind a swirl of uncertainty and dread. Was someone following her? No. Maybe. She couldn't wait to get home and lock the door behind her.

After tossing the paperback and her keys on the counter and dropping her jacket on the floor, she went to the washroom, locking the door behind her. She sat on the toilet and contemplated the tiny little library on Cache Bay and the books she'd borrowed from it. She looked over to the locked door. Why did she lock the door to the washroom? She never did that.

Beatrice washed her hands and face and stared into the mirror. She was being silly. No one was following her or playing tricks with her. It must have snowed since the last time she visited the library. Maybe those tracks were from someone else with the same boots? If finding a new book she wanted to read was so unusual, someone having the exact same boots certainly couldn't be. Still, it was odd and if she told anyone about it, they'd say that she was making it up.

After having a few slices of toast with strawberry jam and another cup of coffee, she settled in at work. The test results from the last lab experiment had come in. It would take her some time to pour over the tables, looking for patterns or anomalies. She loved getting her hands dirty by digging through data, identifying the missing insight.

Beatrice's appreciation for numbers came at an early age. She was able to memorize the multiplication table before other kids. In school she was always near the top of the class in math. Whenever she drove into the city with her parents, she liked to follow the trip on a map, noting each town or highway that was reached. Eventually she developed a desire to work in the food sciences area, where she could satiate the analytical side of her brain.

After she ate a quick lunch, she started *Fahrenheit 451*. The science fiction novel presented a world where literature was banned. "Firemen" didn't put out house fires ... they burned books! Beatrice remembered seeing a copy of the novel at a used book shop a few years ago and was tempted to buy it, but decided not to. It got her thinking about the banning of books, or banning anything for that matter. How was it that some strict cultures didn't allow some of the basic freedoms that she took for granted living in Canada? She could wear whatever she liked on her head. She could own property. Her career choices weren't limited to ones that had been traditionally performed by women.

That's not how her parents saw it. Mother would always release a barely audible sigh whenever the topic of marriage or grandkids came up. Although she'd accepted Beatrice's career and life choices, there was still a yearning for Beatrice to meet a man and settle down. One day Beatrice helped Dad round up a wayward cow. After the cow was led to the barn, he told her that it wasn't too late to leave the silliness of school and do some real work. He said that the Jacob boy two sections over was single and bound to inherit the family farm once his mother passed on.

Sometimes Beatrice wondered if her parents felt resentment towards her for not following their explicit wishes. Did they feel shame as a result of her choice? Some sense of failure? Why couldn't they accept her for the way that she was?

It took Beatrice over a week to finish *Fahrenheit 451*. A rush work assignment needed long hours to complete. The next time she visited the little library she placed it on the very right of the top shelf instead of on the left. As before it looked like only her footprints led to and from the library on the front yard of the house where it stood. She looked around and didn't see anyone else on Cache Bay. She never did.

When she got to the end of the block Beatrice realized that she'd forgotten to look to see if there was another book she could borrow. She didn't want to double back. She could just go tomorrow. It's not like she had to read something immediately.

Later that day, while washing the dishes, she started to feel guilty. Was she starting to take the tiny little library for granted? It had been too easy, too simple. Every time she approached the library it held something that she could appreciate, something that she'd always wanted.

The next morning, she walked the little free library route. Why break up a streak? She turned the corner to Cache Bay and rounded the bend. The large spruce street still stood like a sentinel in the darkness. But when Beatrice passed by the tree, there was nothing on the other side. The little free library was no longer there.

Beatrice exhaled through her mouth, which only served to fog her glasses. What happened to it? Stranger still, there were no footprints in the yard that had held the library. It was like the library was never there.

She turned around in a full circle. Was she in the wrong bay? No, she couldn't be. Cache Bay. It was always Cache Bay, beside the big spruce. Easy to miss if you weren't careful. Maybe the home owner took it down, for whatever reason. Maybe it got knocked down. Could have been kids. Young twerps were always terrorizing the neighborhood with vandalism and pranks.

But the snow looked untouched around where the library should have been. Like no one had ever stepped in the front yard of the home despite it being the middle of December and after several snowfalls. It hadn't snowed all week, though, and certainly not since yesterday morning when Beatrice dropped off *Fahrenheit 451*.

She crossed her arms and stared at the untouched snow near the spruce tree. She stepped off the street and on to the front yard, right to the spot where the library had been on each morning that she'd visited it. She looked down at the snow. Something was sticking out. She bent down and cleared the snow away. A book: *Vision in White*. The same Nora Roberts novel that Beatrice had placed in the little library with *Black Beauty*. It looked like it had been in the snow for weeks.

Beatrice dug further down until she reached the ground. There was no indication that a post had ever been planted there.

She heard a bark and looked up. Someone was walking a large dog at the end of the Cache Bay. They had stopped and the man was staring at her. The dog barked a few more times.

Of course. She must look strange, digging in someone's front yard at 5:30 in the morning. She got up, clutching her romance novel, and walked the other direction to the other entrance of the bay. All along the way her mind raced. How could something be there and then not be? And what about *Vision in White*? It was as if the little library was mad at her and expunged her novel.

Later, at lunch, Beatrice took her car and drove to Cache Bay. She swallowed hard when she turned the corner and saw the large spruce tree. But like this morning, there was nothing other than her own foot prints and the hole she'd dug in the snow.

It felt like she'd lost a friend, a confidant. She hadn't told anyone about the library or thought ill of it, but somehow she'd wronged it. Could it be because she never took another book after returning *Fahrenheit 451*?

The following morning, she walked to Cache Bay with *Vision in White*. The book looked worn and tired. Her heart pounded as she rounded Cache Bay and passed the spruce tree. But the scene looked exactly the same as it was when she drove by the day before: her footprints and a hole in the snow where she had dug.

Like a Pavlovian dog, every day for two weeks Beatrice went to where the little free library had stood, and each time the library was not there. During those two weeks it snowed a few times, concealing any evidence that she had ever walked in the yard with the big spruce tree. By the new year, Beatrice took different routes for her morning walks.

Three months later, after the winter snows had retreated, she decided to venture to Cache Bay for old time's sake. The mornings were now brighter and the air, while still cool, smelled like the promise of spring and a new beginning. She didn't need to wear a mask and liked the warmth of the stronger sun on her bare face.

Beside the large spruce tree there was no evidence that the ground had ever been disrupted. The brown and yellow grass still looked patchy and soggy from the remnants of winter, but it also looked undisturbed. There never was a post erected into the ground.

Back at home, Beatrice sat at her kitchen table with a cup of coffee. Did she imagine everything? Certainly she had read all those books. She remembered specific details of each novel. Someone must have taken down the library. Maybe it wasn't actually lodged in the ground, but on a stand of sorts. She wouldn't have been able to tell from the snow cover. That didn't explain why she only saw her own footprints in the snow, but it was the best explanation she had.

Around when the first buds were beginning to appear on trees, a vaccine was starting to be distributed. It took a month before it trickled down to Beatrice. She was young and able-bodied and had to wait behind society's most sensitive, health care workers, first responders, and others. By the beginning of the summer, masks were no longer required in public buildings although many people, scared by the experience over the winter, continued to do so. She also went back to working in the office. The workplace had changed. A few retired. Others had moved on. Still, it felt refreshing to see faces every day.

While driving home from getting groceries one Saturday morning in August, Beatrice noticed a tiny little library on Birch Street just a few blocks from her own. She stopped the car. The library was different than the one she'd seen in the fall and winter. This one looked like a miniature version of the house behind it, a red A-frame with black shingles. She opened the single glass door. It was filled exclusively with children's books. Nothing to see in this little library.

That night while she lay in bed, an idea germinated. Why couldn't Beatrice put up a tiny little library of her own? She had enough books that she could contribute. After getting permission from the landlord, Google told her that libraries went for about $250 to $400. She could get a kit and build one, but that was beyond her means. She could always ask Dad to put it together. He might like that sort of thing. Then again, she'd have to put up with him telling her what she should be doing with her life. His favorite saying was, "Suit yourself."

The landlord didn't mind as long as Beatrice paid for it and maintained it. He even helped assemble and erect it two weeks later when the kit arrived. While waiting for it to arrive she organized the books she was going to place in the library. She found some children's books by scouring local garage sales and a flea market.

After she loaded books into her little library she took a step back, crossed her arms and smiled. Maybe someone would get inspired by some of the stories from the library. Perhaps a budding future literary novelist will be moved by its offerings.

She kept her curtains open more than she typically did to see if anyone would approach it. Sometimes she would see a young mother with a child or two take a book. She didn't see too many people deposit books. Whenever she checked the contents there always seemed to be less than before. Around September she had to find books to restock her little library. The library she visited the previous winter always seemed to be brimming with books.

One evening in December, she trudged in the snow to examine the contents. There wasn't as much activity in the colder months with its shorter days. The contents looked about the same as when she examined it a few weeks prior. It was also beginning to snow. Light, puffy flakes drifted from the heavens. Back in the house, Beatrice realized that she'd forgotten to add a *Berenstain Bears* book she'd gotten from Eugenia at work. She looked outside and didn't feel like putting on all her winter clothes again and threw the book down on the counter. Maybe tomorrow just before she left for work.

She almost forgot it again the next day and had to re-enter her place just after she'd closed the door. About three centimeters had fallen overnight, enough to put a fresh coat of white over everything. The snow was so light and fluffy, she almost wouldn't need her brush to swish it off her car. After starting her car, she went to her tiny little library and placed *Berenstain Bears* inside with all the other children's books.

Before closing the door to the library, something caught her eye on the top shelf, where the non-children books were housed. There were more books! Someone had made a deposit! She reached in to see the titles: *Black Beauty, Animal Farm, Fahrenheit 451, Hunger Games, The Sisterhood of the Traveling Pants.*

Beatrice blinked and her heart thumped against the side of her chest. She looked at her feet and behind where she had walked. Only her footprints. By the amount of snow that had fallen overnight it would have been obvious if someone had approached the library. Maybe the person came soon after she left the library in the evening and those footprints had been obscured? It didn't seem likely.

She looked in the library again. There was a book she hadn't seen before on the very left of the top shelf, another one that she'd always wanted to read: *The Catcher in the Rye.*

She put the book into her jacket pocket and placed the others back on the top shelf, carefully closing the library door. She was not going to try to understand or explain what had happened. She had to accept it. Just like she had to accept herself and the decisions she'd made in the past. And the decisions she would make in the future. And accept the way that her parents are. And that some people are bad and some are good. And she'll have to quit blaming herself for her faults. Or other people, for that matter.

She read *Catcher in the Rye* over the next few days. It felt like another young adult novel, although it was probably written before the term was coined. Although the main character was male, she felt a type of bond. It was the feeling of not being sure who she was. Of trying to determine her own identity. Of hoping to find some sort of connection. Her life would always be a work in progress and she needed to appreciate it for what it was and that she was in control of it.

Beatrice slipped on her boots and returned it back to the little library. She didn't need to borrow from the library anymore. Besides, it didn't look like there was anything new on the top shelf.

Over the following summer, through the front window, Beatrice would notice the same young woman approach the library every week or so, sometimes more often. Each time she would exchange a book she'd taken from the library for another that she was carrying. On a few occasions, Beatrice could see the woman's surprised reaction, perhaps for a book she hadn't seen before and always wanted to read.

Beatrice made sure the library was always stocked with a variety of books.

Alicia Adams lives in a cabin in the mountains with her spouse, child, and cat. She works as a web accessibility engineer, which, she admits, is pretty tops. When she's not working, writing, or spending time with her family, she enjoys walking through the woods, crossword puzzles, and reading lots of books. She has a deep love for fungi, soil, and the natural world in general.

• • •

In spring 2020 my husband Brian asked me to write him a story for his upcoming birthday. While I had earned an MFA in fiction 10 years prior, it had been a few years since I'd written a full story. The last few years had been a whirlwind of moving across the country, getting married, switching careers, and having a baby. Writing had taken a backseat by necessity.

I wrote this story near the beginning of the COVID-19 pandemic, while the two of us juggled our full-time jobs with our infant daughter at home with us. We were tired and stressed and worried. Even so I knew that I wanted to give him a gift he'd love for his birthday. And in asking for this gift, he gave me the gift of writing again. It's been two and a half years, and I haven't stopped.

LUMINOUS

ALICIA ADAMS

W HEN QUARANTINE STARTED, Jayne thought the world would go quiet. At first, little changed. She still heard the motorcycle zoom by every night at seven as she tried to put the baby to sleep. There was still the roar of leaf blowers as they moved fallen leaves from one side of the sidewalk to the other. The rush of traffic whooshed on.

Somehow she heard more people on the stairs. Up and down. Up and down. All times of day and night. She'd find the packages that were delivered to her doorstep sliced open and gutted, Styrofoam peanuts bleeding out onto the porch.

But it was silently that the neighbors moved out. First the downstairs neighbors. The doormat vanished from out front. Then the door was wide open. A man was in there vacuuming the carpet of the cleared-out living room. She saw him when she went to get the mail. He didn't look up at her as she passed.

Then the next-door neighbor left. She heard big bangs in there, as if there were construction crews demolishing the place. It must have been the movers. When she peeked outside, the doors were open, and the place was empty.

There had been no goodbyes. They had not been close, but she'd thought there would at least have been goodbyes. Now her family was surrounded by empty space. And the noise outside continued.

There had been a glimmer of hope when quarantine started. There would be no time spent commuting to work. No time spent shuttling the baby back and forth from her daycare. She had imagined doing some work from her laptop on the couch, Baby Val playing quietly on the floor in front of her. Of course that never happened. There had not been a single second that she had been able to successfully do work and watch the baby at the same time. And as she and Simon tetrised their schedules into increasingly stranger blocks of work and childcare, the entire day from pre-sunrise to sunset became an onslaught of chaos. When she finally rested her head against the pillow at night, she could hardly keep track of what had happened, how much she'd been able to finish, how much was left undone.

•　　•　　•

It was a Wednesday when her alarm tore through the dark and ripped her from a strange dream. The baby had slept through the night again. A small blessing. She turned off the alarm and shuffled out of bed. Simon stirred in the covers but seemed to recover. What had she just been dreaming? She could remember worms in soil. Or maybe fingers. A feeling of panic. That was all.

The living room was lit a dull gray from the streetlights outside. She started the percolator. Then she searched the living room for the laptop, set it up on the kitchen table, and turned it on. She brought her coffee over to the table, and let her eyes focus in the bubble of blue light. She hoped she was awake enough to get in some quality work before Val woke up.

Simon's alarm sounded two hours later. Somehow she'd only just finished going through her emails. She snuck through the bedroom to the master bath as Simon pushed the snooze button and rolled back over. She had just finished brushing her teeth and hair by the time the alarm went off again. She opened the closet door quietly and stepped inside to find an outfit for the day.

She closed the door behind her and was just about to turn on the light, but she found she could see. There was a faint green glow that illuminated the clothes on their hangers and the shelf of shoes above them. It was a walk-in closet, with a wall for Simon's clothes on the left, and a wall for her clothes straight ahead. To the right were hampers for dirty clothes and bags of clothes to be donated whenever it was safe to go outside again. Along the top of each wall was a shelf for shoes, belts, and hats. Piled up above the shoes were camping equipment, scarves, and tennis rackets they hadn't used in years.

Usually at 7 a.m. the closet was almost pitch black with a sliver of gray light that crept in below the door. She looked around for the source of the new light. Maybe something electronic was plugged into a hidden-away outlet, though she couldn't think of what or why. It was coming from behind her clothes. She brushed the clothes to the left and right, trying to find the source.

And there it was. A little mushroom? Yes, some kind of mushroom or toadstool. Its cap was about the diameter of a nickel. Its stem seemed to come from straight out of the wall.

"Simon! Come look at this!" she yelled. She didn't hear him coming. Maybe he'd gone to the baby's room. "Simon!"

Under the glow, the mushroom looked to be an almost sickly white. The green light (bioluminescence?) emanated softly from it. Her hands looked green in front of her. She watched them as they reached forward and her pointer finger brushed the tiny mushroom cap.

The little mushroom bent beneath her finger. She traced her fingertip over the little stem and then back up under the cap itself and over the little ribs of its gills. *Lamella*, she thought. A word from high school Biology. It felt so fragile. She was sure she could rip it from the wall. She closed her fingers over the stem and considered it. And then for no reason she could recognize, she let go and stepped back.

She grabbed a blouse and pants from their hangers and backed out of the closet.

Simon's alarm was blaring. He thwacked it with his hand and wiped his eyes.

"Two snoozes today?" Jayne said. She heard a little judgment in her voice and felt ashamed. She didn't care what time he woke up. She got the same amount of sleep no matter how late he slept in.

"No, just one," he said. He sat up and pulled on a shirt that had been lying on the nightstand.

"Two," Jayne said. "I came in here when the alarm went off. The first snooze went off as I finished brushing my hair, and the second one just now."

"It's only been one alarm," he said. "If it had been 2, it would be 7:20 by now."

Jayne looked at the clock on her dresser. It said 7:11. *That's weird*, she thought.

•   •   •

She didn't like the conference calls. In person, she didn't have to look at herself. But in her morning meetings she could see the deep-set circles under her eyes. She pulled her hair back into a bun so the split ends were hidden away. It didn't hide the gray.

She could hear Simon and Val in the living room while she had her meetings. That choppy little baby laugh. Jayne wanted to go out and join them. That's all she ever wanted anymore.

When it was finally her turn to take over with the baby, she felt tired and drained. She kissed Simon on his way to the baby's room to work and then set the baby in the high chair. She was still thinking about work as she cut open an avocado and diced half for the baby. She smeared it on a soft piece of bread and cut the bread into tiny squares. In minutes the baby was covered in green.

Jayne leaned over and kissed her baby's cheek. She could taste the avocado on her — light, green, and creamy. Val smiled up at her and then smeared the avocado along the top of her highchair tray.

Jayne wet a washcloth to clean off Val's little hands and face. She pulled globs of avocado from her hair. She lifted little Val in her arms and walked her toward the master bedroom where her playpen was set up for naps. As she passed the window, she wondered how long it had been raining.

Val lowered herself down into her playpen and rested her head against the sheet. Jayne should have gone back out to the living room to get more work done. She was going to. But she thought maybe she'd look at that little mushroom one more time.

She should probably call maintenance, she thought. There could be a whole network of mushrooms in there. They could be releasing toxic spores. She didn't know anything about spores.

She walked back to the closet and closed herself in. Again she saw the faint dusting of green light. It looked like what she'd imagined fairy dust would look like when she was young. When she was little, Jayne would spend full afternoons looking for fairies. She would gently loosen the folds of rose petals in her mother's garden scouting out their hiding places. Under leaves, attached and fallen. In the knots of ragged bark on trees. In piles of small stones. She had imagined when she found one that there would be a glow like this and then a small human form within the glow, tiny dragonfly wings, so delicate you could see right through them.

But this wasn't fairy light. Jayne walked to the back of the closet and pushed her clothes to the side. This time she found the mushroom immediately. It wasn't as tiny as she had remembered. It didn't look so delicate. Its cap was about the size of a quarter now that she looked closely. It was the size of a button mushroom you'd buy in a pack from the store in a little container covered in cellophane.

She touched it again. She almost couldn't help herself. It felt like a button mushroom, too. It was white with green light coming from it. Now that the sun had risen, it wasn't as dark in the closet as it had been. Jayne grabbed a shirt off one of her hangers. It was a dark blue long-sleeve t-shirt with pink swans on it. She stuffed the shirt into the crack below the door to block the light. When she turned around again, the mushroom was brighter, almost electric.

She didn't know how long she spent looking at it. It seemed to be moving. If she watched very carefully, she felt like she could see it grow. Every so often she reached out and stroked her fingers over the cap and then below it across its soft gills.

After what felt like a long time, Jayne convinced herself it was time to go back to work. She moved her clothes back over her little mushroom friend to keep it safe in the darkness. Then she removed the swan shirt and opened the door. When she closed the door, she pushed the swan shirt into the space between the door and the floor to block out the light.

When she looked up, she saw the baby was watching her from her playpen. Her head was on the sheet, but her eyes were open and watching. "Are you ready to get up, Sweetie?" she said. Jayne looked at the time to see how long Val had been napping. But according to the clock, no time had passed at all. As if to confirm, Val blinked twice and then closed her eyes and fell asleep. *That's weird*, she thought.

•   •   •

By the time the baby woke up again, it was Simon's turn to take over. By dinnertime, Jayne was done with her work. She didn't feel so tired tonight. She felt okay. Simon was in the baby's room back to work. Rice was already whistling in the rice cooker. Beans were on the stove with the fire low and the lid on top to keep them warm. Jayne cut up some onions and peppers and heated them in a pan with some oil. She mashed some beans and mixed them with rice for Val. Then she heated some kale from the freezer, chopped it up and mixed it in.

"Here you go, Baby," she said. She loved to watch Val's tiny hands reach for the beans and pull them to her mouth. She lost half of each fistful on its journey, but the fact that she could feed herself at all was such an achievement. Jayne couldn't believe how fast she was growing.

She'd been so tiny when she was first born. Those little hands could barely wrap around Jayne's finger. It was hard to think of this little girl as the same person.

She remembered reading novels to her hoping to expose Baby Val to as many new words as possible, hoping it would make her smart. But it was silly, she thought. The baby had no context for anything. Jayne would read the word "ocean" and then stop and try to explain. "The ocean is a large body of salt water where lots of animals and plants live. It's deep and so big you can't see to the other side of it. Earth is primarily ocean." And then she'd realize that Val had no context for any of that either. "Water is a liquid that we need to live. We can't drink it when it's salt water, though. Animals and plants are other living things. Earth is the planet that we live on." And there was no context for any of that either. Val looked up at her and watched her lips move to form words, and that was the most she got out of it at the time.

When Val finally saw the ocean for the first time a few months later, she couldn't take her eyes off of it. Waves crashed against the rocky cliffside in a spray of white. The water went on and on without end. The air was full of salt and the smell of kelp smashed against the rocks. And this was just what she could see, Jayne thought. There was so much more to the ocean than this.

"Dinner's ready!" Jayne called out. She piled two bowls high with rice, beans, onions, and peppers.

"I'll be there in a minute!" Simon called back.

Jayne soaked a washcloth in warm water and carefully cleaned Val's cheeks and nose. Then she wiped the beans out from between her fingers and let her out of the highchair. Val crawled to a basket of toys and pulled out a bell that she started to ring.

Jayne watched Simon eat. He looked so tired.

The sun was setting over the trees by the time they'd given Val a bath and put her to bed in her crib. The rain had stopped. Jayne brushed her teeth and changed into pajamas. She looked at the portable digital clock. It said 7:35. Then she picked up the swan shirt from the crack below the closet door, opened the door, and stepped inside. She stretched the shirt across the bottom of the door to block out the light from other rooms.

Green. Instant and bright. She pushed the clothes to the side and saw her mushroom. It was clearly bigger this time, and brighter. It had the diameter of a can of soup. She leaned her back against the door and let her eyes unfocus over her luminous friend.

She woke up. She wasn't sure when she'd fallen asleep or how long she'd been asleep. Her back hurt. She looked at the mushroom and saw it had grown again in the night. Now it was the size of a teacup saucer. She went to touch it again. As her fingertips glided over the soft ridges of its gills she pushed it aside enough to see a tiny white toadstool growing beside it.

"Oh hello," she said. But her mind was racing. *Infestation.* If the walls erupted in mushrooms, where would they live? They couldn't move during a pandemic. They couldn't have workers come inside their home, potentially exposing them all to disease. It would be better to rip the mushrooms out now.

But she backed out of the closet and closed the door behind her before giving herself another moment to think about it. She replaced the t-shirt in the crack below the door. Simon came in to brush his teeth.

"You're up late," she said.

He gave her a strange look. Jayne looked at the digital clock. It said 7:36. "Never mind," she said.

• • •

She watched Simon breathing beside her in bed. The sun was down, but the constant city lights from outside glowed in through the blinds in stripes of light and shadow.

She had just woken from a dream. In the dream, the baby had crawled into the closet and the door had closed behind her. By the time Jayne was able to open the door, Val was a teenager with long green hair. She had woken in a panic.

She could see her hands above the covers. There was something not right about them. As she let her eyes focus, she saw that they were ... shining?

This must be a dream, she thought. She got out of bed and looked at her reflection in the mirror. She was like a ghost in a movie. Her skin glowed softly white.

Don't think, she told herself. *Just do it. Rip the mushrooms out.*

She went into the closet and closed the door. The mushroom was huge, the size of a car tire. Smaller toadstools had propped up all around.

How did they grow so fast? But of course, time was meaningless here. Or at least unknowable.

She reached her arms around the mushroom head and pushed her foot against the wall. *Pull it out. Pull it out now. Don't think about it. Pull it out.*

But as she was holding it, she felt peace. She felt *its* peace humming inside of it, generating its glow. *No,* she thought. *It's okay.*

She slumped down and sat beside the massive mushroom. She pressed her face against its face. And she fell asleep.

• • •

Somehow when the sun rose, it was only Thursday. Jayne had been at work for an hour when the light started to shift. Without thinking about it, she slid the blinds shut and continued her work.

By the time the baby woke up, most of the work she had to do was done. She brushed her teeth while Simon got up to feed Val. She made a quick stop to sit in the closet while grabbing her clothes. She noticed that her clothes were pulled to the side, and the mushrooms were left uncovered. She must have forgotten to pull the clothes back over them. Not that they'd be much more concealed.

There were so many now. The big one was, of course, bigger. But the smaller ones were catching up. The tiny mushrooms that had been beside it were now the width of a mason jar, and tiny new growths had sprouted all along the back wall.

After a few moments, she left the closet with her clothes for the day. By the time she was set to take over with the baby, she had finished everything she had to do for work that day.

As she spread almond butter over slices of banana, Jayne realized she felt different. She had forgotten to brew coffee that morning, but she felt awake. She felt a low-key kind of joy, the kind you feel walking outside on a beautiful day.

She looked at the windows and realized she'd left the blinds closed. It was still dark in the kitchen and living room, but enough light came through the blinds that she didn't feel like opening them.

Jayne spent her time chasing the baby around the apartment. She listened to her laugh. She kissed her cheeks and combed her fingers through her soft curly hair.

When Simon came out to take over childcare, Val was napping.

"I'm actually pretty okay with work today," Jayne said. If you have a lot to do, you can keep working.

"I'm actually pretty okay, too," he said. "Have you eaten?"

Simon made them sandwiches, and they sat together on the couch and ate them.

"Is it dark in here?" he asked.

"Yeah, a little."

He didn't move to open the blinds. As she reached for her glass of water she felt his hand on the back of her neck.

"What's this?" he asked.

She felt her muscles tighten. She wasn't sure why.

"What's what?"

"You have a bump on your neck."

Jayne set her sandwich plate on the sofa and stood up. "It's probably just a zit or something. I'll go take a look." She walked to the guest restroom. The mirrored medicine cabinet was on the side wall. If she angled the door a certain way, she could see the back of her neck in the main bathroom mirror.

There was a white bump there. It was whiter than her surrounding skin. It was about the size of a penny. She knew before she touched it that it felt like a toadstool. She pushed it to the side and saw its little stem.

Don't think. Don't think about it. Just pull it out. It's in your body. You have to pull out. It's in your body.

Jayne closed her eyes and gripped the little mushroom head. It was a long slow pull. She tried not to scream through the pain. It felt like she kept pulling and pulling. At last she got the end out. She opened her eyes and saw the tiny mushroom in her hand. Short strands of mycelium clung to the stem like little roots. They'd felt much longer as she'd pulled them out. There was only a little smear of blood.

She wrapped the mushroom in a piece of toilet paper and threw it into the garbage. Then she washed off the back of her neck and put on a bandage.

"It was just a zit," she said to Simon as she walked back into the living room. "I popped it."

"What? You hate popping zits."

"It was a pretty nasty zit."

Simon gave her a look of concern. She wasn't sure why she wasn't telling him the truth. She would eventually, she told herself. Once things started to make sense. Or once she'd made a decision about what to do next. Soon. When it felt right.

•   •   •

She loved giving the baby a bath. Val splashed her hands against the water. Then she slowed down the motion. She slowly moved her hand toward the surface of the water and then through it into the bath water. Then she lifted her hands slowly back out and lowered them in again.

Jayne smiled. She waited for Val to finish before putting shampoo in her hair. She washed her little hands with soap. When the bath was done, Jayne pulled the plug. The water swirled in a mini whirlpool in the drain. Jayne pointed to it, and Val watched the water swirl around and around. She put her hand over it and pulled it off again.

That evening, Jayne didn't go to the closet. She wouldn't go in there until she'd made a decision, she thought.

She could pull the mushrooms out. All of them. She'd pulled one out of her neck. It was possible. The big one would probably offer more resistance. She might need help.

She could tell Simon. Simon hadn't needed to go in the closet for a few days. He was wearing the same clothes over and over. He didn't have conference calls, so there'd been no need to change.

She could let him discover it himself. She could ask him for something in the closet. Maybe he wouldn't see them at all. Maybe time only stopped for her. Or maybe she was going crazy. It was a very real possibility.

Yes, that was a good idea. The next morning. She would ask him to grab something for her in the closet. She would ask him if he saw anything.

Decision made, she went to sleep.

It was 1 a.m. when she woke up to the baby crying. She made a bottle and fed her in the rocking chair in her room. She could feel her eyes lowering as the baby ate. She tried to keep them open. A purple night light lit the room. The mirrored closet made the room look twice as big. A great big purple room. She crawled back in bed at 1:45. At 3:15 she heard people on the stairs. Up and down. Up and down. Why was it always so loud? They woke the baby. She waited for the baby to fall back asleep. By 3:30 it was quiet. By 4 she was back asleep. And by 5 she was up for work.

She kept her eyes half closed as she walked out into the living room to look for her laptop. She had a deep headache. It seemed to pound all the way down her spine.

Just a couple hours, she thought. *Then I'll never go in there again. Just enough for a little more sleep.*

She walked into the closet without thinking and pushed the t-shirt against the crack of light below the door. There were toadstools growing up out of the floor. This was getting to be a big problem. This weekend they'd have to figure this out. They'd have to pull all these mushrooms up. No exceptions. She curled up on the floor and fell asleep.

When she woke, it was still dark. Of course it was. The mushrooms shined greenly from the wall and floor. She noticed that one of the mushrooms on the floor was big enough to sit on. She sat on it. She found it comfortable. *What am I going to do with all of you?* She wondered what would happen if she ate them. She could die. She could become unstuck in time, wandering lonely through an empty house forever. And what if the baby found one and put it in her mouth? She shuddered. Val was always putting things in her mouth. These were dangerous.

But they didn't feel dangerous. Jayne felt calm and rested. She wasn't sleeping through her days anymore. She could get work done and then be there with her family. She was watching her baby grow up instead of passively letting it happen as she continued sleepily on to other things.

She went to work in the dark again. She didn't need coffee. It only took her a couple hours to power through everything, morning meeting included. If she could only be like this every day, she thought. And she could, she realized. When she went to the bathroom and found the new little mushroom growing out of her thigh, she didn't panic. She pulled it out slowly and wrapped it in toilet paper. Then she put on a bandage and went back to work.

•   •   •

Simon had decided to take the day off work. There was a bookshelf near the front door, and he sat beside it reading.

"You can go to another room if you want," Jayne said.

"That's okay. I'm fine here."

In the living room, Jayne and Val were reading board books together. Val turned the pages, sometimes in the right direction. On pages with cutouts, Val pushed her fingers through the holes. Jayne thought it was funny she could be so much more interested in what was left out of the book than what was in it. She imagined Val as a young woman, the two of them sitting down over baby pictures. "You liked to find the empty spaces," she would say. "You wanted to know where the missing pieces were."

Every once in a while, Simon would look out the peephole or open the door, but there would be nobody there. Jayne looked at him questioningly, but he wouldn't say anything. He'd go back to looking at his book.

And then he opened the door and brought a long, thin box inside. It was still taped shut. *He must have been waiting for the box to make sure no one grabbed it,* she thought. He cut through the tape with one of his keys.

"What is it?" Jayne said.

"Curtains," he said. "Blackout curtains. For the bedroom. It gets so bright in there."

"Oh."

He brought the curtains past Jayne and Val and into the bedroom. Jayne heard the blinds clatter.

That night, the bedroom was so dark. Light from the street still crept in under the door, but it was faint. All Jayne could see was outlines of the furniture. She awoke to Simon crawling into bed. She cuddled in next to him and kissed his shoulder. And then she saw it. A little green glow peeking out from beneath the covers.

She pulled the blanket down and found it. Growing between his spine and his shoulder blade was a little white mushroom. It glowed green in the dark. She touched it with her fingertip. It was just a fragile little thing.

There was a rustle of sheets as Simon turned over in the bed. He took her hands and pulled them down into the covers. Her hands landed on another mushroom growing from his solar plexus. This one was much bigger. It filled the palm of her hand. She wondered how long he had known. She felt relief — relief that he did know.

She leaned down and kissed the mushroom head. Under the covers, the glow was bright. But it wasn't just that mushroom. There were more. They grew all along his belly. She brushed her hands over them. There were so many. Simon shuttered. Could he feel her hands through them?

She felt Simon's hands around her, guiding her back up. He kissed her cheek and then her lips. Then he pulled her nightgown up over her head.

She felt his hands travel along her breasts and her back. There was a new feeling, too. She looked at her body and saw that several more little mushrooms had sprouted up. There was one at her collarbone and one on her thigh. One at her ribcage. One behind her knee. As his hands moved up her back, she felt little mushrooms sway beneath his fingertips.

She pushed away the covers and moved her body over Simon's. As she guided him into her, she realized they hadn't done this in weeks. When she came, it was loud enough to shake the walls.

•   •   •

When she awoke, it was still dark. She opened the blackout curtains, but it was dark outside, too. Simon sat up in bed and looked out.

"How long have we been asleep?" he asked.

"I don't know. It feels like a long time." Beyond Simon, she saw a line of mushrooms growing through the floor. "I think time has stopped in the bedroom."

It sounded ridiculous to say out loud, but it felt good to finally say it.

"That's nice," he said.

"Sort of. But what happens if these toadstools spread? What if they reach the whole apartment? What if they get to the baby?" There was a toadstool growing from her jaw. She felt it — it's root-like mycelium fused to bone.

"As far as I'm concerned, this is the best thing that ever happened to us," he said. Maybe it was. But she also felt afraid.

She wondered if she could go out to the living room without him and wait for time to pass. If he was in here, and she was out there, would time pass at all?

She walked out and closed the door. A moment later, he walked out, fully dressed.

"How long did you stay in there?" she asked.

"I don't know. A while. Maybe an hour."

They made food and waited. When the sun rose, she went to get the baby. She was still asleep. Jayne watched her sleeping soundly in her crib. She wanted to wake her up and hold her, but she knew she shouldn't. She opened the blinds to let more light in. The light would keep her safe.

•   •   •

Time passed or it didn't. Jayne didn't know how much or how little. She didn't go back to work or wouldn't if the time came, she knew. There were formidable toadstools all along the line of her jaw. She couldn't cover them for video meetings. She knew that part of her life was over.

She spent all daytime hours by the window with Baby Val. Jayne's skin stung in the sunlight. Her eyes hurt. But the light would keep Baby Val safe, she thought. She opened the blinds in Val's room, even at night. She put in nightlights.

But she couldn't stop Val from touching the many mushrooms that grew from her and Simon. "Don't touch," she'd say as she pulled the little hands away. She did this over and over. When she saw little toadstools grow out of Val's little fingers like little warts, she pulled them out. Val cried and cried. Her face turned bright red as she screamed.

But Jayne admitted defeat when a fleet of toadstools sprang straight from Val's head, fused to the skull. Jayne felt a dull terror for her child but also a sense of relief. They were all in this together, whatever it was, and there was no fighting it now.

She noticed that the sun never rose anymore. They slept and woke in eternal night. She wondered what would happen if they walked out the front door into the cool air. She wondered if the sun would rise or if their timelessness would walk with them.

She didn't think they had to sleep anymore, but they liked to. They slept all together in one bed with the curtains drawn. Even so, sometimes it was hard to sleep. They glowed so brightly, the three of them. And then there were the teeming mushrooms all around them — some big enough to sit on. Jayne had to wear an eye mask to block out the light.

But she wasn't sleeping. Val was snoring lightly between them. She could see that Simon's eyes were open, too. She held his hand in hers.

"How are you feeling?" she asked.

"I think I'm supposed to feel scared or trapped," he said. "But I feel better than I've felt in years. I can't place what the feeling is."

She thought about how she'd felt during her first visits to the closet, her head pressed against a big mushroom, resting against it like a pillow.

"I think," he said, "This is going to sound weird, but I feel, I feel free."

"I know what you mean," she said.

•　　•　　•

She awoke to Simon calling her name. "Bring the baby," he said. Jayne wiped her eyes and sat up. She picked up Val and stood with the baby in her arms.

"Where are you?" she called.

"The closet."

What's he doing in the closet? she thought. They hadn't been back inside the closet since the mushrooms had started growing in their room.

She walked over and looked inside. There were so many mushrooms packed into the closet. They looked like glowing boulders. Clothes and shoes and all other contents of the closet were strewn over them. Simon had climbed over them and stood by the back wall.

There was a bright green crack in the wall. It spanned from ceiling to floor. Simon was pulling out chunks of wall and throwing them to the ground. The hole was getting wider as he pulled the pieces away. It was the same light coming through the wall that came from the mushrooms all around them. She couldn't see past the light into the hole.

Jayne held Val close. Val's little hands were clinging to Jayne's nightgown. She kissed Val's forehead just below the line of mushrooms. She could tell her baby knew what was coming. Just like she knew what was coming without having to ask. They were walking through the wall. They didn't know what was back there or what it would mean for them, but they would do it anyway.

The hole was three feet wide by then. Simon backed up to take a look. Jayne stepped forward to meet him and leaned her head against his shoulder. He wrapped an arm around his wife and daughter. Jayne noticed a thin sheen of sweat on his arm.

"Are we ready?"

"As ready as we'll ever be."

Simon took Jayne's hand. He kissed her forehead, and he kissed Val's forehead. Then he stepped forward into the wall. Jayne squeezed his hand, and he squeezed back. So at least stepping through the wall wasn't immediate death. She looked into Baby Val's eyes. "Okay," she said. "Let's go."

She readjusted Val on her hip, held tight onto Simon's hand, and walked forward into the light.

AFTERWORD

I N MARCH OF 2020, we didn't take the fifteen-minute to two-hour commute into an eight-foot-high cubicle (if you were lucky) on a "campus" or building where the corporate overlords kept us chained to our desks. On this desk were reminders of home and family: pictures, plants, artifacts. This was what we worked for.

In March of 2020, we stayed in the place we worked for — our home. In a closet, on a kitchen table, in bedrooms. Laptops gleamed early in the morning until late at night. The pictures, plants, and artifacts were real, no longer reminders, but part of the décor of our workspace or the background of our Zoom calls. Work invaded the very place that had been our refuge. It *became* our work at all hours and all places of our life.

No matter what, though, we still had to deal with the corporate overlords and culture, this time at a distance and enhanced by technology. There were still the unending progression of meetings and "team building exercises" and unreliable co-workers. But unless they used a filter, we got to see a portion of people's lives that they only let the repairman in to see.

Corporate Catharsis: The Work From Home Edition is a continuation of what's it like to be in corporate lockdown. We survived the Pandemic Days — maybe. Some of us have realized that we can do better than the overlords. Some of us have realized that the real things we work for are more important than their symbols at our cubicles. Some of the Corporate Overlords have realized that they have their claws in our lives, and now we're stuck permanently attached to laptops, tablets, and phones wherever we go.

The stories that are in this collection range from the hilarious to the dark. Muses and gods and demons find their way into our corporate life. Ghosts haunt an office building. A coven gathers for a Zoom call. Pizza gets an additional topping that is illegal in some states.

For the two-plus years we had to work with the limitations of our home internet, cats laying across the keyboard, dogs barking in their sleep at your feet during a Zoom call, kids running in and out of the background because you couldn't set the filter right, and that famous cat-lawyer meme will be considered normal.

Now imagine the supernatural along with that normal.

Welcome to the new normal.

L.A. Jacob
Author, "Grimaulkin" and "War Mage" series

YOU MIGHT ALSO ENJOY

THE FUTURE'S SO BRIGHT

by Water Dragon Publishing

Out of the darkness of the present comes the light of the days ahead ...

With stories from Kevin David Anderson, Maureen Bowden, Steven D. Brewer, Nels Challinor, Regina Clarke, Stephen C. Curro, Jetse de Vries, Nestor Delfino, Gail Ann Gibbs, Henry Herz, Gwen C. Katz, Brandon Ketchum, Julia LaFond, R. Jean Mathieu, Cynthia McDonald, Christopher Muscato, Alfred Smith, A.M. Weald, and David Wright.

Available from Water Dragon Publishing in
hardcover, trade paperback, and digital editions
waterdragonpublishing.com

Ingram Content Group UK Ltd.
Milton Keynes UK
UKHW012019130323
418525UK00015B/300/J